Praise for *New York Times* bestselling author
Lori Foster

"A sexy, believable roller coaster of action and romance."
—*Kirkus Reviews* on *Run the Risk*

"Bestseller Foster…has an amazing ability to capture
a man's emotions and lust with sizzling sex scenes and
meld it with a strong woman's point of view."
—*Publishers Weekly* on *A Perfect Storm*

"Foster rounds out her searing trilogy with a story that
tilts toward the sizzling and sexy side of the genre."
—*RT Book Reviews* on *Savor the Danger*

"The fast-paced thriller keeps these well-developed
characters moving.… Foster's series will continue to
garner fans with this exciting installment."
—*Publishers Weekly* on *Trace of Fever*

"Steamy, edgy and taut."
—*Library Journal* on *When You Dare*

"Intense, edgy and hot. Lori Foster
delivers everything you're looking for in a romance."
—*New York Times* bestselling author Jayne Ann Krentz
on *Hard to Handle*

"Lori Foster delivers the goods."
—*Publishers Weekly*

"Tension, temptation, hot action and hotter romance—
Lori Foster has it all! *Hard to Handle* is a knockout!"
—*New York Times* bestselling author Elizabeth Lowell

LORI FOSTER

ALL RILED UP

ISBN-13: 978-0-373-77806-5

ALL RILED UP

Recycling programs for this product may not exist in your area.

Printed in U.S.A.

www.Harlequin.com

CONTENTS

Dear Reader,

I'm *thrilled* that Harlequin HQN is reissuing these two stories.

The friends-to-lovers story *Trapped!* was so much fun to write that even now, years later, I still smile when thinking about it. Ethan has such a hard time coming to grips with his feelings, but Rosie is relentless, and I loved her for it. She deserved everything she wanted, especially since she wanted Ethan most of all.

Riley features one of my most beloved animals, Brock. My little five-pound Chihuahua has since passed away, and I still miss him—his little kisses, the wonderful way he smelled (not at all like a dog!) and even the cute sounds he made that were so incredibly expressive. Like all our animals, Brock (aka Butch in the book) was a true member of our family. I'm so glad that he'll be remembered in a fun story.

I hope you enjoy reading these stories as much as I enjoyed writing them.

And while you're at it, be sure to read the excerpt from my newest book, *Bare It All,* coming soon. Check my website for more info, www.LoriFoster.com.

All my best,

Lori Foster

TRAPPED!

CHAPTER ONE

ETHAN WINTERS jerked awake with a start. His heart slammed into his ribs, his head ached, his eyeballs felt gritty and his mouth tasted like sawdust. Still, despite all that, he realized several things at once.

Most noteworthy was the woman in his bed. Yep, that very shapely slim leg draped over his belly was definitely of the feminine variety, not to mention the small, delicate hand resting over his heart. Ethan looked at that hand, but with his eyes so fried, it didn't look like any particular woman's hand. Just a hand. A female hand.

Yeah, okay, so he was in bed with a woman. No big deal. He'd figure that one out soon enough. Since he wore no shoes and no shirt, only slacks that were unsnapped and unzipped—he knew that because he could feel her warm thigh on his skin—it stood to reason that the female was only half-dressed, too. That could mean several things, but likely only meant one thing.

So what? He was thirty years old, single, free to do as he damn well pleased, never mind that he didn't remember what the hell had pleased him.

With the sun so bright through the window, he realized it had to be midmorning. A quick glance at the clock showed it to be eight-forty. What time had he gotten into bed?

The incessant pounding on his front door, now getting louder, had probably awakened him, not the soft woman clinging to him.

Groaning with the effort, Ethan raised his head off the pillow to look at her. All he could see was a luxurious tangle of silvery-brown hair. She had her nose stuck close to his side, practically in his armpit, and she wore his uniform dress shirt—a shirt that didn't quite cover the satiny peach panties stretched over a very fine ass.

He didn't remember giving her his shirt and he sure as hell didn't remember either of them undressing. He reached for her hair, ready to brush aside the heavy mass so he could at least figure out her identity, when the pounding on his front door started again.

The woman stirred, then stretched awake, arching her body into his, raising her hands high above her head. Ethan stirred, too, despite being horribly hungover and in pain. Whoever was at the door could just damn well wait. He smiled down at the woman, anxious to see her, to have the mystery solved.

She rolled onto her back with a sleepy little moan.

Ethan leaped out of bed so fast his head spun and he nearly dropped to his knees. No. Hell, no.

His shaky legs continued to try to give out on him and his heart shot into his throat, making him dangerously close to barfing. He grabbed the footboard for support, swallowed hard, found his voice and shouted, "*What the hell.* Rosie!"

The smile faded off her face. Very slowly she peeked open one smoky-blue eye and groaned. "Shut up, Ethan. My head is splitting."

He sputtered, heard the continued noise at his front door, and nearly panicked. "Get out of my bed."

The look she sent his way wasn't nice. Rather than

obey, she rolled onto her stomach and nestled into the pillows. "I need coffee."

Unbound, her hair was glorious, but it wasn't long enough to cover her rump. Ethan stared.

Oh, God. What to do? Rosie. *His* Rosie. His long-time friend, a woman he'd grown up with, his ex-best friend's little sister...

Damn she looked good.

No. No she did not. He squeezed his eyes shut to block out the view of her sprawled in his bed, the sight of her plump bottom turned up for him to see, the long length of those legs. He'd seen her legs before, of course. She wore shorts, even the occasional swimsuit. But he hadn't seen her legs in his bed. Not once. Not ever.

Surely he hadn't... Of course he hadn't. Ethan snorted. What a ridiculous thought. Why, if he'd done anything with Rosie, he'd remember it, and besides, he *wouldn't* do anything with Rosie. She was practically like family. Practically. Not quite, but close enough.

Reassured with his own thoughts, he opened his eyes again—but to be safe he didn't look directly at her. "Stay put."

Rosie grunted but otherwise didn't reply.

Ethan slipped out of the bedroom on unsteady legs and pulled the door shut behind him. Whoever loitered at his front door was making a horrid racket and if he woke up all the neighbors, they'd give Ethan fits.

He crossed the living room, jerked the door open and was met with the sight of Riley Moore, Harris Black and Buck Bosworth. Without being invited, they pushed their way in. Ethan cast a quick glance at the hallway, but all was secure. The very last thing he wanted was for the guys to know Rosie had spent the night.

They wouldn't believe that nothing had happened. Hell, *he* wouldn't have believed it. "What do you guys want? As you can see, you've interrupted my beauty sleep."

Harris snickered. "You'd need to hibernate for a whole winter to improve that mug."

Buck shook his head pityingly. "I knew you were crocked last night, but you must have really fried the old gray matter if you don't remember our fishing day."

Fishing. Oh, hell, he didn't want to fish. Ethan held his splitting head and took two deep breaths. "I've gotta pass today. I can barely stay on my feet."

Riley, the most serious of the three, gave an aggrieved sigh. "I told you last night to quit drinking. I told you to give it up and get over it. But, no, you wouldn't. So now you have to pay the consequences. Go get dressed. We're not leaving without you."

Ethan stiffened. He couldn't credit Riley's nerve, bringing up such a touchy subject. They all knew he didn't want to talk about it. "Go to hell. Me, I'm going back to bed." He winced at his own statement. *Rosie was in his bed.*

"Nope." Riley sat and propped his big feet on the cluttered coffee table, knocking a newspaper and a Chinese food container to the floor. "I'm sick of you feeling sorry for yourself. It's been well over a year. Enough already."

Buck and Harris, both silent, both cautious, looked back and forth while following the conversation.

Ethan clenched his teeth. "Drop it, Riley."

"I will when you do."

"It's none of your damn business." Ethan didn't mean to shout, and, in fact, immediately regretted it when his brain throbbed in pain and his stomach pitched. He rubbed his hands over his face, trying to convince himself he could physically throw Riley out without puking, when a feminine voice suddenly intruded.

"They're your friends, Ethan. Of course it's their business."

Oh, God.

Riley's feet hit the floor with a thud. Buck's and Harris's chins almost did the same. Ethan groaned. Through his fingers, he looked at Rosie.

Bless the supreme powers that be, she'd had the foresight to at least wrap herself in a sheet. His shirt covered her upper parts and her lower parts were covered by toga-wrapped linen. Her hair was wild, though, her blue eyes heavy, her cheeks still flushed with sleep.

All three men turned to stare at Ethan. Their expressions ranged from censure to appalled fascination to extreme curiosity.

That was all it took.

"Excuse me a minute, will ya?" Hoping to preserve what little dignity he still possessed, Ethan forced himself to walk to the bathroom, slam the door and lock it. He needed privacy for the next fifteen minutes while he worshiped the porcelain god, praying it was a dream, hoping against hope that when he emerged everyone would be gone—especially Rosie—and his brain could stop pulsing long enough to let him catch his breath.

He was hanging on to the toilet, his head spinning, when he heard footsteps outside the door.

"Ethan?"

He sat back on the cold ceramic-tiled floor and propped himself against the side of the tub, eyes closed.

Breathing was a chore, thinking more so. He did not want to talk. "Go away, Rosie."

He expected a sharp comeback, a refusal. Hell, he half expected her to knock the door down. Through the years he'd known her, Rosie had shown a knack for doing just as she damn well pleased without unnecessary consideration for what anyone else thought. She was headstrong, opinionated, independent—*and she'd been in his bed.*

After a few expectant moments when nothing happened, Ethan tensed with new foreboding. His eyes opened and he stared at the locked door. Rosie hadn't done anything. Had she actually left when he'd asked her to? Or rather, when he'd rudely ordered her to? Had he hurt her feelings?

Had he had sex with her?

His stomach more unsettled than ever, Ethan pushed himself upright and stuck his head out the bathroom door. He didn't hear a single sound. "Riley?"

Ten seconds passed, then, "What?" Riley leaned around the hallway, looked Ethan over, and made a disgusted face.

"Did Rosie leave?"

"She's making breakfast."

"Oh." That figured. If he wasn't so hungover, he'd have remembered that Rosie wasn't a sensitive girly-girl. In fact, she was pretty damn tough…for a female. So of course he hadn't hurt her feelings.

He hadn't slept with her, either.

"It's not what you're thinking," Ethan mumbled to Riley, who continued to look at him as if he was lower than a worm. "Get your mind out of the gutter, will ya?"

Riley crossed his arms over his chest and flattened his mouth. "She said for you to shower and join us."

And Rosie being Rosie, she fully expected to be obeyed. "Yeah, all right."

"She said you have ten minutes."

Annoyed, Ethan slammed the door. He'd take as long as he damn well pleased, and that was that. Hell, the woman didn't own him. Just because she'd awakened in his bed didn't mean she could start thinking about bossing him around.

'Course, she always bossed him around. And most of the time he let her. Though she was four years younger, they'd been friends forever, through high school and college. They'd remained close friends through the death of her parents, through his long engagement.

They'd even stayed friends after her brother had run off with *his* fiancée, leaving him literally stranded at the altar nineteen months ago.

Naked, Ethan stepped beneath a stinging spray of hot water and clenched his teeth against the surge of discomfort that radiated to his limbs. He braced his hands on the tiled wall, dropped his head forward and closed his eyes.

God, if he'd had sex with her, he didn't know if they could remain friends. Rosie was a marrying kind of woman, not a one-night stand. And he would never consider marriage again.

What the hell had he done?

"How MANY EGGS do you guys want?"

"Two."

"Three."

"Rosie," Riley said with a long, exaggerated sigh, "what's going on?"

Rosie Carrington glanced over her shoulder at Riley. He was a big man, so she cracked three eggs for him, same as Harris. "I'm just making breakfast, Riley. No big deal."

"Yeah, right. Just making breakfast—at Ethan's, dressed in his shirt, probably on the proverbial morning after."

"You're too smart to make assumptions, Riley."

Harris and Buck looked at each other, then snorted. Oh, they'd made plenty of assumptions, all right. Not that she blamed them. It was a rather damning situation.

Riley paid them no mind. "Okay, so what are you doing here? Last I saw Ethan at the party, he was flirting with that sexy redhead and you were fuming mad at him for, as you put it, acting like an ass again."

Rosie concentrated on not overcooking the eggs. Last night…well, she had been fuming mad. Come to that, she was still a little peeved. Most of the time Ethan was the best man around, easy to respect, easier to love. He was hardworking, levelheaded, conscientious. A firefighter with a moral code bone-deep. True, he'd become something of a hound dog, but a good-natured one nonetheless.

Yet whenever people brought up his ex-fiancée, he went from being a great guy to a shallow, chauvinistic jerk who grabbed the first available woman. Rosie assumed he did that to prove to everyone that he was over his fiancée, that he'd recovered. The opposite was true. It showed that he was still hurting—and that hurt her.

It had been over a year and a half, for crying out

loud. She'd had enough. It was time to take matters into her own hands.

Rosie knew the men were uncomfortable to have found her here. If all went as she planned, they'd just have to get used to it. Besides, she was now decently covered—sort of—in a ratty old housecoat that she'd located in Ethan's closet.

"You're being evasive, Rosie."

"Gee, Riley, I'm twenty-six years old. I thought that meant I didn't have to answer to anyone for my personal life."

Harris scratched his head, making his black hair more disheveled than ever. "You and Ethan have a personal life?"

She ignored him as she poked a fork at the pound of sizzling bacon in the cast-iron skillet. Four men, all of them big bruisers, needed a lot of food to maintain their energy levels. "You know, I'm amazed you guys planned to go fishing all day without breakfast. It's the most important meal of the day. You shouldn't skip it."

The men smirked at that ludicrous comment. As firefighters, Ethan and Harris kept in the peak of health. Their jobs allowed nothing less. Buck owned a lumberyard and physical labor was part of his daily work week. He had muscles on his muscles.

And Riley—Rosie peered at him again. Riley was an evidence technician for the police department. A former member of the SWAT team, he now owned a self-defense studio where he taught sparring, grappling, Jeet Kune Do and Silat knife fighting.

Next to Ethan, Riley was the most intriguing, appealing man she knew. He could break a person in two without effort. But more often than not, he was as gentle as a lamb—especially where women were concerned.

There wasn't much call for a SWAT team in the small city of Chester, Ohio, thank God, but Riley had only lived here about five years. Before that, he'd evidently suffered some bad times, not that he ever spoke of it much. He tended to be a very quiet man.

Except for now, when he chose to badger Rosie.

"I think we'll all survive fishing on an empty stomach." Riley's voice was dry, teasing.

"Now you won't have to."

Harris leaned forward, sniffing the eggs. "This'll be better than the pork rinds Buck packed."

Buck shoved him in the shoulder. "I'll just eat them all myself then."

"Hey." Harris acted wounded by Buck's selfishness. "You know I was just placating Rosie."

After wrinkling her nose at the lot of them, Rosie began toasting bread. She had half a loaf out and hoped that'd be enough. Ethan wasn't much on domesticity and therefore didn't have an abundance of groceries. His apartment was a pigsty, his kitchen a disaster and his cabinets all but empty.

She glanced at the clock. She'd give the big coward two more minutes tops, then she'd drag him out of the shower whether he wanted to face them all or not. If he was still naked and wet—well, she wouldn't cavil. In fact, the idea appealed to her.

Dragging him out proved unnecessary when not five seconds later Ethan appeared in the doorway. His mellow brown eyes were bloodshot, his blond hair still wet and only finger-combed, his feet bare. He'd pulled on clean jeans and a gray T-shirt, and to Rosie, he looked better than breakfast.

Her heart felt full to bursting. "You okay?"

He sent her a cautious sneer, hooked a chair, yanked it out from the table and dropped heavily into it. "I'll live, if that's what you mean." His mean, red-eyed look moved around the room to encompass each of his friends. "I'm not going fishing today."

"Of course not."

"We understand."

"You're an ass, Ethan."

That last was from Riley, of course. He seemed to love provoking Ethan. Rosie shook her head. They'd all known each other forever—with the exception of Riley who was late to the group, but had quickly become a good friend. They lived to give each other a hard time, so presumably, they were letting Ethan off the hook this time because of her. Since she and Ethan needed to talk, she didn't object.

Without a word, she set a cup of strong black coffee in front of Ethan. He drank half of it, cursed when he burned his tongue, then glared at her. "You're not my housekeeper or my cook."

"With the way you live, you couldn't pay me enough to be, either."

Harris snickered. Buck held his breath.

Riley said, "You are a damn slob. When was the last time you cleaned?"

"What's it to you, Mom?" He drank the rest of the coffee and Rosie silently refilled his cup. He muttered his grudging thanks.

Riley lounged back in his seat. Because his censure

was so obvious, his silence was more annoying than chatter would have been.

Rosie served the men. When she started to take her own seat, Riley stood to pull out her chair. Ethan growled at him, and Riley growled back.

Men. They could be so unaccountably strange. "Dig in, fellas."

The next few minutes were filled with sounds of appreciation as the men practically inhaled the enormous amount of food she'd set on the table.

In all the time she'd known Ethan, she'd seen him drunk twice—this being the second time.

It amazed her that Ethan could eat such a hardy meal after a hangover. Other than his bloodshot eyes and listlessness, you wouldn't know he'd been so miserable just half an hour before.

Harris finished first. "Damn, that was good, Rosie." He patted his flat stomach. "If I come back tonight, will you cook dinner, too?"

Ethan pierced her with a direct stare. Rosie smiled. "Sure, Harris. Come on by my house around six. I planned on making stew today."

His brows shot up. "Really? I mean, I was kidding, but hell, I'm always up for your stew."

Buck pushed back his empty plate. "If that sorry sack is invited, then naturally I'm coming, too."

"I'll make plenty." Rosie loved to hang out with the guys. Because she'd had a tendency to tail her older brother wherever he went, she'd grown very close to the lot of them. She had very few female friends, thus the guys had become the sum total of her social circle.

Riley shook his head. "You're both mooches. But what would one more matter? Count me in."

Ethan's chair scraped back across the floor. He snatched up his empty plate, caused an awful clatter as he roughly stacked the rest of the empty dishes, then moved to the sink. He kept his back to them all as he scraped the plates before nearly throwing them in the dishwasher.

The men looked at each other, shrugged, then prepared to leave. One by one they gave Rosie a hug and a hardy thank-you, with Riley choosing to go last.

He tipped up her chin. "I'll be back by three. You want to come by the gym? Maybe work off some tension?" He gave a meaningful nod of his head toward Ethan's rigid back.

"I suppose that'd be better than killing anyone, huh?"

Riley laughed. "You're getting good, sugar, but not that good. Not yet."

Ethan jerked around. "Just what the hell does that mean?"

Harris and Buck hunkered out, muttering to Riley that they'd meet him in the truck.

Riley crossed his arms over his chest and faced Ethan. "She's taking lessons."

With an expression of incredulous disbelief, Ethan looked from Rosie to Riley and back again. "What kind of lessons would those be?"

His tone was so suspicious that Rosie laughed. "Self-defense, mixed with some knife fighting." She took a stance and chopped the air with a fist. "I'm going to be lethal."

Rather than appeased, Ethan appeared more livid. "What the hell are you doing that for? Has someone been bothering you?"

She resisted the urge to say *you* and shook her head.

"I just like staying in shape and knowing I can take care of myself. I'm single, remember?"

Ethan's face turned red and he strangled on his reply.

Pulling the tiger's tail, Riley said, "Don't worry, Ethan. I'm real gentle with her."

Rosie thought Ethan's eyes might cross. Instead he fumed in silence for nearly a full thirty seconds before stalking out of the room.

"Oh, boy," Riley rumbled under his breath. He gestured for Rosie to precede him as he headed to the front door. Ethan waited for them there, holding it open, his impatience to be alone with Rosie plain.

Riley walked out into the hallway. "Be good, kids."

"You know I'm always good. But I can't make any promises for Ethan."

He winked at her. "You'll keep him in line."

Ethan snapped the door shut, then turned both locks with a dreadful sense of finality. When he faced Rosie, she decided a strategic retreat was in order; he did not look like a happy man.

In fact, he looked very unhappy. Or maybe "riled" was the word. Yeah, he looked downright riled. She supposed Riley's teasing flirtation hadn't helped matters.

Ethan was used to Harris and Buck razzing her. After all, they'd all grown up in the same neighborhood. The three of them had been best buds with her brother— until her brother had slipped off with Ethan's fiancée.

Riley was new to the mix, and while they all liked him a lot, Ethan apparently didn't take Riley's teasing the same at all.

She'd made it all the way to the bathroom when Ethan caught her arm. "Rosie."

There was so much warning in the way he said her name, she kept her back to him. "Hmm?"

His sigh parted the back of her hair. "Don't play games." He caught both arms and turned her around. "What were you doing here this morning in my bed?"

"Sleeping?"

His jaw worked, his eyes narrowed. Reaching inside the neckline of the housecoat, Ethan fingered the collar of his shirt. His gaze settled on her mouth. "Why aren't you wearing your own clothes?"

Very slowly, realization dawned on Rosie. "Oh, my God. You don't remember, do you?"

An arrested expression crossed his features. His pupils expanded until only a thin ring of light brown remained. His straight, dark brows pulled together. "Just what am I supposed to remember?"

Indignation reared up, followed by humiliation. "Ethan Winters. You have no idea what happened last night, do you?"

He blustered with his own dose of exasperation. "I know damn good and well we didn't have sex."

Rosie gasped, not because he was wrong, but because he was so sure that he hadn't touched her. What was she? Chopped liver? She felt just contrary enough not to reassure him. "Yeah, and how do you know that if you don't remember?"

Muscles tensed, Ethan let his smoldering gaze take a leisurely trip over her—but he only got as far as her breasts. "You were wearing a shirt. And panties. When I have sex with a woman—" his gaze rose and locked on hers "—she's buck naked. Not half-dressed."

Rosie dropped back against the wall with a thud. Her heart had started bouncing around with his first hot look, and his words had nearly brought her to her knees. Oh, she could only imagine what Ethan did when he had sex, but she believed him: the woman wouldn't be wearing clothes.

She cleared her throat, then had to clear it again when he flattened both hands to the wall on either side of her head. At five-nine she was a tall woman, but Ethan stood six-two and towered over her. He leaned in the smallest bit, probably trying to intimidate her—and doing a good job of it, but not for the reasons that he might assume. She wasn't afraid of Ethan and she never would be.

But she was extremely aware of him as a man.

She stared at his sternum and gave an irrefutable reminder. "You were drunk. You couldn't have gotten your own clothes off, much less mine."

Ethan considered that, then smiled. "True. And being that drunk, I doubt I could have gotten a boner no matter what you did."

With another gasp, Rosie shoved him hard—with no visible effect. "I didn't do anything."

"You must have taken off your clothes, because as you just said, I was too damn drunk to accomplish it on my own."

Her eyes narrowed. "Not too drunk to flirt with that redhead."

He stared past her shoulder. After a second, his eyes lightened and the right side of his mouth kicked up. "Yeah, I remember her now. Where'd she go?"

Oh, that was one nasty little shot too many. Rosie stomped on his toes. Given that she was as barefoot as he was, it wasn't an overly painful move. But he did jerk back, giving her a chance to duck under his arm.

She stormed into the bathroom and slammed the door. Hard. She took a lot of satisfaction in clicking the lock into place.

Ethan didn't beat on the door. He just said, "You have to come out sooner or later."

She felt like beating on the door. Or on his head. Instead she took two deep breaths to gather her calm. "My clothes are in your laundry room. Your precious redhead dumped her drink on me, so until you run them through the wash, I can't wear them again. I'd smell like a lush."

Silence stretched until Ethan finally said, "Oh."

"Yes, oh." Inside the bathroom, Rosie stripped off the housecoat and his shirt. "Why don't you throw them in the washer while I shower?"

"Sure thing."

She could hear him whistling as he walked away, secure in the knowledge that nothing of a sexual nature had occurred between them.

But he didn't know that for sure, and no way would she tell him. Let him stew. Let him wonder.

And maybe, just maybe, he'd think about it enough that he'd start to like the idea.

Rosie grinned as she stepped into the shower. She had a plan, and oh, boy, it was going to be fun.

CHAPTER TWO

SHE WALKED INTO the kitchen with his toothbrush sticking out of her mouth.

In the process of shaking out a large plastic garbage bag, Ethan froze. Rosie's hair was still wet, pushed straight back from her forehead and hanging in long twisted ropes down her back. Over *his* housecoat.

Which was now the only thing she wore.

Ethan knew that because she leaned into the laundry room and pitched his shirt onto the pile of dirty clothes, then turned and stuck her folded panties into her purse, which was on the counter. With foamy toothpaste dripping down her chin, she headed back for the bathroom.

It took Ethan a moment to get his eyelids to work so he could blink. When he did, he couldn't help but notice that her behind, without benefit of underwear, jiggled just a little more beneath the terry-cloth robe. He jerked around, grumbling and too warm and feeling somewhat hunted. "Damn irritant." He shoved an old pizza box into the garbage bag.

Five minutes later Rosie emerged again. She gave him a big toothy smile and said, "I used your toothbrush."

"Yeah, I noticed." He would not keep staring at her.

"You don't mind, do you?"

He started to say, *Of course not;* after all, they'd

been friends a long time, shared drinks, once even an ice-cream cone. He wasn't worried about her germs.

But she didn't give him a chance. "I figured after last night, it wouldn't be any big deal."

Ethan went rigid. "Nothing happened last night."

"Did you put my stuff in the wash?" Apparently unconcerned with his emotional turmoil, Rosie pushed in a kitchen chair, closed a cabinet.

Shaking his head to clear it, Ethan said, "Yeah, they should be ready for the dryer in about ten more minutes." He continued to stuff empty food containers and soup cans, plastic cups, newspapers and junk mail into the bag. He shouldn't have felt so awkward with Rosie. He never had before—but then, he'd never slept with her before, either.

He glared when he realized that she intended to help him clean. Not only that, but she'd accomplished more in two minutes than he had in ten. Women, he decided, just had a knack for being efficient with housework.

"Leave that stuff. I'll get it." He glanced around at the remaining mess and for some stupid reason, felt compelled to explain. "I've been on a night shift all week. Had two nasty calls, one right before the banquet. Had to use the Jaws of Life on a guy who got caught in his car. Damn thing was on fire…" At her look of horror, his voice trailed off. He shook his head. "I got behind on stuff, but I planned to clean today anyway, since I have the next four days off."

"You're okay?"

Damn it, she didn't have to sound so anxious. She was a friend, not his keeper, not his sibling, not his wife. "I'm fine."

For a long moment she didn't look convinced, then

she shrugged. "I don't mind helping." She wrung out a dishrag and wiped off the stove. "I've got nothing else to do until my clothes are done, then I have to head into the office. I have a house to show today."

As a real estate agent, her hours varied.

"I don't want you to help."

She blinked up at him with fresh-faced provocation. "Why?"

Damn, she looked cute straight from the shower. Rosie had never, in his opinion, needed much makeup. Her skin was fair, framed by silky brown hair that didn't contain a single hint of red. Her brows were dark, finely arched, her lashes long. Though her eyes were blue, they weren't an ordinary blue. They looked softer than ordinary blue, sort of smoky and smoldering, and when she got annoyed or excited, they turned stormy gray.

Would they turn gray when she was sexually aroused?

Ethan's scowl intensified. "Women always think they have certain rights after cleaning a guy's place."

"Wow, no kidding?" Her brows rose higher. "That's like…really profound. Your grasp on womankind is nothing short of astounding."

She was baiting him, maybe even poking fun at him. "My grasp is astute enough to know you can't be trusted, that you wait for a reason to screw a guy over or to confuse him so that he screws himself over or—"

Rosie stuck her fingers in her ears and said, "La, la, la, lalalal—"

"Stop that!"

She struck an arrogant, annoyed pose, her hands on her hips. "Then stop spouting nonsense."

Ethan shook his head at the gesture, until he realized

that her stance made the robe gap just a little above and below the belt. It showed a length of her legs—which he'd seen a gazillion times, for crying out loud—and her cleavage, which he knew she had but he *hadn't* seen much before now.

Everything male within him went on alert, and he mumbled, "It is not nonsense."

"Are you talking to me or my boobs?"

Flabbergasted, Ethan jerked his gaze up to her face, saw her smile and wanted to shout with frustration. Ruthlessly he beat his male instincts into submission. "You."

"Huh. And here I was certain my ears were on my head, not my chest."

In a ridiculous show of temper, he threw the garbage bag down on the floor. "Damn it, Rosie, what is wrong with you? What are you up to?"

She shrugged, then groaned dramatically. "I need some aspirin."

Dismissing him, she turned to the cabinet and began riffling around until Ethan said, "Here, I keep them over the stove." He shook out two white pills and handed them to her. A new thought occurred to him. "You hungover, too?"

She lifted the aspirin off his palm, tossed them into her mouth and bent her head into the sink to grab a drink of water straight from the tap. When she'd finished, she shook her head. "No, of course not."

He hadn't thought so. Rosie was never much of a drinker. Come to that, he wasn't, either, and he was thoroughly disgusted with himself for overindulging last night. "If you're not suffering from too much drink, then what's your problem?"

"I just have a headache from lack of sleep, actually." She sent him a calculated look. "We didn't get to bed till late."

His chest constricted. Why hadn't she gotten enough sleep? She'd been dead-out when he'd awakened.

The washer buzzed and Rosie stepped into the small laundry room off the kitchen to put her clothes in the dryer, giving Ethan a moment to think.

There had to be any number of reasons why she'd been in his bed, other than the most distressing one. Why she didn't want to tell him, he couldn't say. Sometimes Rosie could be difficult for no apparent reason.

But he'd get the truth out of her, one way or another.

"Hey, Ethan?"

He stayed in the kitchen, unwilling to test his resolve by getting near her again. "Yeah?"

"Did you mean that I couldn't be trusted, or women in general?"

Oh, hell, he didn't want to have this discussion with her. He jammed a carton of sour milk into the bag with more force than was necessary. Just getting the garbage off the countertops and off the floor made his place look much cleaner. Normally it didn't get so bad, but on top of the lousy week, he'd really been dreading the party last night. For days, cleaning had been the last thing on his mind.

"Is this a tough question, Ethan?"

Knowing she wouldn't let it go, he gave her the truth. "I meant all women."

"Really?" The silence was telling. "Including me?" She strolled back in, her eyes a flat gray—not a good sign.

"Rosie, let's drop this, okay?" Ethan could already

tell she was up for an argument. He wasn't. He needed to know that he hadn't… touched her. And then he needed more sleep.

"No, it's not okay." She crossed her arms under her breasts. "You've insulted me."

He stared at the ceiling so he wouldn't be tempted to look at her breasts again. "How about if I just apologize?"

"Not if you aren't sincere." She sighed, sounding a little defeated. "You know, I fully intended to tell you everything."

Everything? He gave up his study of the ceiling and met her gaze. "What the hell does that mean?"

"You know." She flapped a hand. "Why I'm here, what I want, stuff like that."

What she wanted? Ethan tied the bag shut and set it aside. If she kept this up, his head would explode. "Okay, let's get this over with. What do you want?"

Her mischievous smile came slowly, accompanied by a twinkle in her eyes. "Oh, you'd like to rush me through this, wouldn't you? But why? You weren't in a rush last night."

He reached for her and she ducked away, laughing. "I still can't believe you forgot everything from last night."

Two deep breaths didn't help Ethan to contain his temper. "There wasn't much to forget, now was there?"

"There was enough."

His jaw ached from clenching his teeth. "If that's true, then you took advantage of my drunken state—which proves what I said. Women can't be trusted."

"Some women, maybe."

"Like a woman who sleeps with a guy she knows is drunk?"

She winced, pretending to be wounded, but her grin told the real story. "Okay, let's back up. When you spout all that baloney about women not being trustworthy, you make yourself look really pathetic."

"Is that right?"

"Yep. It shows that Michelle really did a number on you and that you let her."

Oh, no, no way. He didn't want to talk about Michelle. He didn't even want to hear Michelle's name. Not now, not ever. "Be smart, Rosie, and keep her out of this."

Of course she didn't listen to him. She wouldn't be Rosie if she did. "Why? That's what this is really all about, isn't it? You got jilted and you've been playing the wounded swain ever since."

"It's none of your business. You're a friend, not my mother, not my confessor."

"Damn right I'm your friend."

She put her hands on her hips again, but this time Ethan was too annoyed to admire her cleavage. Rosie's anger struck him in waves and left him a little awed. He'd only witnessed her fierce temper a handful of times.

"I've had enough of you dragging around with your tail between your legs."

"I don't."

"Don't growl at me, Ethan Winters. What would you call it? You date every single girl within a three-hundred-mile radius—but only once. You make cracks about women all the time—and in case you've failed to notice, I'm a woman."

"I noticed."

That shut her up, even left her bemused, but only for

a moment. Her chin lifted. "Yeah, well, when you be-little half of humanity—"

"The female half. And I don't belittle them, I just look at them realistically. I see them for how they are."

She rolled her eyes. "You make yourself look defensive." Her expression softened. "You make yourself look…well, lovesick."

The humiliation of being jilted in front of half the town and all his friends and family would be burned on his brain for the rest of his life. It wasn't the sort of thing that a man just got over.

It wasn't the sort of thing that Ethan would ever forget.

Rosie took a step closer to him. "Getting drunk and picking up strange women is certainly not the behavior of a hero, a role model for the community."

Because he didn't like the way she looked at him, and he especially didn't like the topic, Ethan backed up. "Screw that. I never asked to be called a hero."

In fact, part of the reason he'd started drinking last night was the ceremony honoring him. It had been every bit as bad as he'd imagined. He'd felt ridiculous, the center of attention for the first time since the wedding. And he'd felt undeserving.

"Ethan." Rosie's tone chastised as she continued to advance, nearly backing him into the pantry. "You're a firefighter and that's heroic enough. But you risked your life to save those people."

He sidestepped away from the pantry and found himself in a corner, next to the stove. "I did what any guy would have done, especially a firefighter. I did my job. That's all there is to it."

"In near-zero visibility? Knowing that the house could have collapsed at any moment?"

Ethan dropped his head back against the wall and stared at the ceiling. Three weeks ago when he'd entered the flaming residence, he hadn't had heroism on his mind. Through the crackle of burning wood and shattering glass, he'd heard people calling, pleading for help. Their voices had been raw from the thick smoke, desperate. Weak. Ethan had simply reacted.

He'd done what he was trained to do.

It hadn't been easy to carry the man out while dragging the teenage son. Everything was ablaze, the smoke so dense he couldn't see his hand in front of his face. He'd made his way through, inch by inch, but he'd managed, and they'd all lived. He was grateful for that—and embarrassed that so much hoopla had been made about it. He didn't ever again want to find himself as the focus of a crowd; it always reminded him of that awful wedding day when he'd been left standing alone at the altar.

Yet there he'd been last night, at the damn ceremony, being applauded by the very people who'd looked at him with pity the night his bride had failed to show. He'd been dressed up then, too, and he'd felt just as numb.

The memories assailed him, churning through his blood, ringing in his ears. He breathed hard, nearly panting, but it didn't help.

God, he was going to puke again.

Rosie touched his chest, gently stroking his right pectoral muscle. Her fingertips grazed his nipple.

It so startled him, the awful memories faded beneath a new emotion. He felt his body stir with sexual awareness.

"I was so proud of you, Ethan, when they gave you

the Fire Commission's Valor Award. But then I'm always proud of you. You risk your life all the time without a second thought. You do what most men won't do—to help others. You're always so tall and commanding and direct. And last night you looked so incredibly handsome in your dress uniform."

Trying to ignore his unwanted arousal, Ethan focused on her soothing voice and eventually on the familiar features of her face. Rosie smiled at him and rested her palm over his heart.

"You know, you owe it to yourself for the person you are, and to the community for the person they see you as, to stop being a self-pitying jerk."

He lurched at the shock of her words, such a contrast to the mood she'd created. Rosie poked him in the chest. Her voice was no longer quite so soothing. "I understand how you feel, Ethan—"

"You can't have a clue."

That seemed to make her angrier. "You're obviously, *rightfully,* embarrassed that Michelle jilted you."

"In front of two hundred people." He hadn't meant to shout, not that it fazed Rosie at all. No, if anything, she stepped closer until he felt her legs against his.

She tilted her head way back so she could stare him in the eyes. "When you carry on the way you do, it looks like you're still pining over her."

Ethan snorted. Personally, he thought just the opposite to be true. People saw him with different women, saw him enjoying his bachelor life, and it proved that he was over Michelle, that he didn't care.

That she hadn't ripped his heart out.

Leaning closer still, until her nose nearly touched

his chin, Rosie said, "But I know you're not lovesick, Ethan. I know, because you *didn't* love her."

Ethan grabbed her shoulders to keep her from getting any closer. He would have moved away from her, but she had him boxed in. That thought almost made him smile. He weighed a smidgen off two hundred pounds, and Rosie couldn't possibly go over one-thirty, yet she did her best to intimidate him with her body.

Her best was pretty damn tantalizing, he admitted, when he felt her soft belly against his crotch.

All humor vanished.

She stared up at him, her eyes the color of an approaching storm. "You want people to know you're over Michelle, that she didn't really affect you? Well, I have a better suggestion than what you've been doing."

Ethan could barely breathe. Her mouth was right there, so close he could smell the toothpaste she'd just used and damn, it looked good. He wanted her, whether he denied it or not, whether he wanted to or not. Unable to move, he growled, "What suggestion?"

"Get involved with a nice girl." Her gaze dropped to his mouth and her voice lowered, went husky in a way he'd never heard from Rosie before. "Quit playing the sexist Neanderthal and get serious again. Stop running scared."

"I'm not—"

She touched his bottom lip, stealing his thoughts, making him tense. She whispered, "Let me love you."

ETHAN KEPT TO THE SHADOWS of the large elms that lined the street, skirting buildings while trying not to look too furtive. He wanted to see her without being seen himself.

He couldn't believe he was doing this.

Actually, everything he'd done in the past twenty-four hours fell into the realm of the "not to be believed," starting with getting rip-roaring drunk, and ending with Rosie in his bed. So what did one more idiotic thing matter?

It didn't. Besides, his curiosity was too keen to keep him away. Luckily, Riley's studio had an enormous front window, so he'd be able to see what kind of lessons Rosie was taking without her knowing he spied.

He could only imagine what she'd think if she knew. The silly goose already thought herself in love with him. If she thought, even for a second, that he returned that overly valued emotion…

Ethan grunted, but deep inside himself something warm had started stirring the moment she'd said those four little taunting words. *Let me love you.*

He knew it was only lust. And no wonder with the way she'd been coming on to him. An ordinary woman he could have withstood, but Rosie…he hadn't wanted to chance it.

Nearly panicked, he'd sent her on her way with the explanation that he loved her, too—as a friend, and only a friend.

He'd looked her right in her beautiful blue eyes and lied through his teeth, telling her he didn't want her sexually, that he saw her as asexual, like a pal. Totally sexless. No sex thoughts involved at all. Sex, no. Friends, yes.

Rosie was not stupid.

She'd sighed, patted his chest in a curiously tender way and told him she'd give him a little time to get used to the idea.

He had a week.

Then she'd dressed and left and he *still* didn't know what the hell had happened last night in his bed. He'd be deranged with curiosity in a week. He had to find out something soon.

The sun was bright, baking down on his head and back. July had started on a heat wave that showed no signs of relenting. Shimmering hot waves rose from the blacktop parking lot. Ethan wore his aviator-style mirrored sunglasses, but still he had to hold a hand up to shield his eyes when he reached Riley's.

There were few people out on this sweltering afternoon, so he stood alone on the sidewalk with only the occasional passerby. Still, he maintained a casual air of indifference so he wouldn't look suspicious. The second he peeked inside, he spotted Riley rolling around in the middle of the mat with someone. It took Ethan less than three seconds to realize the person in the baggy T-shirt, snug shorts, sneakers and headgear was Rosie.

Calm control took a flying leap.

In three long strides Ethan had the door open and had advanced halfway across the gym. He ripped off his sunglasses to better see their shameful behavior. "What in the hell are you doing?" The rafters trembled with his bellow.

Riley, his head stuck between Rosie's thighs, looked up in surprise. His voice was a bit strangled, due to the way she had her legs clenched tight around his neck, when he said, "It's called the North South Position."

He grunted, did a quick flip and ended up on top with Rosie peering at Ethan, her face red with exertion, her head now between Riley's thighs.

Ethan gawked and fought the urge to bodily separate them. "That's...that's *obscene*."

Rosie tried to buck Riley off—and that only made matters worse from Ethan's perspective. His vision started to blur.

"I'm learning...leg...chokes," Rosie managed to gasp around her panting breaths. To Ethan, it appeared her eyes were starting to water.

He was more than ready to intervene when they rolled again and Ethan had to jump to keep from getting caught in the fast-churning tangle of arms and legs. When they stopped, Rosie was on top and she had Riley's arm caught in an awkward position, using her whole body to keep a steady pressure on it. Riley, around his strained laughter, cried uncle.

Rosie jumped up, punched a fist in the air like a world conqueror, and gave a ferocious battle cry. "Ha! Gotcha with a chicken wing."

Riley stood, too, grinning from ear to ear, but he shook his head at her. "You hadn't sunk it good enough. I could have gotten loose if Ethan hadn't been standing here breathing fire."

Rosie gasped in high indignation. "That's just like a man to claim he lost to a woman only because of *another* man."

Riley slipped his arm around her. "We'll keep working on it." He winked at Ethan.

At that particular moment Rosie wasn't the least attractive. Her hair stuck out in crazy clumps around the headgear, some long tangled tendrils loose, some looped in and around the straps. Her face was flushed and there was sweat on her forehead and upper lip. The wrinkled, sweat-dampened clothes she wore couldn't have been less appealing.

And Ethan wanted to throw her over his shoulder, smack her behind soundly, and remind her in no uncertain terms that she'd not only professed her love, but she'd given him a week to get used to it.

Instead, trying to hide his disgruntlement, he said to both of them, "If anyone taped your *lessons,* they could sell them for porn videos."

Cocking one shapely hip and giving him a siren's come-and-get-it smile, Rosie quipped, "Gee, honey, ya really think so?"

The pose should have been ludicrous given her present appearance. Instead, Ethan choked on a surge of lust.

Laughing, Rosie turned and sashayed her way out of the gym, heading for the showers. "Be right back."

The second she disappeared from sight, Riley dropped against the wall and grabbed his shoulder with a loud groan. "Man, she about tore my rotator cuff. She's good."

Ethan stared at him. His eyes narrowed the tiniest bit.

Doing a double take, Riley asked, "What?"

Ethan stared some more, no civil words coming to his mind or mouth.

"Oh, come on, Ethan." Riley pushed his sweaty hair back and grunted. "I'm teaching her to defend herself with legitimate defensive and offensive moves. As a real estate agent, you know she finds herself with male clients in empty houses a lot."

"Well, I hope if a guy attacks her, she doesn't stick her face in his crotch. I seriously doubt that'll deter him."

Riley tried and failed to stifle his laugh. "She's learning different ways to utilize the chicken wing—and as I said, she's getting good at that. She's also learning some good leg chokes. Usually, a woman who is attacked finds herself on her back with the assailant on top. I'm teaching her how to get out of that hold."

It made sense. God knew, Ethan wanted her safe, but still...

"I'm also teaching her the Guard, the High Crotch Series and some Silat knife moves."

"What's the...never mind. I don't want to know." By silent agreement they moved off the mats and to a bench lining one wall. Ethan plopped down, stretched out his legs, dropped his head back against the cool wall and sighed. "Damn, I'm beat."

Totally deadpan, Riley asked, "Long night?"

But Ethan was actually glad that he'd brought up the subject. Slowly, he swiveled his head toward Riley and opened his eyes. "Did Rosie tell you anything?"

"She's not one to kiss and tell."

"I didn't kiss her."

"No? Well, whatever you did, she wouldn't be talking about it. I've never once heard her mention a date or what she might have done on a date, have you?" Rather than wait for a reply, Riley continued. "And you know, now that I'm thinking about it, that's strange, huh?"

Ethan knew he'd rather walk into another burning building than think about Rosie with other men. It never failed to set him on edge. "We didn't have a damn date, and I didn't kiss her."

Rosie reappeared, and Ethan thought she had to have taken the fastest shower in history. Then he realized she hadn't changed, had only removed the headgear and combed her hair.

She was still sweaty.

"You," she said, pointing at Ethan, "don't know what you did."

He snared her gaze with his own and wouldn't let her look away. "So tell me, Rosie. Did I kiss you?"

Her cheeks turned pink and she shrugged. "Maybe I don't remember, either."

Ethan slowly stood to approach her. "Oh, if I'd kissed you, Rosie, believe me, you'd remember."

She squared off, facing him like a prizefighter with her hands on her hips, legs braced. "Yeah? And why's that?"

He jutted his chin forward to match her stance. "Because I'm a damn good kisser."

"Maybe."

"It's true." He reached back to nudge Riley with a fist. "Ask Riley, he knows."

Riley almost fell off the bench. "What are you talking about?" His voice rose to a shout when Riley almost never shouted. "I sure as hell haven't kissed you!"

"Excuse me?"

They all turned toward the front door, and there stood the redhead from the night before. Her glorious hair—Ethan did love the color—was piled on top of her head in loose, very feminine disarray. She wore a pale green, knee-length skirt with a crisp white blouse and very high heels. An enormous satchel was hooked over her arm.

Great, Ethan thought, just great. He needed this like he needed a four-alarm fire.

Much provoked, Riley stood and immediately shouted, "I have never kissed Ethan, swear to God."

Rosie moved with the speed of light to position herself in front of Ethan.

Ethan started to laugh. He couldn't help himself. He was still a little hungover, still very confused by Rosie's recent offer, and horny as hell to boot. Could his life get more muddled?

"It's true," he confirmed. "Riley is as macho as they come. Hell, he's so macho he has hair on the soles of his feet."

"I do not." Riley turned to glare at him. "And don't help me, all right?"

Biting back his smile, Ethan said, "By the way, Riley, I was talking about those twins who wanted to double date, remember? The one told you I was a great kisser and she wanted to test you out to see who was better?"

Riley's frown lifted, a smile started and he said, "Oh, yeah."

The redhead looked beyond confused, on the verge of bolting. Her apparent nervousness kept her shifting her feet and twisting her hands. "Are you open?"

Obviously dismissing Ethan and his memories of the twins, Riley looked her over, crossed his arms and said, "I could be."

Clutching her satchel, Red said, "I need to learn some self-defense."

Riley cocked a brow at that, Rosie scowled and Ethan felt mired in guilt. "Good God, I didn't assault you, did I?" He never should have gotten drunk. He never should have...

"No, of course not." Her green-eyed gaze darted to

Rosie, to Ethan and back to Riley. Her slim brows puckered in a suspicious frown. "Am I interrupting?"

"We were just about to leave." Rosie took Ethan's arm and tried to drag him behind her.

He planted his feet and refused to budge. "If I bothered you last night, I am sorry. I don't usually drink like that."

Red's smile was distracted when she forced herself to look away from Riley. "You were fine," she assured him. "Mostly you just talked about a woman."

Ethan groaned. He felt moronic enough already, but, God, if he'd been waxing poetic about Michelle, he'd have to leave town.

Rosie elbowed him hard to show her displeasure. He grunted, caught her lethal pointy little elbow so she couldn't inflict more damage to his ribs and said to Red, "Again, I'm very sorry. You should have shoved me under a table or something."

"I didn't mind." Red's expression softened. A small smile teased her mouth. "Actually, I thought it was rather sweet that you're so obviously in love with her."

Ethan stiffened, embarrassed and outraged. "I am *not* in love with Michelle."

"Michelle?" Red frowned and again looked around at each person in the room before settling back on Ethan. "But…I thought her name was Rosie?"

CHAPTER THREE

ROSIE DID HER BEST to hide her grin as she turned off the Crock-Pot and dished up heaping bowls of thick stew. She'd gotten home half an hour ago, quickly showered, then changed into cutoffs and a T-shirt. She'd barely finished before they'd arrived.

All of them.

She sneaked a peek at Ethan and felt her heart patter in excitement. He sat at her small round dinner table, behaving like a surly badger, but at least he'd shown up.

He hadn't wanted to. He'd even refused—until Riley suggested to Rosie that they could do a little more practice after they'd eaten. Ethan had immediately changed his mind about dinner, and Rosie was starting to hope that jealousy motivated him.

Just as she finished serving the stew, the bread machine dinged and she carefully removed the hot loaf to a cutting board. The men were all sniffing the air impatiently. Harris even smacked his lips together, making her laugh.

"Ethan, will you pour everyone something to drink? And get the butter out of the refrigerator."

He grumbled an incoherent reply, then fetched a tea pitcher and began filling glasses.

Riley took a long drink and said, "Did you know

that Red is a reporter? She was there last night to do a story on Ethan."

Ethan froze with the pitcher poised over Buck's glass. "Oh, shit."

Rosie dropped the large carving knife, almost removing her big toe.

"Hey, be careful there." Riley frowned at her.

She snatched up the knife and rinsed it in the sink. "A reporter? You've got to be kidding."

"Nah, but she's different from a lot of them. She's real sweet. She said she realized Ethan was drunk, so she's going to contact him for another interview."

Buck nudged Ethan to get him to pour the tea, then peered at Riley. "You like her?"

"Yeah, sure. She's a jumpy little thing, and her imagination is a bit much."

Rosie hated the idea of the woman being alone with Ethan. She wouldn't tolerate it, not since she already knew Ethan found her attractive. When she interviewed Ethan, it would have to be with Rosie present to protect his virtue. "What's wrong with her imagination?"

"She has some goofy notion that people are out to get her. She's a little paranoid, if you ask me."

Harris began buttering a thick slab of bread. "What's her real name?"

Grinning, Riley said, "Get this. It's Regina Foxworth." He laughed. "And she is foxy, but 'Red' suits her better than Regina."

Harris and Buck stared at Riley in complete and total bafflement. It was the very first time they'd ever heard him make such a comment concerning a woman.

Rosie couldn't help but grin. Well, well, well. It would gratify her immensely if Riley staked a claim.

More than anything else, that would ensure that Ethan stayed free of the woman's clutches.

Ethan reseated himself at the table. "Hell, I don't want to be interviewed. Not by her, not by anyone. I had enough of that crap back when the fire first happened."

"It's good for the department." Harris pointed a spoon at him. "Captain is hoping you'll get us new funding."

"The captain can damn well—"

"If you don't willingly meet with her," Riley interjected, "she said she'd be forced to use what information she got at the ceremony last night."

Rosie made a disgusted face. "And that would be what? That Ethan can't hold his liquor?"

"Probably something like that."

Ethan ignored them to dig into his stew. "Mmm. Terrific, Rosie. Thanks."

The others followed suit, showering her with compliments. She thanked them, took a breath, then forged on manfully. "You know, you could all eat home-cooked meals more often if you'd just settle down."

Harris had his mouth full but he still managed to sputter, "I'm plenty settled."

Buck had the good grace to first swallow. Loudly. "No time. The lumberyard is a demanding mistress."

Harris laughed and thwacked him on the back for that quip.

Riley shrugged. "Maybe someday. But not yet."

Ethan remained conspicuously silent.

"You could all start with a nice house. I see terrific deals all the time." She tried not to stare at Ethan. "There's a nice tight ranch not far from where you already live, Riley. One hundred percent financing. New windows, new furnace."

Ethan stood. "Mind if I get some more stew?"

Deflated, Rosie waved at him. "Go ahead. Help yourself."

For fear of not getting seconds, the other guys jumped up and got in line for the Crock-Pot. Rosie tapped her fingertips on the tabletop. They were all so stubborn.

"I'd waive my fee, you know."

Riley patted her head on his way back to his seat, his bowl almost overflowing. "Course you would, hon. It's not that. I just don't think any of us are anxious to get into the home-and-hearth routine."

Squaring her shoulders, Rosie twisted in her seat and faced Ethan. "You used to be. Don't you remember when you were wanting kids and a dog and a house with a picket fence?"

A heavy silence fell around them. Other than a quick look in her direction, Ethan paid her little mind. "It'd be hard to forget, but that was a long time ago."

"Nineteen months. Not all that long."

He pierced her with a lethal look. "Long enough."

Riley cleared his throat and attempted to help Rosie by changing the subject. "So, Ethan, you gonna meet up with Red? You know how reporters are. It's easier not to fight them."

"Yeah, what the hell. I'll talk with her."

"She's probably left a message on your machine by now. Let us know how it goes."

"You know," Ethan said, gesturing with a piece of bread, "a good reporter would be covering something more important, like the damn fireworks. The Fourth is next weekend and I don't know about the rest of you, but I'm dreading it already."

Harris lifted his glass of tea in a toast. "Count me in on that. Every year someone sets a fire or gets burned. Why is it the majority of people who want to play with the damn things are idiots?"

"Are you expecting trouble?" Rosie asked.

"Every year." Arms folded on the table, Ethan glared down at his half-empty bowl. "And with the new bill just passed, a lot of the pyrotechnics we hate most are now legal for adults to use. Only adults aren't the only ones getting their hands on them."

"Firecrackers, Roman candles, bottle rockets." Harris leaned back in his seat. "Did you know about twelve thousand people get sent to emergency rooms every Fourth of July? Over fifty percent of them are kids, and ten percent are permanently injured. It sickens me."

"And," Ethan added, "we have a fireworks dealer in town who's known to be a little less than reputable. I'd love to shut him down, but for now, all we can do is keep an eye on him."

Since Rosie had never heard Harris speak so... passionately on a topic, she was enthralled—and unaccountably worried. By the nature of their work as firefighters, Ethan and Harris faced various levels of danger daily. She'd tried to get used to that, especially since Ethan always seemed determined to be the first man in, the last man out, and the quickest to volunteer. He might not want to admit it, but he had hero tendencies that were as plain as his hair and eye color, there for all the world to see.

But this sounded more lethal than the usual day-today stuff, and she couldn't quite keep the worry from her tone. "Will it be dangerous for you two?"

Ethan scowled over her concern, even as he shook his head. "No, but seeing a kid burned is about the most awful thing in the world."

"I know it's something I'll never get used to," Harris conceded.

Looking thoughtful, Riley said, "Maybe Red can help. She could at least get some of the facts in the paper, right?"

Buck slanted him a look. "Just how well did you get to know her this afternoon?"

Riley shrugged. "We talked about an hour. I told her what the lessons would cost, how often she should come in—stuff like that. She wanted a starter lesson today so we spent another hour on that." He stretched. "I worked up quite an appetite, I can tell you."

"Hell," Ethan muttered, "if you showed her the same stuff you were doing with Rosie, the two of you might be having kids soon."

Riley laughed out loud at that, and Rosie blushed.

"We've seen." Harris grinned at her, and his blue eyes were glittering with mischief. "Wanna wrestle, Rosie?"

"No." She stood and collected bowls, hoping no one noticed her heightened color. "Anyone want ice cream for dessert?"

Buck and Harris both cackled at the way she tried to change the subject.

Ethan wouldn't let it go. "What do you mean, you've seen? You two have been down there watching?"

Buck nodded. "Hell of a show." He and Harris clicked glasses.

Flustered, Rosie smacked them both in the back of the head. "Now you two just quit it. And you, Ethan. You're making a big deal out of nothing. Why, Riley's the one teaching me the moves and he doesn't laugh about it."

She glanced up in time to see Riley wipe the grin off his face. "All right, that's it. Forget dessert. You can all go home now."

Immediate apologies followed, along with a lot of schmoozing hugs and entreaties. Rosie could barely catch her breath, they were all talking so fast and squeezing her so much.

"Enough already! All right, you can stay." Her eyes narrowed. "But no more razzing on my lessons. Understood?"

After they'd all dutifully nodded, Ethan stood. "I'll get the ice cream. One of you lazy slugs get the bowls."

Together, the men managed to serve themselves since Rosie was still peeved and it showed in the way she crossed her arms tight and kept her mouth flat.

The bowls were no sooner filled than the phone rang. Glad for something to do, Rosie answered it on her kitchen wall phone, but then excused herself from the guys to take the call in private. No one seemed to mind that except Ethan, who scowled and asked, "Who is it?"

"A client, nosy." She started to tell them not to wait for her, then saw that Buck already had his mouth full and Harris was soon to follow. "You're all social misfits, do you know that?"

They shrugged. Rosie shook her head and walked out.

The interruption was timely, in her opinion. She needed a few minutes to form her next plan of attack.

Bringing up home and hearth hadn't worked, so she'd have to hit Ethan on a more basic level.

Damn it all, she was going to have to seduce him.

THE SECOND ROSIE was out of hearing, Ethan said, "Finish up and get out of here. I want to talk to Rosie alone."

Riley bit his upper lip, but refrained from saying anything. Buck wasn't so subtle. "You two hooked up now?"

"No, we're not 'hooked up.' What the hell's wrong with you? Rosie is a friend and you know it."

Harris rolled his eyes. "A *female* friend, and that's all the distinction she needs far as I'm concerned."

"That's about it," Buck agreed.

Riley set his spoon aside. "Have any of you ever thought of Rosie in a...you know, sexual way?" He saluted the air with two fingers, giving the first admission, and Harris and Buck quickly lifted their hands, too.

Ethan gawked at them. "You can damn well stop thinking of her that way right now!"

"Impossible."

"No way."

"Sorry."

Ethan shoved his chair back. "You're all..."

"Normal? Healthy?" Riley laughed. "Gifted with perfect eyesight?"

Buck added, "Male."

And Harris tacked on, "Single."

"I don't believe this."

Unconcerned with Ethan's escalating temper, Riley took another bite of ice cream. "You know, Ethan, you're thumping your chest over nothing. Rosie has al-

ways treated us as just pals." He pointed his spoon at
him. "'Cept for you."

"Lucky bastard," Harris mumbled with feigned but
good-natured envy.

Stone-faced, Ethan paced away. Damn it, he was
losing his mind. Ever since he'd awakened with Rosie
draped over him, he'd been unable to stop thinking
about her. But for the most part he'd forcefully kept
those thoughts chaste, not carnal. *For the most part.*

But now, with his best friends putting thoughts in
his head, well, how the hell was he supposed to *not*
think about it? The woman was plain hot and that was
all there was to it.

Rosie didn't help any, prancing around in those Daisy
Duke cutoffs with her rounded ass and long legs on
display. Oh, yeah, he'd noticed the other guys stealing
a peek every few minutes. Course, they did that to all
females. But still— This wasn't just any female. This
was Rosie.

His Rosie, damn it.

Riley dropped his spoon into his empty bowl with a
resounding clink, catching Ethan's notice. "She seems
a little different since this morning, huh?"

Emotions roiling, Ethan asked through his teeth,
"What do you mean?"

"It's like she's on the make or something. The way
she's watching you—her body language."

His throat constricting, his eyes burning, Ethan re-
peated, "Body language?"

"Yeah." Riley turned to his cohorts. "You two've
seen it, haven't you?"

"Yep." Buck gave a decisive nod. "She wants him."

"Bad."

"Stop it!" Ethan paced again, more furiously this time. But he couldn't outrun his own thoughts. It was too late. Their words were already bouncing around in his brain, making him sweat, causing his muscles to cramp. Last night he'd done…something with her. This morning she'd been so warm and soft and his bed still smelled like her, sexy and female and utterly Rosie.

He breathed hard, walking faster 'round her kitchen, the three stooges looking on. He couldn't banish the images of Rosie seducing him, touching him, kissing him…

"That's it." Ethan grabbed up their bowls and put them in the sink. "Go home. Go away. Just go."

Harris made no effort to hide his laughter. Buck had to quickly grab for a napkin as Ethan shoved him toward the doorway.

Riley hung back, grinning like a fool. "One thing, Ethan."

"What?" Ethan could barely breathe and seriously doubted he could manage a chat with Riley.

Somber now, Riley crossed his arms over his chest and stared at Ethan. "Don't do anything to hurt her. Remember that she is my friend and I care about her."

Ethan struggled for control. More than anything he wanted to knock Riley on his ass. How dare he act territorial now when seconds before he'd been all but throwing Rosie at him? He looked at Harris and Buck and they nodded, too, equally protective, equally serious about it.

Riley wasn't done. "She's a real nice woman, Ethan, with a huge heart. Don't use what her brother did against her. She had no part in that."

"Goddamn it," Ethan exploded, infuriated that Riley

thought such a warning was necessary. He would never hurt Rosie and Riley should have damn well known it. "How dare you bring that up?"

Rosie stepped around the corner, the disconnected phone held loosely in her hand. She frowned in worry, her gaze darting back and forth between the men. "Bring what up? What's going on?"

Refusing to back down, Riley continued to watch Ethan. Harris and Buck moved to flank Rosie—as if she needed protection.

From him.

"Leave," Ethan said to all three of them. "Or I will."

Rosie bit her bottom lip. "Ethan? What's going on?"

Riley stepped away from Ethan. His expression changed when he tugged Rosie up against his chest for a long hug. "Just guy stuff. Nothing important."

"Don't give me that." She shoved back, her eyes filled with annoyance. "You guys are—"

"Drop it, Rosie." Ethan waited, his temper growing more fractured by the second as each of them took a turn embracing Rosie. Harris even sighed. Buck touched her cheek with poignant regret.

You'd think she was a virgin they'd decided to sacrifice to some evil spirit! Hell, he cared about Rosie, too, always had. Even during his engagement, she'd remained one of his closest friends. The night his fiancée had jilted him, it was Rosie he'd gone to because he'd been too shamed to face anyone else. He could talk with her, just *be* with her, easier than he could anyone.

Looking back on it now, he realized there was significance in their complete and total trust of one another. There'd always been a special bond between him and

Rosie. She liked all of them, hung with all of them, but only he shared that extra closeness with her.

He was the only one she wanted in the sack.

Oh, hell.

Ethan strode to the door and jerked it open. "Enough, all ready. Violins are going to start playing if you guys don't stop being so melodramatic."

As they filed past Ethan, they all grinned and winked and bobbed their eyebrows suggestively. Riley clutched his heart and pretended to swoon. Now these were the guys he knew and loved. He even laughed a little at their antics. "Idiots."

He closed the door behind them, leaned back on it and surveyed Rosie with new eyes—and undiluted male interest.

She looked worried. "Uh…what's going on?"

Ethan pushed away from the door. Just thinking about getting her into bed now, about doing everything he hadn't done last night, made him hot. Holding her gaze, his hunger growing, he murmured, "God, I've been dense."

She took a step back, her eyes wide, locked on his. "Yeah, so what's new?"

Her sarcasm couldn't quite hide her nervousness. Ethan felt like a superior male, ready to gentle the little woman, ready to give her what she evidently wanted, what he now knew he wanted.

"No more games, Rosie."

Her chest rose and fell with deep breaths and she planted her feet, done with backing up. "Okay."

"Do you want me?"

She blinked hard, twice. "You mean…sexually?"

Just hearing her say it nearly tipped him over the

edge. His voice turned husky. His chest constricted. "Yeah."

Silky brown hair shimmered around her shoulders with her nod. "I have for a long time now."

"Is that right?" Ethan didn't want to know how long—it might kill him. He stopped two inches from her. "Nothing happened last night, did it?"

"No."

"Not even a kiss?" He wanted it confirmed that if he'd kissed her, she'd damn well know it.

"No." She stared down at her feet. "Your redhead accidentally dumped her drink on me, so I had to leave. You were too drunk to drive and so you asked me to call you a cab." She looked up, determination darkening her gaze. "I decided to take you home myself to be sure you made it safely, and well...I didn't want to leave."

"I see."

She rushed to add, "I did refrain from taking your pants off you." She made it sound like a huge concession on her part.

Ethan smiled. "I appreciate that."

"You do?" She started wringing her hands and frowning at him in confusion.

"Oh, yeah." Her uncertainty in the face of the bizarre circumstance was rather endearing, Ethan decided. It was rare indeed to see Rosie suffer such a human emotion as self-consciousness. "I damn well want to be sober when I lie down with you, so I can remember every little detail."

Her eyes widened like saucers. "I was going to seduce you," she blurted.

"What?"

She nodded hard. "I was. But it's your fault."

"My fault you were going to seduce me?" Following Rosie's train of thought proved impossible, especially when he was already so horny.

"Yes. You were being so stubborn about it, refusing to see me as a female and—"

"I've always known you were a female, Rosie." He wouldn't lie to either of them. "Not once did I ever confuse you with Riley or Harris or, God forbid, Buck."

Her mouth fell open, then snapped shut. "Really?"

She sounded so hopeful, Ethan's heart turned over in his chest. He'd always considered Rosie a very special friend. Now he realized she was very special—in all ways. Especially as a woman. "Hell, yeah." Then he scowled. "So have the other guys."

"What other guys?"

The way she asked that made his worries disappear. She wasn't aware of their interest. And she'd made it clear she wanted him. It was enough. "Never mind."

"But…"

"Shh." He took hold of her shoulders and gently caressed her, hoping to calm her and himself. She felt so soft, so warm. He'd touched her shoulders before, for crying out loud, but this was the first time he'd done so with sexual intent. It was different. How he felt was different.

Rosie deserved the best he could bring to her, and that meant not jumping her bones and dragging her down to the carpet, even when that was what he most wanted to do. He needed to be gentle and considerate. And slow.

Ethan closed his eyes. It was going to be a close call, but he thought, all things considered, he'd manage.

"Being that we're both here, alone, and finally in agreement about what we want to do, maybe we should—"

She didn't give him a chance to finish. With an exclamation of delight, Rosie launched herself at him.

Taken off guard, Ethan staggered under her weight, but quickly righted himself. He was already half hard with expectation and now, feeling Rosie hugged up tight to him, her breasts against his chest, her belly against his groin, he lost what little control he'd been hanging on to. "Damn."

"Ethan." She caught his face and kissed him, awkwardly at first but with so much enthusiasm, he groaned. "Ethan," she said again, his name almost a wail.

"Easy," he tried to tell her even as he stroked his hands down her back to that perfect heart-shaped bottom. Her shorts were very short and it was nothing for him to slip his fingers under the frayed edges to tease her firm, rounded cheeks. Her skin was so silky, he felt sure his blood would boil.

Rosie bit his bottom lip. She wasn't overly gentle, either. He jerked, but she knotted her hands in his hair and brought his mouth back to hers so she could suck his lip into her mouth, tease it with her tongue.

"Jesus, Rosie, slow down."

"No." She sealed their mouths together and Ethan tilted his head so he could take over, thrusting his tongue into her mouth, swallowing her moan. It was the first deep kiss they'd ever shared, and boy, it was good.

"Wait." She shoved him back and reached for the hem of her shirt. "I want you to touch me. I've been thinking about you touching me for days."

Oh, no. Hell, no. In very Rosie-like fashion, she was running the show. Ethan couldn't let her do that. She probably had no idea that she drove him wild, that he might lose control at any moment. She'd never driven him wild before, so how could she know?

He caught her wrists and held her still, even when she struggled against him. "Damn it, Rosie. Give me a second." He panted, trembled, while she continued to fight him. He should have expected as much; Rosie wouldn't accept any man's control easily, not even a man she wanted. Above the lust, that struck Ethan as funny, and he laughed roughly.

Rosie glared at him. "What?" she demanded, still pulling against his hold.

"Let's go into your bedroom." Maybe if he could get her pinned beneath him on the mattress, he could slow her down a little.

"The bedroom? Oh, okay." She tried to turn and hurry in that direction.

Ethan pulled her up short, a little desperate. "Honey, this isn't a race."

She turned around and yelled right into his face, "You'll change your mind!"

She looked so vulnerable, so unsure of herself. He'd been a pig, not seeing what was right in front of his face. "No," he told her very softly, smiling to reassure her. "Not a chance."

"Then why—?"

"Ever since I woke up with you this morning, my imagination has been in overdrive." He touched her slightly parted mouth with trembling fingertips. "Hell, Rosie, thinking about you, wanting you all day, has been like indulging in foreplay for hours and the result is that I'm working with a hair trigger here."

Her eyes darkened to a deep gray. "You've been thinking about me?"

"About getting you naked and under me, yeah." Saying it made him see it, and his stomach cramped with need. But she deserved to hear everything. "I've also been jealous as hell."

"Jealous? Of who?"

Ethan released her and rubbed his face. The need to laugh struck him again, lightening the urgency—at least for him—just a little. Rosie could be so single-minded in her determination she noticed nothing beyond her objective. Of course, he'd been the same, blind to the fact of his friends' interest.

But no more.

Ethan caught her hand and led her toward the bedroom. "Everyone. Any guy who looks at you."

"Really?"

"Especially that damned Riley." They entered her bedroom and Ethan pushed the door shut. "He knew it, too, and kept egging me on."

Disbelief had her wrinkling her nose. "Riley?"

Ethan stared down at her, so overwhelmed with tenderness—with newfound love—he could have choked on it. "And Harris and Buck."

"You've got to be kidding."

"No." His smile came naturally. So did the love he felt for her, until it filled him up, making him feel whole for the first time in ages. Loosely looping his arms around her, Ethan kissed her temple. "I knew all along that I thought you were hot, but they think it, too."

She snorted. "They do not."

"They do." He smoothed her cheek, her silky-soft

brown hair. *Rosie.* He couldn't get over the shock, or
the rightness of it. "But you only want me, right?"

She stared at him a long minute before squeezing
him tight. "I'm not her, Ethan. Of course, I only want
you. Michelle was the biggest fool alive to walk out on
you. And as much as I hurt for you when it happened,
I was so glad you didn't marry her."

Ethan closed his eyes, cut by her words. He hadn't
meant to bring that up, hadn't even been thinking in
that direction. Hell, the humiliation Michelle had in-
flicted couldn't possibly invade his thoughts, not now,
not with Rosie in front of him, ready to take him to her
bed. He took one breath, then another, but it didn't help.

Leaning back, Rosie saw his pained expression and
flattened one hand on his chest. "You didn't love her,
Ethan. I know you didn't."

"Rosie…"

Her small hand smoothed over his chest then down
his abdomen, and lower. He caught his breath.

Still staring up at him, she touched his fly, gently,
curiously. He was fully erect, straining his jeans, and
Rosie traced her fingertips up and down his length.
"I'm not a fool," she said. "How could I want any other
man but you?"

"Yeah," Ethan murmured, barely able to think much
less discuss the past. "Right now."

Her smile affected him as much as her touch. "I'm
ready."

She stepped back and this time when she reached
for the hem of her shirt, Ethan didn't stop her. He stood
there, every muscle in his body tense, as Rosie disrobed
as naturally as if she'd been baring herself to him for a
lifetime. She threw the shirt aside, unhooked her bra,

and still he stood there, just watching—and catching on fire.

With slow precision, playing the tease naturally, she unsnapped her shorts, slid down the zipper, and bent to push them off, taking her panties with her. When she straightened, she was beautifully naked.

A slight blush colored her cheeks when she lifted her face and looked at him. Shaking, Ethan closed his hands on her waist and brought her up against him.

"Rosie," he whispered, and he took her mouth as he lowered her down to lie flat on the mattress. He'd waited long enough.

He couldn't wait a second more.

CHAPTER FOUR

ROSIE FELT HIS MOUTH on her throat, open, damp, hot. One big hand rested on her ribs, just beneath her right breast. He laid half-atop her, heat pouring off him, *and he wanted her.*

She closed her eyes and luxuriated in the moment. She loved him so much she hurt with it, and now finally she could tell him.

His long rough fingers slid gently over and around her breast, teasing, making her skin prickle, before he cupped her fully. She could feel his hot breath against her shoulder, near her ear, disturbing the fine hairs at her nape. His breathing was rough, uneven, sounding so sexy, so male. He continued to place openmouthed kisses here and there, until Rosie couldn't catch and hold a thought.

She was already squirming, unable to stay still, when his thumb brushed over her stiffened nipple once then returned again and again. The effect was startling, wonderful. Her heart raced and everything she felt intensified to an acute ache.

Rosie looked at him, and all she could think was that this was Ethan, finally. He was hers. "Ethan…"

He groaned, lowered his head and took her nipple into the wet heat of his mouth.

An overwhelming wave of sensation made her thighs stiffen, her toes curl. "Oh, Ethan..."

She arched hard, but Ethan held her steady. "Look at you," he murmured, and his breath drifted over her wet nipple. "So pink and soft. So sweet."

He switched to the other breast and Rosie thought it was almost too much. She'd wanted this, wanted him, for as long as she could remember.

"Take your shirt off, too, Ethan. Please." She barely recognized her own voice, but Ethan understood. He came up to his knees, straddling her hips, and yanked his shirt up and over his head. He started to return to her breasts but she flattened her hands on his shoulders and held him back.

"Let me touch you," she whispered with wonder. She'd seen Ethan without his shirt before. They'd played softball, gone swimming, and he'd helped her move in. Each time he'd pulled off his shirt, as most of the guys had. It had been so hard not to stare, not to let her love for him show through. All of them were impressive, but they all weren't Ethan.

Now he was here, with her, and she intended to get her fill.

Slowly, savoring the moment, she smoothed her palms over him. He felt perfect to her, hard and sleek and hot, with soft, crisp hair lightly scattered from pectoral to pectoral. His body hair was shades darker than his blond head, a rich brown, matching his brows and lashes. A very sexy line of silky hair teased down the middle of his abdomen and disappeared into his low-riding jeans. Awed, Rosie shoved him onto his back.

He smiled up at her, eyes twinkling with amusement. "You are so pushy, Rosie."

This time she straddled his hips—and he shut up as she settled atop his erection. "I can feel you beneath me." Her eyes closed, her breath caught. "I can't wait until you're inside me, Ethan. Until I can feel all of you."

Heat flared in his eyes and he growled, "Come here."

She evaded his hands and moved to the side of him. "You need to take off your jeans." She flipped the snap loose and grabbed for his zipper.

"Rosie, wait." His long fingers curled around her wrist. She looked at his face and saw that his pupils were dilated, his nostrils flared. Arousal colored his high cheekbones.

He wanted her, and she loved him. It was more than enough.

She bent and kissed his navel.

Ethan stiffened, but Rosie continued to kiss him, each rib, across to a hipbone—the hard ridge of his erection through his jeans. His stomach tautened until each muscle was defined. "Rosie, honey…" He gasped and his hands fell to his sides.

Satisfied, she licked the hot, taut flesh of his abdomen as she carefully lowered his zipper. "Raise your hips," she murmured, so anxious to have all of him that she couldn't stop trembling.

He did as she asked and she worked his jeans down his muscled legs, then his underwear. It took her a moment to work off his shoes and socks, and then finally he was completely, wonderfully naked. Like a feast laid out in front of her, Ethan was irresistible and she couldn't stop devouring him with her gaze. She heard a rough, rumbling purr and realized the carnal sound was her own.

Relishing each broken breath he took, the way his

strong fingers fisted in the sheets, Rosie reached out her hand and touched him. The feel of his penis amazed her, warm velvet over flexing steel, alive, pulsing. Ethan made small desperate sounds as she explored him, but she barely paid him any mind, too intent on what she wanted.

She bent toward him again and his rough fingers tangled gently in her hair.

"You smell so good." Nuzzling into him, she breathed deeply, filling herself with the wonderful musky male scent.

With the smallest nudge, Ethan guided her mouth to his straining erection, and she obliged, anxious to taste him as she'd so often dreamed of doing.

She wasn't disappointed with his reaction. The first touch of her tongue on him and he froze, his powerful body shaking. "Oh, damn."

Rosie stroked her tongue over him, licking along his length then up and over the broad head. With a rough growl, he tried to pull away. "I'm going to lose it, honey," he warned.

"Okay," she purred, and opened her mouth, taking him in. His taste was delicious, turning her on even more. She heard him moan again—and she sucked.

A great shudder went through Ethan; his fingers clenched in her hair to hold her closer and his hips lifted with a small, unintentional jerk. She took more of him, sucking gently, moving her wet tongue over and around and...

"Enough." His strength took her by surprise as he pulled her away and up to his chest. "Rosie, baby, that's enough." Before she could protest, he turned and caught her beneath him. His mouth covered hers and he

kissed her with rough determination, his tongue wild, his hands stroking everywhere.

Wanting him now, Rosie opened her thighs for him, but instead of accepting her invitation he slid down a little and again kissed her breasts. He wasn't so gentle this time, sucking strongly at her nipples, nipping with his teeth. She cried out, stunned by his urgency, which made her own need escalate, but still he didn't stop. He slid lower and one hand moved between her thighs.

The shock of it had her stiffening, but he didn't seem to notice. They both paused and she heard Ethan groan as he carefully began exploring her, his fingertips gliding through her curls, pressing in, parting her. It seemed the oddest caress, so intimate, so hot and stimulating and, judging by the hungry sounds he made, Ethan enjoyed touching her as much as she enjoyed his touch. She didn't know what she had expected, but the gentle, insistent way he continued to stroke her made her wild.

His five o'clock shadow rasped against her belly as he turned his face inward to kiss her, leaving small, tingling love bites. By slow degrees, he went lower and lower until taking a single breath was too difficult to accomplish.

Rosie struggled to assimilate all the new feelings— and then he pushed one finger into her and she jerked, her eyes rounding, her body rioting with sensation. "Ethan."

"You're tight." His voice was nearly soundless with arousal. "And wet."

She bit her lip to keep her groans to herself, but she couldn't stop the automatic rise and fall of her hips. Ethan had large, hard, wonderful hands.

"Yeah, that's it. That's what I want." He worked another finger in, stretching her, just as his breath touched her most sensitive flesh.

"Ethan?" This was all very new to her, though he couldn't know that. "I…"

With his fingers buried deep inside her, he covered her with his mouth. The scalding heat struck her first, then the gentle damp rasp of his velvet tongue. The sensation was so intense she couldn't bear it, but she couldn't stop him, either. No matter how she twisted, how she moaned, Ethan didn't stop.

If anything, he pressed closer, holding her motionless with the weight of his broad shoulders, and then his mouth closed around her clitoris, suckling at her while his fingers pushed, withdrew and sank in again.

Her climax hit her without warning. Rosie had thought about this moment so many times, about how she'd act feminine and sexy and she'd lure Ethan so that he wanted to have sex with her again and again.

Instead she shouted like a crazy person, her body arching hard, uncontrollably. His hold tightened and he drove her until every nerve was alive, tingling.

As the spiraling explosion faded, she heard Ethan moan, felt his hands settle on her hips, tenderly squeezing. When she lay flat again, stunned and more or less quiet, he pulled away.

Rosie couldn't move. Her legs were sprawled around him, her thoughts scattered. She simply hadn't expected such a thing, such a wild bombardment on her senses.

Ethan rested his cheek on her belly and hugged her. She still gasped for breath, astounded by what had just happened, when he whispered, "I love you, Rosie."

Her heart slammed to a halt. It took her two tries to catch her breath, to believe he'd actually said those special words, and then she started to sob. She didn't mean to, but once the tears started, she couldn't stop them. And damn it, she wasn't a pretty crier. She wasn't very quiet, either.

Ethan lifted his head to look at her, and his smile was lopsided, a little silly. "I've never seen you cry, Rosie."

"Shut up." She sniffled, wiped at her eyes and stretched her arm to the nightstand for a handful of tissues.

Watching her with that endearing grin in place, Ethan said, "So surly."

"I'm embarrassed, all right?"

"Why?"

"I'm not very dainty about crying." Her brother used to tease her that she sounded like a drunken walrus when she wept.

"You're not very dainty about coming, either, but hey, I'm not complaining." He stood beside the bed. Rosie froze in the middle of blowing her nose.

Dear heaven, he was gorgeous.

He lifted his jeans from the floor, pulled his wallet from the back pocket, located a condom and, casual as you please, opened the package and put it on. Rosie bolted upright in fascination. She'd never seen an erection in a raincoat.

Then she remembered she'd never seen an erection—not up close and personal anyway.

She started to comment on the process, but then Ethan was there, pushing her back down on the bed, crowding over her.

He kissed her cheek, up to her damp eyelashes, to her temple. Very softly he said, "I love the way you cry, and I love the way you come." He cupped her face. "I love *you*."

The tears came again, this time in a torrent. *"Ethan."* She wrapped her arms tight around him and bawled. She felt stupid for her loss of control, but she couldn't count the nights she'd lain awake and prayed that someday he'd say those three special words to her. Now that he finally had, her heart wanted to burst.

In a butterfly caress, he kissed her shoulder—and nudged her thighs wider apart so he could settle between them. "Shh," he rumbled lowly, sounding indulgent. "You'll make yourself sick."

"I don't—"

He pushed into her.

"—care!" Rosie clenched down hard as his cock slid deep inside her. It burned a little as he filled her, and felt so good she lost her breath again. "Oh, my— Ethan. *Ethan.*"

He actually laughed. But the laugh trailed off into a groan. He kept his hips flexed, straining against her, maintaining the pressure, pushing deeper and deeper. "Relax for me, honey." He kissed the corner of her mouth. "I want you to take all of me."

All of him? Rosie bit his shoulder, trying to silence her roar of pleasure as he rocked against her, slowly giving her more, then more still. Without thinking about it, she lifted her legs and locked them around his waist— and he sank in another inch.

Just when she thought it would be too much, he stopped and rested against her. "Rosie?"

She swallowed, shivered and finally choked an indistinct, "Mmm?"

"You were a virgin?"

There was only one answer she could give. "I've never wanted anyone but you."

Ethan didn't tease her, didn't crow about his conquest, he simply gathered her closer against him, kissed her mouth in a long, slow, deep kiss—and began moving.

The friction proved beyond incredible. Ethan kept kissing her. Long, lazy, consuming kisses. Hot, frantic kisses. He started to move faster and his breathing deepened, his muscles tightened.

Suddenly he levered himself up on stiffened arms. His thrusts were hard, slow, deep. Rosie stared at him, enthralled by the sight of his corded neck, the bunched muscles in his shoulders and biceps. His narrowed eyes were golden brown, bright, fevered. His jaw clenched.

And then she knew he was coming. She watched him through a haze. Their labored breaths mingled and she moaned with him, so excited to see him like this.

Moments later Ethan dropped sluggishly onto her, his face in her neck. Her legs went slack and slipped to the mattress. He was still inside her. It wasn't easy, but Rosie managed to lift one hand to stroke the nape of his neck down to his sweaty shoulder. "I love you, too, Ethan."

He gave an incoherent reply and tightened his arms.

Smiling, happier than she ever thought possible, Rosie asked, "When can we get married?"

He stopped breathing.

One second he was sucking air, sounding like a marathon runner, the next he was perfectly still. She barely felt his heartbeat—until it started drumming madly against her breast.

He raised his head, eyes agog. *"Married?"*

He appeared so horrified by the idea that Rosie considered slugging him. "Don't say it like a dirty word, Ethan."

"Well, no, but...*marriage?*"

Oh, she didn't feel like crying now. She was spitting mad and very determined. "I'm marrying you, Ethan Winters, so you might as well get used to it right now. And, by God, we'll live in my house and plant flowers in the summer and get a damn dog and eventually have some kids and—"

The shock cleared from his face and he started to laugh. Rosie shoved at him, but he didn't seem inclined to stop. "You think me being a mother is funny?" she demanded.

"No," he gasped around his chuckles. "No, I swear."

"Buffoon! Get off of me."

Instead he dropped his whole weight on her and got his chuckles under control. He wore a tender smile and his eyes were twinkling when he said, "Rosie."

"Don't you 'Rosie' me!"

He kissed her, but it was a funny kiss because she was fighting him and he was snickering again.

"I love you," he reminded her when she tried to twist his arm behind his back. "Ow, ouch. Rosie, I love you! Now stop that."

Mulish, a little hurt, she let him go but glared at him.

He still looked entirely too close to hilarity. "Honey, I *love* you." He touched her mouth, teasing. "You just took me by surprise, that's all."

He sounded sincere, she had to admit. "I've always known I loved you, Ethan."

"Yeah, well, I've only had it figured out for a few hours, so how about just giving me some time?" He cupped her face, kissed her again, a tickling teasing kiss.

"And time will make you realize that we need to be married?"

He tried to sound somber when he said, "I'd consider myself a shallow ass if it didn't."

Relief washed over her and she found her own smile. "All right."

With one last kiss, Ethan moved away from her. "Stay put. I'll be right back." Naked, gorgeous and far too sexy, he went out into the hall and then she heard water running in the bathroom.

Ethan loved her. The rest would come. It had to.

ETHAN TOOK HIS TIME removing the condom, finding a washcloth, soaking it with warm water. *Marriage.* Damn, but Rosie only knew one speed—Mach.

She'd left him in the dust that time for sure. He'd been doing his best to reconcile the fact that he loved her, that she'd been a virgin, that she was a regular wildcat in bed—and bam! She'd planned out their whole lives, complete with a dog and kids.

But now that she'd brought it up, the idea appealed to him. He did love her, no doubt about that one. Once he'd admitted it to himself, the feeling had expanded and grown and all but consumed him. He couldn't believe it had taken him so long to realize what was firmly rooted in his heart. The strength of what he felt for her was even a little scary.

Ethan knew he couldn't bear the idea of any other man touching her. So far, no other man had. If he played his cards right, no other man would. She was his in every sense of the word—and by God, he'd keep her.

If that meant marriage, then so what? It wouldn't make him care more for her, but if she needed that, then he'd give it to her.

A quiet little ceremony, with only two witnesses... yeah, he could do that. He wouldn't like it, and he assumed some pretty ugly memories would plague him. But Rosie was worth any emotional discomfort.

He took a steadying breath, wrung out the washcloth, and headed back to the bedroom.

She hadn't bothered to cover herself.

Ethan almost tripped over his own feet. He'd always known Rosie was pretty, and that she was built nice. But naked, stretched out on a bed, she was about the sexiest thing he'd ever seen.

Her head turned toward him when he stopped in the open doorway. Her hair was tumbled around her face, her body still flushed in selective places—such as her breasts, her belly, her silky thighs.

Damn, he was getting hard again.

Ethan cleared his throat and sat beside her on the mattress. "I'm going to clean you up."

Now she moved, darting under the covers so fast she was a blur. "You most definitely are *not*."

Ethan grinned. "Wanna bet?"

"Don't even think—"

He had the covers completely off the bed in a flash, which left Rosie squawking and ready to tussle. He obliged. Wrestling with Rosie wasn't at all like wrestling with other women. For one thing, she refused to understand that she was the weaker sex. Instead, she fought hard, determined to get the upper hand. By the time Ethan had her hands pinned above her head and his hips settled firmly between her spread thighs so she couldn't kick him, they were both panting from exertion.

And he was fully aroused again.

He grinned down at her, but she didn't smile back. No, her eyes had turned all molten and she was staring at his mouth. The way he held her left her breasts on display and Ethan had a hard time keeping his gaze off her tight pink nipples and on her face.

He lowered his forehead to hers. "You're distracting me, Rosie."

"Good." She lifted her hips in an undulating roll, stroking him with her body. "Let's do it again."

Hell of an idea. "You're not too sore?"

She shook her head. "No. Well, maybe just a little, but...no." She lifted her long lashes to stare up at him. "I want to watch you come again. You are so sexy."

Feeling a little self-conscious with her bold statement, Ethan laughed. "You don't act like a virgin, you know that?"

Her thighs closed around his waist. "If you stay the night with me, I'll try to act more virginal." Since she made that promise while leaning up to nip his chin, Ethan could only nod his agreement. It felt damn good to be wanted so much, especially by Rosie.

"You have more condoms?" she asked.

"Just one," he told her.

"Then let's make it last." She pulled her hands free, pushed him to his back, and Ethan groaned as she climbed atop him.

Loving Rosie was going to be a lot of fun.

As the night wore on, so did Ethan's determination to legally bind her to him. The rest of his life wouldn't be long enough to love her. He'd discuss it with her in the morning, and then they could make plans. With any luck, they could get the marriage business over with on his next day off.

WHEN ETHAN AWOKE, he found Rosie at her dresser, putting in earrings. He smiled, thinking how delightful she looked standing there in her slip and nylons, her beautiful hair twisted atop her head.

He scooted up in the bed and stretched. Rosie turned to face him, smiled, and came to him for a good-morning kiss.

"I've got coffee in the kitchen if you want some."

He pulled her onto his lap. "I was hoping to find you naked in bed beside me, not half-dressed."

"Sorry." She pushed away and checked her hair to make sure he hadn't messed it up. "I have to see a client in about half an hour." Absently, she stroked his chest hair, and her gaze warmed. "You look good in my bed, Ethan."

"Is that a hint?"

"That I'd like to see you here more? Absolutely." She stood and went to the closet to pull out a tailored dress, which she stepped into and buttoned up. Next she slipped her feet into medium-heeled shoes and she was done.

It felt right to watch Rosie dress, to be privy to her little morning rituals. He should have awakened in time to shower with her. Tomorrow he would.

Ethan swung his legs over the side of the bed, stood and scratched his chest. When he reached for his jeans, he realized that Rosie was just standing there, staring at him, and he grinned.

"You know," he said as he pulled on the jeans, "I was thinking about this marriage stuff."

Her breath caught. "And?"

"I think it's a hell of an idea."

She stood still for almost fifteen seconds before she let out a squeal and bounded around the bed to reach him. Ethan caught her, whirled her around once, then laughed out loud as she choked him with a tight hug. "I knew you'd be reasonable!"

Still laughing, Ethan said, "It has nothing to do with reason and everything to do with loving you." He cupped his hands over her bottom and kissed her. "Do you think we could get it done next week on my day off?"

"Next week?" Her face went blank. "Of course not. I have to order a dress and rent a hall and find a preacher and invite everyone…weddings take time, Ethan."

His heart sank like a stone into his stomach. "Rosie." Gently he set her away from him. "I want no part of a big, fancy wedding. I thought we could just go to a justice of the peace and be done with it."

"But…I don't want to just 'be done with it.'" She looked stricken, a little pale. "I want a big wedding." She tried a smile that went flat, and teased, "I'm only getting married once, you know."

Ethan couldn't bear to see her hope. He turned away, stalking to the window to look out. Her small backyard was immaculate, perfect for the dog and kids that she wanted. He gave a muffled curse.

The silence behind him was suffocating, but damned if he could think of anything to say to her. The idea of a fancy wedding with guests staring at him…no. He couldn't do that.

"Ethan?" She touched his bare shoulder. "I *love* you."

"I know."

Her arms came around him from behind. "I would never do anything to hurt you."

"I know that, too, Rosie. But I swore I'd never again put myself in that position." He turned to face her. "If we had a big wedding, you know what everyone would be thinking? They'd be remembering the last time, how I was left standing there looking like a goddamned fool when your brother ran off with my bride."

Rosie backed up a step. Her chin lifted. "You weren't the only one humiliated that day, Ethan Winters. Every person at that wedding wanted to ask me about it, too, to see if I'd known what my brother was planning."

"Did you?"

Her eyes narrowed, her mouth trembled. "I'll pretend you didn't ask me that."

He rubbed his face. "Shit. I'm sorry."

"You weren't the only one to lose someone you loved, either." Her voice got shaky, her eyes a little liquid. But she didn't look away, didn't lower that stubborn chin. "I haven't seen my brother since. With Mom and Dad gone, he's the only family I have left, but until you forgive him, until you let everyone know that you're over Michelle, I have no one."

Ethan hadn't thought of it that way, and now he felt sick. "You have me."

She didn't smile. "Yes I do, and I love you. But… maybe that's not enough."

She waited, and he knew what she wanted. Rosie never bothered with subtlety. But Ethan couldn't relent.

With a resigned sigh, Rosie glanced at her watch. "Wow, look at the time."

"Rosie…"

"Darn it, I have to go or I'll be late." She tried to look chipper—and failed.

"I'm off today," Ethan told her. "I'm going to see if I can get the interview with Red out of the way early this afternoon, then I'll come back here. We can talk more tonight." He hated to give her false hope about a big wedding, when just the thought of it made him break out in a cold sweat and sent cramps to his stomach. But he also hated to send her out the door when she was upset.

"All right." She turned thoughtful, and Ethan had the faint suspicion she was plotting something. "I'll be back around five. Make yourself at home, okay?"

"Coffee first, then your shower." He touched her cheek. "Could I have a key?"

This time her smile was natural. "On top of the fridge in the basket. I had it made for you months ago."

Ethan slipped his arm around her and started her toward the front door so she wouldn't be late. "I appreciate your confidence in my intelligence. You knew I'd wise up, didn't you?"

Rosie laughed. "I couldn't bear to think otherwise."

CHAPTER FIVE

AT ONE O'CLOCK, Rosie parked in front of the entrance to the park where she'd set up a meeting with Regina Foxworth. The reporter said she'd be in the area to talk with a fireworks dealer located nearby, then at two, she would be interviewing Ethan over lunch at the diner across the street. She agreed to give Rosie half an hour first, plenty of time to set the record straight.

Rosie had rearranged her schedule, but still it had been difficult to get to the park by the designated time. Luckily, when she shaded her eyes and looked around, she found Regina just seating herself on a park bench in front of a decorative fountain.

Rosie strode forward, a woman on a mission. Ethan might be resistant to the idea of a big marriage now, but she'd get him around that somehow. In her heart, she knew he was over Michelle. She just needed him to know it, too.

Regina was another matter entirely. She believed Ethan when he said he loved her, but he'd also made his admiration of the reporter plain. Rosie had waited too long to have Ethan to take chances now. She wanted Regina to understand that Ethan was already involved in a relationship. "Hello, Regina."

The pretty redhead smiled up at Rosie and extended her hand. She was dressed in a chic summer-weight suit and a camera hung from a wide strap around her neck. "Nice to see you again, Rosie."

"I appreciate you making the time for me." After a friendly handshake, Rosie sat beside her on the bench. Though the day was hot, the park buzzed with life. Children were playing everywhere and she could hear the occasional happy bark of a dog chasing a Frisbee. Someday in the near future she and Ethan would bring their children here and watch them on the swings. She sighed.

"No problem." Regina crossed her legs and smiled. "You've got me curious, so I wanted to meet with you first. When I interview Firefighter Winters, I don't want to be distracted."

Rosie clenched her teeth. Jealousy was new to her and she didn't like it at all. "Please, call him Ethan—I know he'll insist."

"All right."

A man and a woman jogged by. Regina waited, not saying anything more, leaving it up to Rosie to explain herself.

She got right to the point. "Why do you want to interview Ethan?"

Regina's brows rose. "Just the obvious reasons. Ethan has a history of heroic deeds and he was rewarded for it. The ceremony was a big deal and I got some great photos, but obviously Ethan wasn't up to an interview then."

Remembering how foolishly Ethan had behaved chasing the woman beside her, Rosie scowled. He'd thrown himself at her and the only surprise was that Regina hadn't jumped on the chance to be with him. Rosie would have.

"The paper has already done a couple of articles on him," Rosie pointed out.

"True. But in a town this size, a man like Ethan quickly becomes a role model. Pride for one of their own is top-notch news. Everyone wants to hear about him, about the ceremony the other night, his past good deeds and what's happening with him now."

"What do you intend to ask him?"

If Regina thought her questions intrusive, she didn't say so. "You're protective of him, aren't you? I can understand that. His behavior at the ceremony was..." She searched for a word and finally shrugged. "Well, as big and strong and capable as he is, he seemed vulnerable to me."

That startled Rosie. "He was drunk."

Grinning, Regina said, "That he was." She tipped her head. "Does he drink often?"

"No. Almost never, actually."

"But he drank too much that night." She nodded. "I think that's because he was so ill at ease. Being uncomfortable in that situation is a startling contrast for a man who enters burning buildings without a qualm."

Regina sounded far too admiring to Rosie. "Ethan doesn't like all the fuss made over him."

"Maybe." She watched a butterfly flit by, turned her face up to a warm breeze. The seconds ticked by and finally she shrugged. "I'm sure you know Ethan better than I do, but I don't think that's it." She turned toward Rosie. "I think it's the ceremony itself he didn't like."

Regina sounded so sure of herself, Rosie grew uneasy. "Why do you say that?"

"I skimmed some of the other articles done on him the last few weeks, just to get a bare-bones history on him, and in every case he spoke freely about his duties as a firefighter, posed for the occasional picture, even ribbed his chief a little. He was totally at ease, comfortable. He didn't mind the one-on-one attention at all, or the publicity in the papers. No, it was the crowd, everyone looking at him and making him the center of attention at a formal affair that got to him."

Rosie dropped back against the bench, stunned by how blind she'd been. And she'd accused Ethan of being dense. Realization pounded through her, causing her heart to ache. Knowing she might have hurt Ethan with the awful way she'd pressed him for a big, elaborate wedding was a weight on her chest. She'd been so insensitive.

Regina reached over and patted her hand. "Forgive me for sticking my nose in where it doesn't belong, but...well, I *am* a reporter." She grinned at that. "I couldn't interview Ethan the night of the ceremony, not because he was so drunk, but because all he wanted to talk about was you."

She'd said that at the gym. At the time Ethan hadn't given her a chance to ask Regina any questions. He'd rushed Rosie out of there so fast her feet had barely touched the floor. "What did he say?"

Ticking off comments on her fingers, Regina said, "You're funnier, sweeter, pushier than any other woman he knows. You drive him nuts with your smart mouth, smother him with your mothering tendency—he grinned when he said that, by the way. You're honest, loyal, a great cook with a big heart and..."

Rosie covered her face and groaned. "Oh, God."

Sympathetic, Regina patted her again. "He hadn't mentioned this Michelle person until I saw you both at Riley's gym. And seeing you both side by side...well, it didn't take a genius to figure out you're in love."

Rosie had few female friends and she wasn't close with any of them, not like she was with the guys. But she found she liked being able to confide in Regina. The woman wasn't at all as she'd first assumed. "He was engaged to Michelle. I thought…I thought he was still upset because of what had happened between them."

"I found articles on that, too. She jilted him—in front of the whole town." Regina shuddered delicately. "I can only imagine how that would affect someone like Ethan. It'd be tough on any man, but firefighters are naturally arrogant and more proud than most and to be humiliated that way…I'm sure it wasn't easy for him."

Rosie found herself wringing her hands. She needed to see Ethan, to make it up to him, to assure him that having him for her husband was all she ever really wanted. "You're not going to ask Ethan about that at the interview, are you?"

"Heavens, no. For one thing, I try very hard to be fair and up front in my reporting. That means sticking to pertinent facts." Then she wrinkled her lightly freckled nose. "Besides, I imagine Ethan would walk out on me if I invaded his privacy that way."

When Rosie just sat there, pondering her own guilt and how she'd tried to coerce Ethan into a big wedding just to prove he was over Michelle, Regina cleared her throat. "Was there anything else you wanted to talk to me about?"

Rosie considered it for only a moment. "Yes. Would you like to come over tomorrow night? I was going to invite Riley and a few of our other friends, as well. Ethan will be there, too." At least she hoped he would. She had to get home to him and apologize first. "I know you're new to town and I think we can be friends."

A little surprised, Regina smiled. "I'd like that. Thank you."

Just then a young man came barreling up behind the bench, his attention on the ball he meant to catch. He collided with the bench and nearly toppled over into Regina's lap. Rosie steadied him with both hands, but Regina gave a short scream, whirling around in what could only be described as near panic.

With the ball safely captured, the man turned fiery red and apologized all over himself. When Regina seemed incapable of replying, Rosie told him not to worry about it, and he ran off, glad to escape.

"You okay?"

Nodding jerkily, Regina pressed a hand to her heart and closed her eyes.

Watching her, Rosie remembered Riley claiming that Regina was "a little paranoid." Seeing her now, Rosie understood. She was white as a sheet. "What's going on?"

"Nothing. I'm sorry." She opened her eyes, looked around again and, somewhat distracted, checked her watch. "I should be going if I hope to make it back here in time to meet Ethan at the diner. The address I have for the fireworks dealer is supposed to be in this area but I'm not sure where exactly and I don't know how long it will take me to find him."

Considering all the insight she'd just gained into Ethan, Rosie felt she owed the other woman. This would be a good way to repay her in part. "If you don't mind the company, I'd be glad to walk with you to the address. I'm a real estate agent and can pretty much find any building."

"You're sure?"

"I've got an hour free."

Regina looked vastly relieved. "Thank you. It shouldn't take me long. I've already found some background information on the guy, so mostly I just need to ask a few questions and take some pictures."

"He agreed to be interviewed?"

Regina winced. "Not exactly. At least not until I told him I'd run the story with or without his input. He, uh, well, he wasn't happy with my persistence. But with the Fourth almost here, and this guy's reputation not quite aboveboard…"

Rosie fought a smile. "It's okay. I can be persistent, too, when I want something."

"This job is important to me. Riley told me how Ethan and the others feel about all the illegal fireworks that show up every Fourth of July. He suggested the public could do with a little more knowledge on the subject, and I agreed. So…" She made a face. "I'm going to do something of an exposé."

"He does know you're coming, right?"

"He knows. But under the circumstances, I'll understand if you don't want to join me."

"No, I'll go." Now Rosie felt honor-bound to help protect Regina from the surly man. Besides, it felt like an adventure. As they started on their way, Rosie said, "Do you hope to uncover some illegal activities on his part?"

Regina laughed. "I wish, but it's doubtful. It's just that I found out from Riley that Ethan is concerned over this guy. It seems he's had several violations over the years. No fire alarm, narrow aisles. He didn't have a guard posted at the door last Fourth of July and someone lit an exposed fuse. There was a small fire that could have been really bad. He waits to get cited, *then* he fixes the problems."

"Why does he need a guard?"

"To make sure no one carries a lighter or matches into the store, so that there won't be any fires. State safety regulations have been strengthened over the years. But from all accounts, this guy's something of a shady character and he walks a fine line on keeping his shop legit. And since he's a nasty-tempered fellow, too, he'll make a good counterpoint to Ethan's natural heroism. When I interview Ethan, he can add to the discussion on fireworks safety. I think my editor will run the articles side by side as a special feature."

To Rosie, it did sound interesting.

They had no trouble finding the building, but once they did, Rosie stared in dismay. Though it was only two blocks away, she felt as though they'd crossed over into another city. The atmosphere of the industrial area was very different; darker, more desolate from that near the park. There were no children around, no joggers, only a few ominous, shadowed silhouettes hanging in deep, open doorways.

This was not an area of town for two women alone.

The buildings were spaced close together and included an abandoned factory and two warehouses. Large trucks were parked on the street and in alleys. A wolf whistle came from somewhere. Rosie admitted to feeling a little apprehensive.

The fireworks store sat between two other two-story brick buildings, one selling risqué novelties, the other a pawnshop.

Rosie stared at the front door of the fireworks store

with its crooked Closed sign and frowned. "It's awfully rundown for a business, isn't it?"

Regina shrugged. "I'm told he sells mostly to companies that put on displays for large groups. I guess he considers this a warehouse of sorts."

"It's closed."

Regina gave her a telling look. "Doesn't that seem strange to you? It's the middle of the afternoon, surely part of his business hours."

A pane of glass was missing from one of the upstairs windows, but darkened curtains blocked any view to the inside. A profusion of weeds grew in a narrow patch of dirt between the street and the building. The front stoop was littered with debris.

"It's an eyesore, but that'll only make it a better contrast." Regina took several photos of the front of the shop, all the while glancing around nervously. "Let's try around back."

The narrow alleyway was overgrown with some type of scraggly vine that spread up the brick walls, into the gutters, and across every surface. They had to step around broken pieces of glass, empty boxes and garbage overflowing from a Dumpster. The gate to a rusted chain-link fence hung from one hinge and squeaked loudly when Regina pushed it open.

They rounded the corner and saw that the tiny backyard was nearly filled with a gigantic oak tree planted too close to the structure. The tree had likely never been trimmed; branches spread out over the roof and kept everything so shaded that not a speck of grass grew on the small square of spongy ground. The back door stood open. Rosie could hear men caught in a heated debate.

Regina took a breath and approached the door, cautiously stepping over twisted, exposed roots from the tree. "Hello?"

No one answered. The voices were farther away, down a hall. There was no door blocking the interior doorway, only a thin curtain tacked up and pushed partly open. The women looked at each other, but when Regina went inside, Rosie followed.

They were apparently in a back storage room and despite Rosie's untrained eye she saw a catastrophe waiting to happen. Open crates overflowing with firecrackers were stacked to the ceiling against one wall. Opposite that was a narrow flight of stairs lined with boxes of sparklers and snakes and other gimmicky fireworks. To Rosie, it appeared someone had been riffling through the boxes, given how some of the packages had been opened and products cluttered the floor.

Regina lifted her camera and snapped off several quick shots, getting a close-up of the exposed fuses. Rosie stepped around some boxes and moved to the stairs. There was a small bathroom built beneath the stairs and Rosie stared at it in disgust. Beyond being filthy, it also held several bottles of cleaner and a rag mop and bucket. Regina caught Rosie's wave and took more pictures.

At the very top of the stairs, Rosie could see more boxes. She couldn't tell what they were, but they looked different from the ones downstairs. She was ready to investigate when a large man came bursting into the room. He stopped in the curtained doorway and glared darkly at Regina.

"Here now! Just who the hell are you? You ain't allowed in here to take pictures."

Frowning at his tone, Rosie took two steps forward.

Regina quickly attempted to introduce herself. "I called earlier. I'm a reporter with the—"

Suddenly a loud crack sounded like the blast of a gun, and the man whirled around. "What the hell!" His eyes rounded at something Rosie couldn't see and he shouted, "What are you doing? No!"

A whoosh of fire shot through the doorway, caught the curtains and flared up into his face. Cursing, he staggered backward and jammed into Regina. They both went down.

"Regina!" Rosie tripped over a box and almost fell, too. She fetched up against the wall, bruising her arm. Before she could straighten herself, the burning curtains fell to the floor and the fire spread to lick around the crates of firecrackers. Seconds later, they began to explode, the sound almost deafening.

Horrified, Rosie saw that Regina had hit her head and was badly dazed. The man, who had started to run out without her, apparently thought better of it and quickly threw Regina over his shoulder. He raced out the back door, leaving Rosie inside, alone. She tried to call out, tried to scream, but the roar of the fire and the noise of the fireworks swallowed up any sound she made. The man hadn't seen her, so he hadn't even known she was inside.

The fire spread too quickly, and Rosie's alarm was almost as choking as the smoke filling the room. Hot flames blocked the back door, leaving her only one other way to go. Up.

Praying, Rosie quickly scaled the stairs. She had only a second to see that the upper floor was congested with bottle rockets, flares and Roman candles—then she saw the window and lurched toward it. She struggled to get it open, but her fingers felt numb in her fear; the window refused to budge. Behind her, the roar of the fire grew, angry and menacing. Tears ran down her face from the blinding smoke, but she brushed them away, forcing herself to think. Finally she pulled off a shoe and smashed it against the windowpane until all the sharp shards of glass were gone.

Leaning out to gulp in fresh air, she looked for Regina, but she couldn't see her or the man. However, about four feet in front of her, a thick sturdy branch from the oak tree reached out like a lifeline.

Several explosions sounded below, making her jump in terror. Rosie covered her ears before new determination gripped her. She'd just gotten Ethan, damn it, and no way was she going to let some stupid fire keep her from him now. Thanks to all the lessons she'd taken with Riley, she was strong, agile. She would save herself.

She kicked off her other shoe, crawled onto the window ledge and stretched out her hand. She couldn't quite get hold of the branch, no matter how she tried. There was only one thing left to do. She's have to jump to the tree—and pray she didn't miss.

HIS THOUGHTS HAD centered on Rosie all day. He had to be the biggest fool alive not to have realized earlier how much he cared for her. She was his best friend, his better half and his perfect match sexually. When he considered all the time he'd wasted, he wanted to kick himself.

When he remembered how sexy she was in bed, how soft she felt and the way she held him when she came... he could barely breathe. Rosie did everything with an abundance of energy and involvement. Lovemaking had been no different. Damn, he was lucky because out of all the men in the world, she wanted him.

She also wanted a big, formal, fancy wedding. Ethan closed his eyes and groaned.

He needed a distraction in the worst way and his appointment with Regina Foxworth would serve as well as any other. He was just starting into the diner when he heard the explosion and saw the smoke in the sky. It wasn't far away, and he knew fire engines were probably already on their way. Still, before he even knew it, he was halfway there, his long legs eating up the distance. The closer he got, the thicker the smoke grew.

He reached the industrial area and pushed his way through a wall of people lining the street, watching the flames consume the old building. He recognized it, of course. This was the shady fireworks dealer he'd mentioned to Rosie. He wasn't surprised by the fire, all things considered, but he prayed no one was hurt.

"You people should back up," Ethan told them as his training naturally came to the fore. "At least go to the other side of the street." He got people moving even as he heard the sirens start off in the distance. Reluctantly, the crowd parted and shifted—and then he saw Red.

But…she was supposed to be at the Diamond Diner, waiting for him.

She sat on the curb, a thin trickle of blood running down her temple, her clothes dirty and torn. "Hey?" Ethan crouched in front of her. "Are you all right? What the hell happened? What are you doing here?" As he spoke he pulled out a hanky and dabbed at the blood on her head.

She opened vague eyes and blinked at him. "Ethan?"

"Yeah, it's me." Ethan wondered if she had a concussion or if she was in shock. Either way, he needed to move her a safer distance away from the fire. "Can you walk, Regina?"

Appearing desperate, she clutched his hand. *"Rosie..."*

"What?" Frowning, sure she was delirious, Ethan took her shoulders. "What about Rosie?"

She shook her head as if to clear it, then tried again. "Oh, God, I think…I think she's still inside."

Ethan stiffened; the bottom fell out of his stomach. *Still* inside? He looked at the flames dancing out every window, coloring the sky crimson. He took in the billowing black smoke that clung to everything, stinking up the air. "She's at work."

"No." Big tears clouded Red's eyes. "She was with me."

Numb incredulity gave way to rage. Ethan wasn't aware of roaring, wasn't aware of charging the building, but suddenly men were holding him back and no matter how he fought, he couldn't get loose. No, no, he wouldn't accept it. He hit someone, kicked someone else.

Riley appeared, though that didn't make any sense. "Ethan, damn it, no."

"Let me go," he snarled, fighting for his life.

Riley wrapped his arms around him and they fell to the ground ten feet from the building. Intense heat washed over them, and there was another loud boom. Half of the roof caved in. With Riley holding him flat on his back, Ethan twisted his head to stare at the destruction. He couldn't breathe, couldn't even really see. The smoke was so goddamned thick…

Then he heard her calling his name. At first he thought he imagined it even as hope sprang alive inside him. None of it seemed real. Why would Rosie even be here? And Riley?

He pushed Riley aside as if he were no more than a gnat. Before he'd taken two steps toward the building, Riley grabbed his arm and swung him around. "Ethan, there! There she is."

With his fist cocked back, Ethan hesitated. He heard her call him again and then he followed the direction Riley pointed. Two buildings down, Ethan saw her. She'd lost her shoes, her hair was singed, but she was running toward him and, damn it, he couldn't manage a single step. He started desperately sucking air two seconds before his knees gave out.

"Ethan." She stumbled to a halt in front of him, grabbed his arm and tried to haul him to his feet. "We have to move," she panted. "The place is full of stuff—bottle rockets and Roman candles and…I don't know. All kinds of explosive things."

Slowly his vision cleared until he could see again. Belatedly, his instincts kicked in and he struggled to his feet. "We have to move."

Rosie blinked at him. "That's what I was saying."

"Come on." He wrapped her protectively in his arms and together they jogged to the opposite side of the street, away from harm. Riley walked up to stand beside them, holding Red in his arms. Ethan hadn't even noticed him picking up the other woman, yet there she was, cuddled against Riley's chest. They all sat on the curb.

The men shared a look. "This is going to be one hell of an interesting story." Riley glanced down at Red and shook his head.

Beyond confused, still rattled with lingering fear and

embarrassed over his reaction, Ethan scowled. "Just what the hell is going on? Why are you here?"

"I was just..." Riley glanced at Red, frowned and shrugged. "I was just checking up on her. She was so damn jumpy yesterday and..."

Red, still holding Ethan's hanky to her temple, lifted her head. "You were worried about me?"

Riley looked disgusted. "Yeah."

"But I thought you didn't believe me."

He glanced at Ethan. "I believe you now." Suddenly he looked furious. "Damn it, Red, when I suggested you do a story on fireworks and safety, I didn't mean for you to go skulking around this part of town."

"I'm a reporter," she insisted, but with her face white and streaked with blood, her indignation was ludicrous.

Riley took the hanky from her and dabbed at her cut. "You're a fool." She started to protest and he pushed her head back to his shoulder. "I know why I'm here, but, Rosie, what are you doing here?"

Ethan's grip on Rosie was bruising, but he wouldn't, couldn't, let her go. She patted his chest in a bid to soothe him. "I was with Regina."

Ethan stared down at her. "Why?"

"I didn't want her to try to steal you away."

He looked thunderstruck, then outraged. "Of all the idiotic..."

Red lifted her head. "But I don't want him."

Rosie looked at Riley. "Yeah, I know that *now*."

The fire engines arrived with a lot of flashing lights, noise and fanfare, drowning out any further possibilities for conversation. Men ran to the surrounding buildings, evacuating people, moving others to safety.

Without being told, Ethan and Riley strode farther

away. Ethan kept Rosie tight to his side, and Riley still carried Red. Other members of the crowd weren't so easy to sway, and Ethan had to wonder at the idiocy of spectators. If the building should explode again, anyone close by could be hit with debris.

The firefighters went to work, pulling out hoses, surrounding the building and fighting the fire from the outside in an exterior assault. One look told Ethan that it wasn't safe to do anything else.

A concerned firefighter approached Rosie. "Was there anyone else inside?"

Her voice raspy from the smoke, she said, "We—Regina and I—heard two men arguing. Only one came out to talk to her, though. I don't know about the other man."

Riley gave her a sharp look. "What do you mean, he talked to her? What about you?"

"He didn't see me. I was by the stairs."

She leaned on Ethan and he pressed his face against her smoke-scented hair. All his training, everything he knew, had disappeared with his panic. But then, no woman had ever loved him the way Rosie did. She was his, and if he lost her...

When she continued, her voice was softer, a little frightened. "I had to go upstairs because the fire just... spread. Like a whoosh."

Ethan held her back. "Do you think it was deliberate?"

Rosie looked at Regina. Both women looked upset. "Maybe."

Regina nodded. "I saw a flash of fire, then I fell and hit my head. I'm sorry I can't be more help."

Riley patted her back. "Shush. Just rest."

Bemused by Riley's behavior, Rosie had to force her gaze back to the man questioning her. "The fire blocked the door where we'd entered and it was all around these boxes of firecrackers, and they were all spilled everywhere and half-opened so that the fuses were sticking out almost like someone had set it up on purpose. Regina took a lot of pictures but…" Her babbling came to a halt. "Regina, where's your camera?"

Regina looked down at where the camera had hung around her neck, then stared for several moments in disbelief before saying, "Well, damn." She glared at Riley as if it might be his fault. "It's gone!"

Rosie scowled. "I bet the man who carried Regina out took it. He did seem mad that she was using the camera. I don't know where he went but I did see him leave with her."

"You said you went upstairs?" Riley didn't seem in any hurry to put Red down.

Rosie nodded, sending her frazzled hair to bounce around her face. "I climbed out a window, into that big tree behind the building. The fire blocked the alley so I had to go two buildings over to cut back to the street."

The firefighter touched her arm. "Thanks. I'll want to talk to both you ladies later. In the meantime, if you see that man, let me know right away, okay?" He waited for her nod, then headed off to once again force onlookers back.

Rosie lifted her face and touched Ethan's mouth. Her fingers were trembling, her eyes a little red. "I'm so sorry if I scared you."

"Scared me? I was more than scared, Rosie." He kissed her gently. "I love you, damn it."

"I don't want a big wedding."

Not sure he'd heard her right, Ethan frowned. "What?"

She fisted her hands in his shirt and tried to shake him. "We're getting married at a justice of the peace as soon as possible, and that's that. Do you understand me?"

Ethan looked at Riley, who raised both brows and shrugged. Against his throat, Red murmured, "They're in love. They're getting married."

"I see." Riley kissed her ear. "Let's let the paramedics take a look at you, okay?"

"But I'm fine."

"We'll do it anyway."

Disgruntled, she said, "All right, but at least let me walk."

"No." Riley headed for the ambulance that had just pulled up.

Ethan watched him carry her off, a little surprised though he didn't know why. Riley was…well, he was more dangerous than any modern man should be. He'd joined their group after they all met on a fishing trip. Since then, they'd been good friends, but Ethan was always aware of Riley's sharper edge and thinly veiled civility. He hid it well, but there were times, such as now, when his primitive instincts shone loud and clear.

Ethan had seen hints of it with the way Riley fought, how he remained alert at all times, the precise gentleness he utilized in his everyday life, as if he had to concentrate on that because it didn't come naturally.

This was the first time he'd seen his armor crack around a woman. Interesting.

Shrugging away those thoughts, he gave his attention back to Rosie. "Honey, we can get married any way you want. It was stupid of me to—"

"You heard me, Ethan Winters." The rest of the roof caved in with a thunderous crash. Rosie jumped, gripped him tighter and raised her voice accordingly. "It'll be a small wedding, damn it, just us and the guys and well…maybe Regina." She looked worried, and watched him with a frown. "You won't mind that, will you? I like her and I kind of think Riley does, too."

"You kind of think, huh?" Ethan glanced over at the ambulance where a paramedic tried to convince Riley to set Red down. Ethan grinned, knowing Riley had just claimed a woman in the most elemental way known to man. No way would he relinquish his hold on her. "I'd kind of say you're right."

"I do love you, Ethan."

He sat—or rather his knees gave out—but he caught Rosie on his lap. "As long as I get you and the house and the dog and the kids, nothing else matters to me."

She beamed at him. Ethan pushed her singed hair away from her face and kissed her. "You're making me old before my time."

She sighed. "Well, as long as I'm the only one making you, I can live with that."

EPILOGUE

ROSIE LAUGHED AS SHE GOT OUT of the limousine Ethan had insisted on hiring. They'd ridden to the small church with Harris, Buck, Riley and Regina. Her white dress was knee-length, simply cut, but it was lovely, the bodice overlaid with lace and pearls. The look on Ethan's face when he'd seen her in it had made her feel more beautiful than any traditional wedding gown could have.

The church was another thing he'd insisted on. And Rosie loved him too much to argue. Only two weeks had passed since the fire, which was still under investigation. They'd found the man who had carried Regina out, but no one else. He denied taking her camera, denied any wrongdoing, and claimed the other man Rosie had heard was just a customer.

He did agree that someone had deliberately set his place on fire. Unfortunately, he wanted to blame Regina.

So far, the fire was a mystery, but Riley was now convinced that Regina had reason to worry—and he'd taken it upon himself to keep an eye on her.

Rosie started for the front door of the church, but Ethan sidetracked her. "We need to go in from the back."

"We do? Why?" Everyone kept watching her, making her very suspicious. "What's going on, Ethan?"

His smile made her heart do flips.

"You're so difficult, sweetheart. Come on." He caught her hand and she had to trot in her high heels to keep up with him. Regina carried her bouquet for her—a beautiful creation of roses and baby's breath and lilies. There was a strange hush to the air as they traversed the cobblestone path to the rear. Rosie hesitated when she saw the flower-covered trellis, but Ethan didn't give her a chance to balk.

They stepped through the trellis—and into an elaborate setting of orange blossoms, crepe paper and hundreds of chairs filled with guests. A multitude of trees had been decorated with ribbons and a white outdoor platform, complete with a smiling minister, had been erected on the immaculate lawn.

Thunderstruck, her mouth hanging open, Rosie scanned the crowd of grinning faces. She recognized her neighbors, all the people she worked with, Ethan's relatives and co-workers and friends and…almost the whole town.

And there, right in the front row where her family belonged, was her brother with Michelle at his side. He looked at her for a long moment, his expression poignant, tender, then he grinned like a rascal and winked. Michelle gave a small, happy wave. Emotion choked Rosie and she started gasping, unable to catch her breath.

"Hey." Ethan slipped his arm around her. "Don't faint on me now."

She stared at him through a haze of tears. "Oh, Ethan…"

He caught her chin and tipped her face up to his. "I love you, Rosie."

She covered her mouth with a shaking hand, gulped, but it didn't help. Darn it, she never cried.

Ethan turned them both so that he blocked her from view with his body. Smiling, he used one fingertip to wipe the tears away. "You're going to ruin your makeup, sweetheart."

"But I thought you didn't want this." She sniffled, tried to pull herself together without much success. "Ethan, it's wonderful, it really is. But you're all that's important. Nothing else matters to me…"

"It matters to me, Rosie. I used to think if I did this, everyone would see me and remember how I'd been jilted." His mouth curled in a crooked smile. "Now I know what they're really thinking."

"What?"

His thumb rubbed under her chin, teasing her, keeping her face turned up to his. "That you're beautiful, and that I'm the luckiest man alive." He bent and kissed her to the roar of their guests. When he lifted his head, he grinned. "And I want the whole town to know that you're mine."

Rosie heard soft music begin, saw the guests all smiling and the flash of a camera capturing the moment.

Regina rushed up and handed her the bouquet.

Rosie stopped crying. She had everything—because she had the perfect man. Forever.

She caught Ethan's hand and dragged him to the platform. To the surprise of the other guests, Harris and Buck and Riley all whooped, cheering her name and swinging their fists in the air. But then, they were used to Rosie and her pushiness.

Once they were standing in front of the minister, Ethan pulled her close. "Love me forever, Rosie."

She laughed and threw her arms around him. "I already have."

* * * * *

RILEY

CHAPTER ONE

"RAISE YOUR KNEES."

Wide-eyed, breathless and straining, she said, *"No,"* in such a scandalized voice that Riley Moore grinned. That was the thing about Red—she made him laugh, made him feel lighthearted when he hadn't thought such a thing would be possible ever again. Not a bad start.

But he had other things to accomplish here besides smiling.

"I'm not letting you up till you do." Hell, he'd be happy to stay put for hours. Not only did she amuse him, she also aroused him more than any woman he'd ever known. Her body was slight but very soft, a nice cushion under his larger, harder frame. And the warmth he felt in the cradle of her thighs could drive him over the edge.

Her big green eyes darted left and right. "Riley, people are *watching.*"

"I know." He decided to taunt her. After all, this was important. She needed to learn how to handle him. No sense in wasting all his instruction. "They're waiting to see if you've learned anything through all these lessons. Most of them think not. Others are pretty damn doubtful."

New determination drew her slim auburn brows down into a frown and turned her green eyes stormy.

Suddenly her knees were along his sides, catching him off guard with the carnality of it. While his mind wandered down a salacious path, she bucked, rolled—and onto his back he went.

Proud as a peahen, she bounced on his abdomen and cheered herself. *Wrong move, sweetheart,* he thought, and deftly flipped her straight back and into the same position that she'd just escaped, except that this time her legs were trapped around his waist. With the wind temporarily knocked out of her, she gasped.

Half frustrated, half amused, Riley straightened. Because he knew his own ability, even if most others didn't, he always utilized strict control and caution. Especially with women, and most especially with Red. He'd sooner break his own leg than ever bruise her.

He pulled her upright, forced her arms straight up high to help her breathe, and shook his head. "When you get the upper hand on an attacker, honey, you do not stop to congratulate yourself."

Seeing that the display was over, the crowd dispersed, going back to their own training. Riley stood and gently pulled Regina Foxworth to her feet. She wasn't necessarily a short woman, but next to his height, she seemed almost puny. The top of her head reached his shoulder. Her wrists were like chicken bones. Narrow shoulders, a delicate frame...and yet, she wanted him to teach her self-defense.

Riley snorted. Hell, whenever he got this close to her he had things other than fighting on his mind. And the fact that, regardless of what he'd tried to teach her, she still ended up on her back with him in the mounted position put all kinds of considerations in his mind.

Like what it'd be like to have her situated that way,

with no clothes between them and without her attempting to escape.

Soon, he promised himself. Very soon.

In a huff, Regina promptly jerked away and began straightening her glorious red hair. If the woman thought half as much about applying herself as she did about her appearance, they'd make more progress.

For her lessons today she'd restrained her hair in a braid as thick as his wrist that hung to the middle of her back. Already silky tendrils had worked loose, giving her a softened, just-laid look. Riley shook his head in awe. He worked with other women and they just got sweaty and rumpled. Not Regina. Somehow, no matter what, the woman always managed to look more appealing.

Watching her tidy her braid sent tension rippling through his muscles. A man could conjure quite a few fantasies over that hair, not to mention the delicate, ultrafeminine body that came with it. Hell, he even found the sprinkling of freckles over her nose adorable.

Riley snatched up a towel. "Quit pouting, Red."

"I'm not." But her bottom lip stuck out in a most becoming way. Normally a princess like her wouldn't have appealed to him. But Red had guts beneath the fussy exterior. And in the time he'd known her, he'd also realized she was gentle, compassionate, understanding, and damn it, he wanted her, had from the very start.

If that had been his only problem, he'd have coaxed her into bed by now. But it was more than that. He hadn't thought to ever want involvement with another woman, but he wanted it with Red.

Riley slung his arm around her shoulders and headed her toward the shower. Not that she needed to shower.

The natural fragrance of her skin and hair was warm and womanly. His body tensed a bit more in masculine awareness, on the verge of cramping. "We're wasting our time with these lessons."

"I need to be able to defend myself."

True enough. Three weeks ago, Regina had been caught in a burning building while on assignment for the *Chester Daily Press*. As a reporter, she liked to stick her cute little freckled nose into places where it didn't belong, and that particular building had been in a disreputable part of town. That should have been her first clue not to be there. The fact that the fireworks dealer had already had trouble in the past should have been her second.

She'd forged on anyway and had come damn close to dying for her efforts. Most were inclined to call the fire an accident due to the shoddy management of the owner, who left opened pyrotechnics scattered around. But there was more to it. Long before Red got caught up in that fire, she'd been afraid. Riley first met her while she attempted to interview his friend, Ethan, for commendable work as a firefighter. Even then, she'd been as jumpy as a turkey on Thanksgiving morning. She'd seemed so strained, Riley had expected her to scream at any minute.

The day after the interview, she'd come into his gym and asked for lessons to protect herself. Unlike most of the women who approached him with the same request, Red had seemed more desperate, as if she needed the lessons for an imminent threat, not for general assurances.

Before the fire, he'd discarded her claims of endangerment, as had the county police where he worked as an evidence tech. *They* still didn't believe her, but at thirty-two, through life and some hard lessons, Riley had learned to read people, to sift real from feigned. Red was afraid, and he'd bet she had reason.

Someone was after her. She didn't know why. He didn't care why.

The day she'd almost died in that fire, he'd staked a claim. Little Red just hadn't figured that out yet. But no way in hell would he let anyone hurt her.

"Why don't you shower up and we'll talk about it?"

"Again?" She gave her long-suffering look. "There's nothing more to say. The police don't believe me, nothing else major has happened—"

Riley jumped on her choice of words. "What do you mean, nothing major? Has something minor happened?"

She shrugged, which did interesting things to her petite breasts. Dressed in snug biker shorts and a matching sports tank, there wasn't much of her body left to his imagination. But then, he'd wrestled with her enough and studied her in such detail that Riley already knew she had a discreet rack. Her breasts were small, firm and a definite draw to his eyes.

He could span her waist easily in his big hands, but from there she flared out. Her bottom was fuller, nicely rounded, as he liked. Not that it mattered. He already knew you couldn't judge the woman by the package. A facade of innocence, of kindness, or honor, meant nothing, less than nothing.

Regina could have looked a dozen different ways and he'd still want her because her draw on him went deeper than appearances. He felt an affinity to her, a vague basis he could trust in and that, more than anything, appealed to him. It seemed the moment he'd met her something had sparked.

So far, she'd shut him out.

"My apartment door was vandalized the other day."

Riley stopped dead in his tracks, right in front of the entrance to the women's shower. In a voice low with annoyance and disbelief, he growled, "Why the hell didn't you tell me?"

"I'm telling you now."

"Now is too damn late." He felt like shaking her, but she was so dainty a good shake would rattle her teeth.

"There were three other doors that got egged, so I figured it was random, not personal. And really, there's no threat in an egging, just an aggravation."

"Unless someone is trying to bug you enough to make you move." The fact that she lived in a nice apartment building with good security and lots of neighbors around reassured Riley many a night. It was the only thing that had kept him from forcing his pursuit of her. Because he felt she was safe at night, he intended to let her get used to him at her own pace. Little by little, he'd make his intentions known.

Still, he felt compelled to point out the facts. "I don't care what *you* figured, Red. From now on, tell me everything. I'm the expert here."

Her gaze dipped over his chest, now damp with sweat so that his T-shirt stuck to him. Wrestling with her hadn't caused any exertion, but he'd been in the private studio all morning giving lessons. Besides, just being near Red fired his blood. Having her open and vulnerable beneath him brought out a possessive sweat. He'd conquer her—in his own time.

"Yes, you're an expert, Riley." Staring up at him,

her big eyes full of serious regard, she added, "At a lot of things."

"At a…" His voice trailed off. Was she coming on to him? 'Bout damn time. He crowded closer to her, letting her feel the heat of his body, instinctively over-powering her with his size and masculinity and inter-est. "Just what does that mean, Regina?" He sounded gruff, half-aroused, but then she had that effect on him.

Head tipped way back to meet his gaze, she sighed. "You're an amazing guy, Riley Moore. That's all I meant. I don't know any other man who used to be part of a SWAT team, now serves as a crime scene evi-dence technician, *and* owns his own gym."

Deflated, mouth flat, Riley said, "No."

With a ludicrous show of innocence, she blinked. "No, what?"

"No, I won't do the damn interview." He should have seen right through her. He was good at deciphering mo-tives, but his perspective was blown around her, clouded by lust. She'd been after an interview for over a week now, but his past was just that: the past. He wouldn't dredge it up for anyone, not even Little Red.

"But—"

At that moment, Rosie Winters shoved her way out of the showers, forcing them both to back up. Now Rosie, bless her, knew how to work out. She got sweaty, red-faced and hot. *Not* more appealing. She cursed, grunted, struggled, and she gave it her all, showing constant improvement without a single thought to her hair or audience.

Like Riley, Rosie fought to win and she was now good enough that she just might stand a chance against a man without Riley's special training. But as ex-SWAT,

Riley could be lethal when necessary. His job had taught him how to come out the victor in any scenario. But long before that, when he'd still been a kid, nature had taught him that he didn't like to lose.

At anything.

As one of his best friends, Rosie had been coming to his gym a lot, much to Ethan's dismay. She and Ethan had married last week, but that hadn't slowed down Rosie. Nothing slowed her down. The newlyweds supplied endless hours of entertainment with the way they clashed wills, and the way they loved.

"Hey, Riley." Rosie gave him a resounding smooch on the cheek before turning to Regina. Her brown hair, still wet, hung down her back. "I lingered in the shower so I could talk to you."

Regina lifted her brows. "Really? What about?"

"Prepare yourself," Rosie warned with a lot of suspenseful anticipation. "Your loan went through. You're all set to close on the house!"

That announcement seemed to set off both women. Regina squealed as females are wont to do, and Rosie, who never squealed, laughed heartily. But around Regina, Rosie often got pulled into the more feminine mannerisms. Like now, with Regina holding her hands and dancing in circles and bouncing around.

Watching them, Riley crossed his arms and leaned back against the wall. He just adored women, the way they reacted, their expressions, their unique mindset that was so different from men's. Rosie and Regina couldn't be more dissimilar in most ways, yet they had similarities, too, just by virtue of being female.

It gave him pleasure to listen in—until it dawned

on him what Rosie had said. He shoved away from the wall. "A house? You bought a house?"

They quieted, but both still grinned hugely. "It's adorable," Regina confided. "Just the right size for me."

"And such a great bargain," Rosie added. "Because it's empty, she can have immediate occupancy."

"Immediate occupancy?" The words emerged a dark whisper. "As in alone in a house, unprotected, immediately?"

Rosie paused. "Oh. I hadn't thought of that. I mean, it's in a nice quiet neighborhood with half-acre yards—"

"Great. Just great."

Regina gave him a level look. "Really, Riley. You act like I'll be camping in the open with wild bears all around me. I can lock my doors and windows." When he only narrowed his eyes, she added, "I'll even buy an alarm system, okay?"

"It's a lousy idea. Have you two forgotten that someone recently tried to burn you alive?"

Rosie shuddered. "I'll never forget." She'd gone with Regina that day, and damn near died because of it. "But the police seem to think that it was either vandalism that got out of hand, negligence on the part of the owner, or at the very worst, vengeance aimed at the owner, not at us."

Regina watched Riley closely. "They think we were innocent bystanders."

"Right. And that's why your camera was taken and the owner has disappeared?"

Looking guilty, Rosie turned to Regina. "Maybe he's right."

"No, he is not right. I have to live somewhere, so it might as well be my own house." She patted Riley on the chest. Though she did it negligently, without a single sign of awareness on her part, he felt the damn pat clear through to his masculine being. "I'll get an alarm system *and* a dog. How's that?"

Seeing that he wouldn't win, Riley gave up that particular argument. At least she wanted to take steps in the right direction. A big, well-trained German shepherd or Doberman would certainly be a deterrent to anyone thinking to harm her. In the meantime, he'd just have to see about advancing his courtship. Once she gave in, he'd have the right to keep her close, to watch over her.

And all her spare time would be spent in bed, giving her less time to get into trouble.

With Ethan and Rosie's rushed wedding plans, they'd been forced together more frequently than otherwise. Adding to that her lessons at the gym, he'd seen her almost daily for the past three weeks. Their time together had been platonic because he couldn't possibly wrestle with her and have romantic thoughts without embarrassing them both, and possibly breaking a few sexual harassment laws. He felt certain a boner would have been out of line.

But he knew how he felt. Maybe it was time she knew, too.

It wouldn't be a bad idea to live with her until he felt secure that she'd be safe alone. The benefits to that scenario were more than obvious. To both of them.

"When's the closing on the house?"

Rosie winced.

Resigned, Riley asked again, "How soon, Rosie?"

"Weeeelll…" Rosie cast a quick look at Regina, but she was too busy smiling over her good news to share Rosie's uncertainty. "Because the house was empty and her credit impeccable, I sort of rushed it through. We have a date set for the middle of next week."

Regina squealed again, but with Riley so subdued, she quickly quieted. "You're being such a stick in the mud, Riley. Can't you be just a little happy for me?"

If it weren't such bad timing, he would be. But he worried about her enough already without her being off on her own, away from the safety of the apartment complex. In his mind, she was already his. He wanted to protect her, not leave her safety dependent on a dog and alarm.

He studied her for a long moment, deciding how best to proceed without making her more skittish. Then he realized his stare alone had her squirming uncomfortably. He tried a smile, but it felt more predatory than anything else. "I'll take you to dinner to celebrate." He made it a statement rather than an invitation, on the off chance she thought to refuse.

Her hesitation fell heavy between them. "I don't know..."

Riley took a step closer. "Say yes, Regina."

Rosie's gaze bounced back and forth, watching them with great interest.

A blush tinged Regina's cheeks. "The thing is, I wanted to get my dog today. I figure I might as well potty train him at my apartment so he won't mess up my house."

Riley didn't let her off the hook. He waited, still watching her intently until her unease was palpable.

Finally, she sighed. "If you can come over around six, I can cook dinner at my place."

Now that sounded promising. Much better suited to his purpose than being in a crowded restaurant. "I'm on vacation for the next two weeks, so I'm at your disposal." He realized suddenly that Rosie had a vacuous grin on her face. She knew him better than Regina did, so she'd probably already realized how territorial he felt.

Glancing over his shoulder at the workout area of the gym, he said, "I have to get back on the floor. I have three more hours of personal instruction before I'm free." He touched Regina's cheek. "Promise me you'll be careful, Red."

She blinked, then stepped out of reach. Her laugh sounded forced. "It's the middle of the day. I swear, Riley, you're more fretful than I am."

That's because he knew firsthand the danger that could befall a woman alone. He shook off that dark thought and raised her chin. "Promise?"

"Cross my heart." With a last platonic pat on his chest, she said, "Don't be late."

Riley watched her disappear into the shower room, spellbound until Rosie started snickering. When he gave her his attention, she clutched her heart and pretended to swoon.

"Brat." Riley put her in a chokehold and knuckled the top of her head. Though she was gorgeous and sexy, Rosie was like a pal, permanently safe from any lecherous intentions, especially since she'd married Ethan.

"Hey," she gasped out, "no fair. I don't want to get messy again. I have a showing this afternoon."

Riley released her and got a sharp elbow to his middle. He grunted while Rosie quickly backed away. "Sucker," she said with a grin, then she turned and jogged toward the door.

Riley laughed. He did love Rosie, but he didn't want her. He didn't burn for her.

Not the way he did for Ms. Regina Foxworth.

REGINA KNEW it wasn't the wisest decision she'd ever made. And for a woman who prided herself on only making wise decisions, she should have been appalled at herself. She only had so much money for decorating her new house and putting in the alarm system that she'd promised Riley.

She tried to talk herself out of it, she really did. But as she stared at those big brown eyes, she fell madly in love. He was so cute with the way he laid his enormous ears back on his little round head, how he stared at her with bulging eyes, shivering with uncertainty. He probably wasn't the type of dog Riley had in mind, but the man said they were loyal pets, dedicated to their owners.

"I'll take him." Sometimes things just felt right. Like being a journalist. Like buying the house.

Like being near Riley.

This felt right, too. Now that she'd met this dog, no other would do, so she shelled out the six hundred dollars that she really couldn't spare. Love was love and it should never be denied. Not that she knew a lot about love. But she did know that she wanted it more than anything. And to get it, you had to give it, she reasoned. She could really love this dog.

While she carried him outside, he continued to shake and stare at her with those big, watchful eyes. She'd never seen such a pathetic look in her life. She wanted to crush him close, but he was so puny, she didn't dare. Gently, she stroked his skinny back and rubbed his soft neck.

She'd never felt a dog so soft. He had bunny fur, so cuddly and silky. And he didn't smell like a dog either. She rubbed her nose against his neck and got a tiny lick on the ear in return.

Once in the car, secured in the carrier, his teeny tiny mouth formed an O and he began to howl.

It was both hilarious, the way he looked, and heart-wrenching the way he sounded. The mournful baying continued until Regina was in a near panic. "Shh. What's wrong?" Did he want her to hold him? "I have to drive, sweetie," she explained. "It wouldn't be safe. Soon as we get home, I'll cuddle you again, I promise."

At the sound of her voice, the dog quieted and inched to the edge of the small cage to sniff the air near her. His spindly little hind legs quivered and he continued to look sad, but trusting.

"Awww…" He was just so adorable. Big tears filled her eyes. She *had* made the right decision. Sticking one finger through the carrier, Regina rubbed behind his ear. "You're as soft as a baby bunny, did you know that?"

He cocked his head, listening to her, his ears still down in a woebegone display but he made no sounds of dismay.

"What should I name you?"

The ears came up. Regina marveled at his many expressions.

"How about…Elvis?" His ears pricked, then flattened again and he gave her a sideways look. "No? Then maybe Doe? You do look like a little deer, you know. Hmm. That doesn't appeal to you either? Something more manly then. I know. Butch. Or Butchie when you're being so adorable."

Soothed by her banter, he gave an excited yap of agreement and Regina nodded. "Butch it is."

For the rest of the ride home, Regina alternated her attention between her driving and the dog. She constantly scanned the road and surrounding area, still spooked from the time someone tried to run her off the berm. To calm herself and the dog, she spoke to him, being sure to use his name as the breeder suggested, so he could get used to it.

By the time they pulled into her apartment complex, he was looking around with interest, animated anytime she spoke to him. He continued to shake though.

People were coming and going, keeping the parking lot alive with a safe, surrounding crowd. Feeling secure again, she carried Butch, along with his paraphernalia, into her apartment. She'd bought bowls, food, chew sticks, a toothbrush, leash, collar and a cozy fleece-lined bed. She set Butch down first, watched him cower there on the floor, and decided he needed some encouragement.

Her apartment was small, only one bedroom, a bath, kitchenette and living area. "I'll be right back, Butch." She went to the kitchen to unload all the items, then came back for him. She found him sprinkling her couch.

"Oh, now that's just not right, Butch."

He slunk toward her, his head down in apology.

Regina's heart melted. "Honey, it's okay." She cuddled him close, got a tentative lick on her cheek. He was the most precious perfect dog, she decided, and carried him into the kitchen since that was where he'd spend most of his time. With a kiss to the top of his round head, she put him in his bed, then went back to clean her couch. When she returned to the kitchen, she found three more wet spots. Butch looked so very contrite, she couldn't hold it against him. She understood that he was nervous and needed reassurance. Instead of chastising him, she hugged and petted him some more, trying to let him know he was safe and secure and well loved.

By the time she had dinner going and Riley was due to arrive, Butch had relaxed enough to play a little. He followed Regina everywhere she went, sometimes bounding here or there, sometimes turning excited circles. Charmed, Regina had to keep stopping to pick him up, kiss him and hug him.

Because she was on the second floor, she put a litter box on her small balcony for him to use and in no time he got the hang of going to the glass patio door to scratch. She used a short leash that kept him from reaching the edge of the balcony so he couldn't accidentally fall off and get hurt. He did his business like a trooper and came back in.

Of course, he marked his territory everywhere inside the apartment, too. Regina wasn't yet sure if he was uncertain of his boundaries, stubborn or just not very bright. She hoped the first, because the second and third didn't bode well for her peace of mind.

The chicken was done, the potatoes already mashed, when the knock sounded on her door. She recognized Riley's knock right off. Decisive, firm, just like the man himself.

Though she hated to admit it, she felt that familiar leap of her heart whenever he was near. They'd known each other three weeks now, and so far Riley had been attentive, courteous and understanding.

More important than that, he believed her somewhat wild stories about stalkers and threats when no one else would. Of course, Regina thought his belief just might be attributed to boredom. Riley used to be SWAT, for heaven's sake. He was used to excitement and danger.

In Chester, the most excitement he got was photographing old man Tilburn's house because the neighborhood rascals had toilet-papered it once again. For a man like Riley, a man of his skills and background, that had to add up to a lot of frustration. Even chasing Regina's ghosts had to be better than that.

But she wouldn't complain. Regardless of what motivated him, she needed his help, so she'd take what she could get.

She expected the thrill that skated through her when she started to open the door.

What she didn't anticipate was Butch going into a complete hostile frenzy. He transformed from tiny shivering dog into Tasmanian devil right before her eyes.

Riley called out, "Regina? It's me. Open up."

"Just a second." She picked up Butch, but holding the snarling, rigid, four-pound mass of meanness was nearly impossible. Outrage stiffened every muscle in his lean little body and he fought her to be free—so he could attack her visitor.

What a courageous dog!

Using one hand, Regina turned the locks on the door and then struggled to maintain her hold on Butch while Riley stepped inside. The dog broke free. Regina almost dropped him but managed to get him to the floor, head first.

He rolled, landed on his feet and like a shot, went after Riley.

Riley stood there, brows high, expression arrested, while Butch tried to tear his pant leg off. "What the hell? Is that a rabid squirrel?"

Indignant, Regina closed the door and crossed her arms. "Of course not. It's my dog, Butch."

"*That's* a dog?" Incredulity rang in his voice. "Are you sure?" His head tilted down at the wriggling fury hanging from his leg. "How can you tell?"

Offended on Butch's behalf, Regina huffed. She pulled the dog free and went about soothing him. "Shh. Butchie, it's okay. He's allowed in. Such a good dog. So brave."

Riley looked like he might puke. "That *is* a dog. What the hell is wrong with it?"

Regina sat on the couch. "Nothing. He's perfect."

"He can't weigh more than four pounds."

"He's four exactly." She rubbed Butch's belly and he rolled to his back, his skinny legs falling open, his eyes half-closed.

Riley pulled back. "Good God."

Regina didn't take him to task for that comment. After all, Butch was showing his equipment with no evidence of modesty whatsoever. She cleared her throat. "The breeder said I should have him neutered."

"He'll only weigh three pounds if you do." Grinning at his own joke, Riley took the seat beside her and reached out to pet the dog. Butch went berserk again, his doggy lips pulled back tight, rippling with menace, the whites of his eyes showing. One second he looked so innocent and sweet and the next he appeared like a vicious gnat.

"He needs time to get used to you," Regina explained in a rush, and hoped that was true. If Butch continued to act so contrary, what would she do?

In his usual calm manner, Riley surveyed Butch. "What kind of dog is it?"

"He's a pure bred Chihuahua. His beautiful coloring is very unique." She certainly thought him beautiful. "Red with black brindling."

Riley only nodded. "How much bigger will he get?"

"Oh, he's full-grown." She rubbed Butch's ears and watched his bulgy eyes narrow in bliss. "Isn't he just precious?"

"No." Riley frowned at her. "Please tell me this isn't your idea of a guard dog."

"But he's perfect," she said by way of answer. "You saw how he attacked you."

"And you saw how I held real still so I wouldn't accidentally hurt him."

She had noticed that. Riley was always so cautious with people, so careful. She knew a lot of that had to do with his training and his ability. It would be so easy for him to hurt someone, that he naturally tempered himself in almost all situations. Others might not be aware of his restraint, but Regina had seen it in his intense blue eyes, and she'd felt it during her lessons.

She'd also noticed that he hadn't been startled by Butch's attack. Most people would have jumped, maybe even screeched.

Not Riley. She couldn't imagine anything unsettling Riley enough to wring a screech out of him. With unparalleled calm, he'd taken in the situation and then reacted, without haste, careful not to hurt Butch.

Such an incredible guy.

Nodding, she said, "I did notice. Thank you."

Lounging back in his seat, Riley put one arm along the couch back, almost touching her shoulder. Without leaving Regina's lap, Butch slanted a mean gaze his way, his rumbling growls a warning. Riley continued to watch the dog while speaking to Regina. "When do we eat? It smells good."

Flustered by the compliment, she came to her feet,

holding Butch like an infant—which he seemed to
enjoy. "It's ready now. We have to eat in the kitchen. I
don't have a dining room. Once I get moved in I'll have
a dining room, and we can use it then. I mean, if you're
ever over for dinner at my new house…." Turning her
back on Riley and rolling her eyes at her own rambling
nonsense, she rushed into the kitchen. Hostesses should
not ramble. They should feed their guests.

Riley followed. "Regina?"

"Hmm?" She turned after setting Butch in his bed.
He came right back out of it, still watching Riley, inch-
ing closer for a sniff. Now that Regina no longer held
him, he was jumpy enough to lurch back a step each
time Riley moved.

"We'll be having plenty of dinners together."

The sneaky way the dog advanced distracted her.
"We will?"

Butch was at Riley's foot now, his sniffing more
purposeful. Knowing what Butch probably intended,
Regina scrambled to find a chew stick. In no way did
she want Butch to mark Riley. He was not part of the
permanent territory and unlikely to become so.

Riley crouched down and held out a hand to Butch.
The dog gave his fingers a thorough inspection, donned
an angelic expression complete with big innocent eyes
and a small doggy smile, and even allowed Riley to
rub under his chin. Teasing, Riley said, "You sure he
wasn't bred with a rat?"

Regina, too, bent down to hand Butch the rawhide
chew. The second she got near, Butch did an about-face.
He snapped at Riley in warning, squirmed up close to
Regina and accepted the chew.

"Contrary dog," Riley commented while standing up straight again.

Butch retreated to his bed to work over the chew. "He's getting used to you already."

Riley caught her hand and pulled her upright in front of him. Her heart pounded when his strong, warm fingers laced with hers, palm to palm.

"What about you, Red? You getting used to me, too?"

Oh boy, there was a load of innuendo in the way Riley said that. And truthfully, she was so used to him that when he wasn't around, she missed him. Dumb. Regina Foxworth did not allow herself fanciful infatuations. She thought to tell him that yes, she was used to him and why shouldn't she be? He was no different from any other man. But with his callused fingers holding hers, words stuck in her throat. She barely managed a shrug.

With his gaze holding her captive, his hand opened, slid slowly up her arm, over her shoulder and the side of her neck, along her jaw until his fingers curled around the back of her neck. Where he'd touched, gooseflesh sprang up and she trembled.

Softly, Riley whispered, "Wrong answer."

Her startled gasp emerged just as he urged her to her tiptoes. "Riley?"

"You need to accept a few things, Red."

She felt spellbound, uncertain. Anxious. But if she hesitated much longer, her chicken would burn and then she'd make a bad impression. She forced herself to say "Like?"

"Like this." He bent and kissed her.

CHAPTER TWO

THE TOUCH OF HIS MOUTH was brief, warm, firm. Regina barely had time to appreciate his taste before he lifted away the tiniest bit.

"Oh." Tentatively, thoughts of chicken obliterated, Regina laid her hands on his chest. He'd dressed in casual chinos and a polo shirt, but the domestic clothes couldn't hide the true nature of the man. The soft cotton fabric served an enticing contrast to the hard muscle, long bones and crisp hair underneath.

His eyes were more gray than blue now, glittering with heat. There was nothing even remotely domestic in the way he watched her. "More than anything," he rumbled low, "I'd like to carry you into your bedroom right now, strip you naked and make love all night." He closed his eyes a moment, drew a breath. When he looked at her again, some of that intense heat had been tempered. "But we've got a lot to get cleared up first."

Regina faltered. Make love all night? *Strip her naked?* They hadn't known each other *that* long. Regardless of her strong attraction to Riley, she wasn't the type of woman to leap into an affair. Responsible people utilized caution and thought before making that type of commitment.

Stepping back from him, she gestured to her tiny two-seater table. Her hand shook and she had to clear her throat twice before she could speak. "Sounds like we have a long talk ahead." Thankfully, her voice was only a little shaky. "Sit down while I serve dinner."

Riley watched her with indecision before silently agreeing. Regina could feel his gaze on her rump when she bent to pull the perfectly browned chicken out of the oven. Martha Stewart would be proud. Ms. Manners would applaud her.

As the delicious scents of stuffing and chicken wafted through the air, Butch perked up, his little nose raised and quivering with interest. Regina looked at him, but Riley said, "I wouldn't. Once you feed him table food, you'll never be able to stop. And it's not good for him anyway."

"Right." She knew that, and since she always tried to do the right thing, she hoped her dog would do the right thing as well. Giving Butch an apologetic shake of her head, she filled his bowl with dog food. Appeased, he began to eat while Regina carried the food to the table. The chicken was placed perfectly on a platter, the potatoes looked fluffy in a decorative bowl, and steam rose from the broccoli with melting butter atop it. She lit a scented candle in the middle of the table and everything was complete. Beautiful.

"What can I do to help?"

Regina stared at Riley, and he stared back, studying her. She'd expected him to sit and admire her dinner preparation skills, not watch her every move. But if he wanted to help...wasn't it a man's job to carve? She'd never had a man around long enough to know, and her father certainly hadn't been the type to worry about how food was cut. He was more a grab-and-stuff-it-in-your-mouth kind of guy.

Regina handed Riley the butcher knife and fork with a flourish. "Iced tea, milk?"

"Tea is fine." He stood to begin slicing apart the chicken. Regina noticed that he did an admirable job. He glanced up at her. "Why are you so nervous, Red?"

"I'm not."

"You are."

She sighed, unable to deny the obvious. "No more so than usual. That is, I'm always nervous." It was a complaint she often got from men. But now, with the man being Riley, she felt doubly unsettled. Add to that some unknown assailant who had tried to hurt her several times and might just try again, and to her way of thinking she had plenty of reason to be nervous.

"Because you're worried?"

"Yes." She poured the iced tea, sat, remembered she wanted music and popped back up. "I'll be right back." Seconds later, the stereo in her bedroom played low, adding soft sounds to the clink of china and silver.

Riley waited for her to return. He held her chair, but when she sat, he didn't retreat. Instead he bent down and kissed the side of her neck. Oh Lord, she'd never get used to this spontaneous kissing of his. At Mach speed, he'd taken them from acquaintances, maybe friends, to something much more intimate.

Fighting the urge to gasp again, she stiffened. Where he'd pressed his mouth, her neck tingled and felt damp. A strange but pleasant warmth rippled through her.

Riley spoke softly into her ear, adding to her awareness. "You need to be comfortable being alone with me, Red."

The way he said that, all seductive and low, made her stomach flip-flop. "I do?" At this rate, she'd never be able to eat. It'd look like she didn't appreciate her own culinary skills.

"Yeah." He brushed her nape with the back of one finger, then circled the table and sat in his chair, facing her, casual as you please, as if he hadn't just been teasing her, turning her on.

"Um…why?"

He picked up his fork. "Starting today, we're going to be alone together." His gaze caught and held hers. "A lot."

THE FOOD WAS DELICIOUS. He'd had no idea that Regina was such a fine cook. For long moments, they ate in silence. He waited to see what Regina would say to his statement, but she just sat there, watching him cautiously, occasionally nibbling on her food.

He didn't want to spoil her dinner, so he sat back and studied her. "I guess you want me to explain?"

She cleared her throat. "That'd be nice, yes."

A starched linen napkin had been placed beside his plate. Since it was there, Riley used it to pat his mouth. "All right. You're not showing much improvement at the gym."

Her shoulders sank the tiniest bit. Riley wasn't sure if it was disappointment or relief. "I know. I'm not a very physical person."

He intended to hold all judgments on that until he had her in bed. Then he'd see just how physical he could coax her into being. "You don't need physical strength, Regina. But you do have to stop worrying about other people watching you."

She winced. "I know. It's just that I hate looking like a fool."

"Once you know what you're doing, you'll look like a pro."

"Yes, of course," she quickly agreed. "I'll try harder, I promise."

He didn't believe that for a minute. "Regina?"

She glanced up at him, her brows raised quizzically.

"I'm going to give you very private lessons from now on. Just the two of us." He looked at her mouth. "All alone. No spectators."

She stared at him for three seconds. "You are?"

Riley nodded, a little put out that she questioned every damn thing he said, like she couldn't believe it or doubted it to be true. He wasn't a liar, damn it.

Stunned by that mental statement, he shook his head and made a quick amendment: he wouldn't lie to *her,* and not about this. Other lies, lies from his past, were well buried.

Holding on to his patience, Riley continued his explanation. "There's not much room here at your place, so we can't really get going tonight."

Her mouth opened. In anticipation, shock or horror? Riley couldn't quite tell. "You can either come to my place, or the gym after hours."

She held perfectly still. Tonight she had her thick hair twisted at the back of her head and held in place with a fancy gold clip. It had been somewhat loosened by the kiss he'd given her earlier. The florescent overhead lights brought out the deeper reds and lighter golds, mixed in with the auburn. It also reflected the wariness in her green eyes.

She wore a freshly pressed sleeveless green V-neck shirt and low-riding cotton slacks. Her sandals showed off her meticulous pedicure.

From the top of her head to the tips of her toes, she was polished to a shine. She'd even managed to do dinner with no additional mess, putting things away as she used them so that no empty pans sat on the stove and no seasonings were out.

Riley wanted to see her mussed.

He wanted to see her sweat.

He wanted to hear Ms. Suzy Homemaker crying out in raw sexual excitement without a single thought as to how she looked, concerned only with the deep, driving pleasure.

Damn, he had to stop that train of thought or he'd be seducing her right now.

Finally, she nodded. "Thank you." Her voice sounded a little raspy. "It does embarrass me. I think it'll be easier without others watching. But, Riley, mostly it's you that I worry about."

"Me?" Sipping his iced tea, he watched her, thinking it wasn't such a bad thing if he unsettled her. It meant she held at least a small amount of awareness for him as a man.

She pleated her napkin. She straightened her fork. Suddenly she blurted, "Are you attracted to me?"

"Yes."

She seemed surprised by his immediate answer. Then she chewed on her lips. "I'm attracted to you, too."

She made that admission with the same regret she might have given a murder confession.

"I know." He hadn't known. He'd hoped. He was pretty sure. But he'd wanted confirmation.

Now he had it.

"It…bothers me, the idea of you seeing me all messy and sweaty."

Hearing her say it sharpened his desire. "Eventually, I'll see you every way there is." He toyed with his iced tea glass, his gaze never wavering from hers. "When we have sex, you'll definitely be sweaty. Messy, too. That's the way it is with good sex. But I'm willing to bet you'll look hot as hell."

Her breathing deepened and her brows puckered in thought. After a long hesitation, she said, "You, um, you treat Rosie like a pal."

"Rosie is a pal."

"But she's also a very attractive woman."

Leaning back in his seat, Riley nodded. "Agreed."

"And yet you never have romantic thoughts about her because she's become your pal."

Riley had no idea where she was going with this. Women could be so confusing, even to a man who prided himself on getting past the surface stuff. Oh, he could detect some of her thoughts. She was uncertain, interested, wary. But he wanted to know *why* she felt so uncertain.

He eyed her, then decided a little truth couldn't hurt the situation. "Who says?"

Confusion left her face blank. "Who says... Well, Rosie said. She assured me that she loved Ethan and—"

"She does." It had recently become very clear that Rosie had always loved Ethan—she'd just been waiting around for him to come to his senses and realize that he loved her, too.

"—and that Ethan was a good friend of yours."

"He is." With Harris and Buck, they made a regular foursome, but he and Ethan had more in common. They were all friends, but if Riley ever had his back to the wall, he'd trust Ethan more than any other man.

"Then—"

"You think because we're friends, I shouldn't have sexual thoughts about her?" He stretched out his long legs beneath the table and bumped into her small feet. "You and I are friends, and I have plenty of sexual thoughts about you."

Her eyes widened comically. "Plenty?"

It was his turn to smile. "All day, every day, as a matter of fact."

She stewed on that for a bit before speaking again. "But see, that's just it. I thought you felt about me the way you feel about Rosie, except you're closer with her."

"Not a chance."

"You're not close to her?"

"Very close. But the way I feel about you is on the other end of the scale. I don't intend to ever sleep with Rosie." He let his gaze drop to her breasts. "You, however, I intend to get naked with just as soon as it can be arranged."

Her eyes dilated in shock, but he also saw reciprocal interest in the way her breathing deepened and how her skin warmed. Despite all that, she shook her head. "You should probably know, Riley, I don't sleep around."

"You're a virgin?"

More color stained her cheeks and she frowned. "No, I didn't say that." Then she added in a mumble, "For heaven's sake, I'm twenty-eight years old."

"So you're saying you don't want to sleep with me?" He knew damn good and well that wasn't true. But would she be honest?

"Of course I do."

He grinned.

"I mean, I do, but I'm not going to. Not anytime soon, that is. We barely know each other."

He'd known her long enough to understand exactly how he felt. "We've known each other better than three weeks now. That's not exactly a sneeze. And because of the lessons, we've been physically close."

"You're keeping count?"

She was clearly astonished by that. Hell, it still stunned Riley a little, the depth of what he felt. But he didn't want her panicking on him, so he backed off. "Let's finish eating, then we'll talk about it more. By the way, you're a hell of a cook. I'm impressed."

Relieved by the change of topic, she nodded. "I wanted you to be. Impressed, I mean." She caught herself and her gaze jerked up to his. "That is, I try to impress everyone."

"Yeah? Why is that, Red? You don't think just being yourself is good enough?" There was so much he still had to learn about her. Funny how appearances meant nothing to him because they weren't something you could trust. Yet, they meant the world to her.

The contrast in their views might have discouraged him, but he figured he was at least making headway now.

"Maybe." She propped her head on her hand, realized that wasn't the proper way to sit and jerked upright again. "Actually I've thought about this a lot, about why I'm the way I am. Every so often, I wish I could be different because sometimes it has the opposite effect and just drives people nuts."

"What people?"

"Co-workers, friends. Men."

He didn't give a damn what other men thought of

her. If they steered clear, hell, he was glad. "Rosie and Ethan and Buck and Harris like you fine." He smiled. "I like you more than fine. But I am curious why you're so worried about what other people think. That is, if you care to talk about it."

She pleated and fussed with her napkin. "It's silly really. Maybe something of a habit left over from when I was young."

"You were a fussy child?"

His teasing put a self-conscious half smile on her face. "Yes. Very fussy, I guess. See, I came from a…a dirty farmhouse." She wrinkled her nose with that confession. "And when I say dirty, I'm not exaggerating. It's awful to admit, but we lived like pigs."

Not sure that he understood, Riley asked, "You were poor?"

"Poor and slovenly are not the same thing, but yes, we were poor, too. I've never been certain if it was necessary, if they just couldn't make enough money or if they simply mismanaged what they made." She shrugged. "My parents sustained us from paycheck to paycheck. If we ran out in the middle of the week, or something came up—as things always do—they'd borrow or beg."

The expression on her face twisted his heart. Softly, he said, "That had to be rough."

"I hated it and it embarrassed me."

The emotional plethora took Riley off guard. Being a private man, he couldn't imagine discussing so much of his personal background. "So you've worked to change your life. There's nothing wrong with that."

"It was never my life." She sipped her tea, scooted her broccoli around on her plate with the edge of her fork. "It was my mother's, my father's and my younger brother's. But not mine."

No, Riley couldn't quite imagine her ever being comfortable in those circumstances. She was so prim, proper and precise now, that it must have been almost painful for her.

"You didn't accept the circumstances of your youth."

"For as far back as I can remember, even as a young kid, I tried to make it different. Everything I owned was old and stained, but I did my best to always keep it clean and pressed." She glanced up at him and gave a low laugh. "My brother used to make fun of me for being so meticulous. The other kids we knew.... They liked to call us names and poke fun at us."

Riley hated that anyone had hurt her feelings, even though it had happened long ago. And her brother... It was ridiculous to be angry at him when he'd been no more than a boy, too. But that didn't change how Riley felt. "Kids can be pretty cruel when no one is teaching them better."

"Maybe. But if you'd ever seen our farm or car or how my parents behaved in public, you'd understand why the kids treated us the way they did. I understood it. And I knew my family would never change. After I graduated high school, I moved away, got a job as an errand girl with a small paper and worked my way up to reporter."

Riley smiled. Reporter was a bit of a stretch considering the small pieces she wrote. Then again, her human-interest stories for the local paper were always entertaining. She'd done a stellar article on Ethan that had made the fire department, as well as the whole town, proud.

Riley thought about it and decided selective sharing was good. It forged a bond that would bring them closer together, and that was his ultimate goal. There were parts of himself he could discuss, parts that weren't buried deep and that wouldn't reveal anything beyond the surface.

He mentally skimmed a variety of topics and settled on his safest bet—family. "My mother isn't immaculate or anything."

Her interest obvious, she glanced up at him with a smile. "No?"

"She keeps the place tidy, but it's always well lived in. I have two younger brothers, one older."

"Four boys? My goodness."

"Yeah, Mom felt the same way." He laughed. "The others still live near to home and they drop in a lot with their broods. Between the three of them, I have ten nieces and nephews."

"Wow. A big family."

He acknowledged that with a shrug. "Mom is old-fashioned, the type who wants to feed you the minute you show up and fusses around you the whole time you're there. I haven't been home to see her in a while." That was something he should remedy, Riley decided. Funny that he hadn't much considered how long it had been until Regina started discussing her family.

Wondering how Regina would react to the casual mess around his mother's house, he pushed his plate away. "Maybe next time I go, you could come along with me."

Her eyes shot wide. "You want me to meet your mother?"

She sounded as if he'd asked her to swim with sharks. "And Dad, too. You'd like them."

She had nothing to say to that so Riley pressed her. "What about your folks? Do you visit with them at all?" He wouldn't really be surprised if she'd broken all ties, but it'd be a shame. When all was said and done, family should be there for you, and vice versa.

"They're gone now." There was a wistful, sad note to her voice. "Mom died years ago from cancer and Dad passed away from a stroke two years after. The farm was sold and my brother and I split the profits. That's how I bought my house. I've been sitting on that money for a while."

Riley had wondered about that. He didn't imagine a small-town reporter earned much income. "I'm sorry."

"It was a long time ago. I loved them, but I was never very close with them. We had a...strained relationship." She hesitated, and Riley wondered if she'd pull back now, if she'd return to being evasive. Instead, she shrugged. "They thought I was snooty."

With almost no prodding at all, she continued to open up to him. In his experience, reporters pried into anyone and everyone's life, but clammed up when it came to their own personal issues. He couldn't help wondering if her openness was a compliment reserved for special people. Did she feel safer with him? Did she trust him?

"Snooty, huh?" He pretended to study her head to toe, then nodded. "Circumspect, yes. Meticulous, maybe. But not snooty."

"Thank you." She tucked in her chin to hide her smile. "My brother still accuses me of thinking I'm better than them."

"Do you?"

"Think I'm better? No. But I'm certainly wiser about how I handle my life." Her long look seemed like a warning, one he fully intended to ignore. He would have her, and soon. "My parents had a great farm that they let go to ruin because they refused to do any real work. It should have been worth five times as much, but they'd never taken care of it. The house was so run-down it had to be demolished. There wasn't a piece of furniture or a dish to be salvaged."

"No mementos at all?"

"A few photographs that my brother and I split. My folks didn't believe in cherishing the past or planning for the future. They had the barest medical coverage and of course, it wasn't enough. Now my brother seems just like them. He flits from one job to the next, one woman to another."

Sounded like a lot of guys Riley knew, men who wouldn't grow up and so, at least in his opinion, weren't really men.

"He's already spent his inheritance and doesn't have a thing to show for it. I asked what he intended to do when he retired, but he just laughs and says he has a lifetime to worry about it. He hasn't learned at all."

"But you have?"

"Absolutely." She met his gaze squarely. "The house is an investment in my future, but I have others as well. If I get sick, I'll be able to take care of myself, not rely on others or end up in the care of the state. I'm careful about everything I do and I don't give in to impulses."

Impulses like sexual desire? Did she hope to deny the chemistry between them? Riley didn't correct her but he knew different. He could be persuasive and he never gave up easily.

At his long silence, her chin lifted. "What about you?"

"What about me?"

She looked self-conscious but forged on. "Do you have a retirement plan? And you mentioned your place. Do you have your own house or are you renting?"

The inquisition so surprised him, Riley laughed. "Tell me, Red, are you curious for personal reasons, sizing me up as husband material, or are you mentally working on that damn article?"

She stiffened, but she didn't lie. "A little of each maybe, though it's certainly too early to be thinking about anything serious between us."

"You really think so?"

Her face went blank, then pink with confusion. She forged on. "And I wouldn't write the article without your permission. It's just that the whole community hero angle worked so well with Ethan, I know people would eat up a life story on you."

He ignored that because his life wasn't anybody's business. "But you're personally interested, right?"

She chewed on her lips again. "We're not involved, Riley, so it's more curiosity than anything."

"I want to be involved."

She pressed back in her chair. She blinked, studied his face, then looked down at her hands. "You know, Riley, it occurs to me that this could get pretty muddled."

"How so?" Riley felt strangely sated. He'd had a delicious meal, cozy conversation and the sight of Regina seated across from him. It was the kind of setting he could get used to—the kind of setting he hadn't wanted again until he'd met her.

He knew exactly how he'd like to end the day, but after everything she'd confessed, he had his doubts about her cooperation. He could be patient, especially since all indications led him to believe he'd eventually win.

"You say you believe me about the attacks."

"I do."

"Then don't you think we should keep the personal and the professional separate? Won't it be hard for you to be objective if we're...well, sleeping with each other?"

Objectivity had flown out the window within hours of meeting her. He drank the last of his iced tea and nodded at her plate. "What I think is that you should eat some of this great dinner you fixed."

"I am eating." She took two more bites, then went on in a rush. "Why would you believe me when no one else does?"

"It's easy enough to understand. You finish eating and I'll tell you a story, okay?"

"All right."

She still only picked at her food, but he felt better knowing he hadn't completely ruined her meal. "Back when I was a new evidence tech, before I became SWAT, I got called to the scene where a guy had broken into his seventeen-year-old girlfriend's house. The mother had forbid the girl to see him anymore, but when she left to go shopping, he snuck over. When the girl tried to send him away, he got unreasonably furious, choking her and banging her head on the wall a few times."

Regina's head came up, a broccoli floret dangling from her fork. "Dear God."

"The mom got home in time to pull him off her,"

Riley assured her, but as usual, the bitter memories filled him with anger. Too many times, he hadn't been able to make a difference. "The detectives got there just before me, but the boyfriend had already fled. They were speaking with the mom and daughter, and the dad who had just arrived home. Patrol tells me that the mom wants to prosecute the guy, but the daughter doesn't. When I explain that her boyfriend committed a Felony One—aggravated burglary—which carries the same sentence as murder, the mom starts backing up, too."

"But her daughter…"

"Has purpling choke marks on her neck and bruises on her cheek and temple. Still, she just kept saying, 'But I love him. He didn't mean to hurt me.'"

Regina threw down her fork. "Well, what in the world did he think would happen when he manhandled her that way?"

"Men like that don't concern themselves with the victim. And with the daughter spouting all the classic I-have-no-self-esteem phrases that you get from abused women, there wasn't much we could do. The dad was noticeably silent, only occasionally saying, 'I think I just need to have a talk with the boy.'"

"Unbelievable."

"No, honey, unfortunately it's all too believable and cops run into that crap every day. We had to leave with no charges filed because the victims wouldn't prosecute. I was pissed, the other detective was scratching his head and then the female officer says, "I can tell you what's going on in there. Dad's beaten Mom up a few times and the daughter knows it. Mom doesn't want to say anything because she might get another beating and the poor girl thinks this is normal behavior because she's lived with it for years."

Riley's hands fisted on the tabletop. He wouldn't tell Regina that eventually the girl had run off with the jerk—and died because of it.

Subdued, Regina left her seat and came around to Riley's side. Immediately, Butch did the same. He ran from his bed, stretched up with his paws on her thigh and begged to be held. Regina scooped him up close, rubbing her nose against his soft fur but speaking to Riley. "I'm sorry."

Riley gave her a one-arm hug, pulling her into his side. Because he was still sitting, his face was level with the subtle swell of her breasts. Well, her breasts and a fuzzed-up, irritable Butch who didn't want Riley to touch her.

The dog was too territorial, but Riley understood how he felt. "Yeah, me, too." He forced his gaze to her face. "But you know what, Red? It taught me something. There are all kinds of perspectives and things we never see. And women, God bless them, are pretty damned intuitive. If you say someone is after you, I'd be an idiot not to take you seriously. And, believe me, I'm not an idiot."

She gave a small, tremulous smile. "Thank you. It… Well, it feels better, safer, just knowing someone isn't writing me off as a nut."

Riley pushed back his chair and came to his feet. Oh yeah, he knew exactly how Butch felt because the urge to hold her was nearly overwhelming. "Tell you what, Red. Let's put the dishes away, then go to the living room and you can tell me everything that's been going on."

"Everything?"

"From the beginning. Maybe we'll be able to sort things out." He put his hand at the small of her back and urged her away from the table. "Do you think Killer can entertain himself a few minutes?"

The dog managed a sideways glare and a roll of his lip, but when Regina put him in his bed, this time he circled, dug at the bedding for a few seconds, then plopped down to sleep with his nose noticeably close to his rump.

Her kitchen was so immaculate, it didn't take any time at all to put things away. The leftovers went into matching containers in the fridge. The dishes were rinsed and put in uniform order in the dishwasher. Regina was so orderly, so clean, it unnerved Riley a bit.

Would she expect everyone to be that tidy? Curious as to how judgmental she might be, Riley said, "You've been to Rosie's place before, right?"

"Yes, why?"

"How'd you like it?" Rosie was tidy, but nowhere near as big a neat freak as Regina.

She thought about it for a moment, then smiled. "From the first time I stepped into Rosie's house, it felt cozy, like a home." She gave a soft laugh that sank into him. "But Rosie's that way. Very warm and open and friendly. I like her a lot."

Satisfied by her answer, Riley smiled. "Yeah, me, too."

Together they washed the pans, Regina cleaning and Riley drying. Damn, but he had a good time doing it. Just being with her calmed something turbulent inside him, making him feel more at peace with himself and his life. But slowly the serenity of the moment expanded into heightened awareness. He wanted her, and not having her was torture.

When her hands were completely submersed in soapy water, Riley moved behind her. Holding her waist so she couldn't slip away, he deliberately pressed in, relishing the feel of her full bottom against his groin. A short groan rumbled in his chest.

One day soon, after she'd accepted him, he'd take her this way, from behind, sinking deep, feeling her buttocks on his abdomen and thighs. He'd be able to cover her breasts with his hands, toy with her stiffened nipples, slip his fingers down her belly to her...

"Riley?"

He ignored the hardening of his body, the surge of lust, to nibble carefully on her ear. Without intentional thought, he further aroused her, letting his breath tickle her ear, using the edge of his tongue to tantalize the sensitive nerve endings along the tendons in her neck. "You don't want to sleep with me yet, Red, but you will soon. In the meantime, a little kissing won't hurt anything, right?" Before she could answer, he dipped his tongue into her ear, then gently sucked her earlobe. His accelerated breaths fanned the delicate, baby-fine hairs at her temple.

"No." Her hands went still, just dangling over the edge of the sink, not quite in the water, not quite out. She tipped her head back to his shoulder and closed her eyes.

Riley leaned around her to see her face. "No what, honey?" He pressed one hand from her waist to her belly, spreading his fingers wide in masculine possession. His thumb dipped into her navel through her clothes, pressing gently, symbolic of so much more. Few people understood the erogenous zones of a woman's body, how small touches, when combined just right, could elicit carnal reactions.

In his training, he'd learned a lot about pressure points that could cripple, but the reverse was also true. He knew the places where exquisite, almost unbearable pleasure existed.

He could make her come, right here, right now, without undue effort, and that knowledge had his entire body straining in need. But he didn't want to push her. The constraint cost him, making him tremble and turning his voice hoarse. "No, you don't want me to do this, or no, there's nothing wrong with it?"

"There's nothing wrong with it."

A shudder rippled through him; she'd seemed so wary of sexual involvement with him that any capitulation now felt like a major triumph.

Suddenly she turned and plastered herself up against him, breasts to abdomen, belly to groin. "I want to kiss you, Riley. I just don't want you to expect it to lead to bed."

"All right."

Her green eyes narrowed with mingled surprise and uncertainty. "All right, what?"

He settled his hands on her hips, urging her closer still, so he could feel the rounded, feminine contours of her body. "All right, you can kiss me. Go ahead."

"Oh." She looked at his mouth, licked her own, and Riley nearly lost it.

"Hurry up, Red."

"Okay then." With her soapy hands sliding around his neck, she went on tiptoe and her mouth touched his.

Riley waited, his heart thundering, his erection

straining, his testicles tight. With ruthless determination, he gathered his control around him and kept his
stance relaxed, his expression calm, when in reality his
emotions bordered on savage. He'd never wanted any
woman the way he wanted Regina.

Her warm velvet tongue licked out again, this time
over his lips. "Riley?"

"Yeah?"

"Open your mouth for me."

That did it. As carefully as he could manage considering the tumultuous raging of his libido, Riley gathered her fully against him. With her heartbeat echoing
his, he opened his mouth but didn't let her take the lead.
His tongue slid in, deep and slow, mating with hers,
teasing, showing her with his mouth how he wanted
to take her with his body. Their hot breaths mingled,
their hands clutched. Her body relaxed and sighed into
his, so soft and fluid and feminine; his grew more taut
with pounding lust.

He'd promised himself only a few kisses when he
started this, but then he hadn't counted on the effect of
her full and enthusiastic involvement. Before he'd even
had time to think it through, he had a small breast in
one hand, a firm, lush cheek in the other.

Their groans sounded at the same time.

Her nipple stiffened against his palm, a plea that
he couldn't ignore. Using only his open palm, Riley
brushed his hand over her again and again, abrading
her nipples, giving her only so much. Her fingers tightened in his hair. She pulled her mouth away to gulp for
air. "Riley?"

She said his name as an invitation, an appeal for
more. "Regina…"

The sudden furious yapping of the dog startled them both. As if he'd only just then realized their physical closeness, Butch ran wild circles around them, snapping at Riley's leg without actually touching, making his discontent with the situation well known.

It hit Riley that his control had definitely slipped. For that brief moment, he'd lost all sense of himself, acting solely on need. It was an awesome, almost frightening admission. No one, not even his wife, and not even the worst imaginable scene, had so much as caused a flicker of loss in his innate control. He'd considered it an unchangeable part of him, like his height and bone structure.

One glance at Regina's hot face and he wanted to curse. "I'm sorry."

She shook her head. "No. No reason to apologize." She smoothed her hands down the front of her blouse, realized they were wet and tucked them behind her. Her smile was entirely false and self-conscious. "Would you like coffee?"

Strangely insulted, Riley stared at her. They'd shared a killer kiss, he'd had his hands all over her, and she wanted to continue playing proper hostess. "What I'd like," he muttered under his breath, "is to finish what we started."

"Excuse me?"

"Nothing." He needed a distraction and fast. The obvious distraction was now chewing on his heel while growling like a banshee. Riley reached down for Butch, but with his expression so dark the dog tucked in his tail and scurried away with due haste. Issuing a grievous sigh, Riley caught Butch with one hand and held him up close. Regina stood next to him like a fretful mother while the dog tried to brazen it out, grumbling, snarling and looking to Regina for rescue.

"Shh," Riley soothed while stroking the narrow back with one finger. The dog was smaller than his foot, his legs no thicker than Riley's baby finger and he fit fully into one hand. Butch quieted just a bit, giving Riley a suspicious look reminiscent of Regina's. "Good boy. See, I'm not so evil, huh? I saw that you weren't actually biting me, just trying to scare me off. You don't trust me with Regina. But you're going to have to get used to me touching her, buddy, because I intend to touch her a lot."

Regina said, "You do?"

Riley slanted her a look. "Since we're done here, let's go into the living room. The sooner I can figure out what the hell's going on with your attacker, the sooner we can get beyond it."

Regina dried her hands, neatly folded the dish towel to hang over the bar and hurried after him. "And then what?"

"And then I can concentrate on just you." He smiled at her over his shoulder, a deliberate smile, hot and suggestive. She stopped dead in her tracks, blinked twice, then followed him into the room.

And damned if she didn't wear a coy little smile of her own.

CHAPTER THREE

"IT STARTED AFTER MY assignment in the park."

The second Regina sat beside him, Butch snapped at Riley again and jumped over into her lap. Traitorous dog. "What park? Around here?"

"No, where I used to work before moving to Chester." While she spoke, she absently petted the dog and within minutes Butch was sound asleep again. "It was a new park opening. There'd been a lot of problems with it because some of the bigger businesses wanted to use the area for a parking lot. The arguments were pretty good on both sides: beautify the land with a park to draw visitors to the area, or use it to provide adequate parking so people would come to the stores to shop, thereby actually spending money."

"So I guess the park won?"

She nodded. "It was in the news every day. City hall got more action than it'd seen in months. The mayor had started to look pretty harried before everything got settled. The paper I worked for ran regular articles about it, then they sent me there to get photos and to do a write-up a week before the park officially opened. It was my biggest feature, a two-page spread."

Riley smiled at her enthusiasm. Sitting so close to her, seeing her so animated, made it impossible not to touch her. He reached toward her, and Butch came off her lap like a whirlwind. Riley didn't duck away. He held his hand out while Butch pretended to bite. He came close, but never actually closed his teeth on Riley.

"Just like I thought. All bluster." He kept his tone soft so he wouldn't upset the dog more. "You're ferociously defensive, aren't you, squirt? I like that." And then, despite Butch's complaints, he rubbed his ears. Butch gave up and enjoyed the attention. "So what happened at the park?"

"Everything was going well at first. I took some pictures of the elaborate fountain, the new swing sets, the pond with ducks and geese. It really is a beautiful spot." She glanced down at Butch and blushed. "I even got to meet my favorite politician."

"Yeah? And who's that?"

"Senator Welling. He was there with an intern, doing the same thing I was doing, checking out the park. He'd supported it, you see. He always supports the conservation of land whenever possible. I've admired him so long, I even took a few pictures of him. He waved to the camera for me."

Riley sighed. For a reporter, she sure had a hard time getting around to the point. "So what happened, Red? Did someone attack you in the park? Did the good senator try to come on to you—"

"No! Senator Welling isn't like that." She looked genuinely annoyed by his teasing remarks. "The reason I admire him so much is because he's such a dedicated family man. He's a wonderful politician, too, of course, and I agree with most of his political stands, but it's his dedication to his wife and children that's his real appeal."

Personally, Riley thought the man was a schmooze,

but then he wasn't about to get into a political debate with Regina. "I'll take your word for it."

Still disgruntled, she said, "He politely posed for my pictures, even did one with him and the intern standing on either side of the fountain. He walked me to my car *and* opened my car door for me."

Maybe he'd been coming on to her after all and Regina was just too naive to realize it. "So what happened at the park that made you feel threatened?"

"Oh, it was as I was leaving the park. I was almost to the main road when some jerk sideswiped me."

Riley straightened. "What do you mean, he sideswiped you?"

"I drive a little silver Escort, and this fancy SUV tried to pass me, but he didn't clear my hood before cutting back into my lane. His rear end hit my front bumper and my car went into a spin, then off the road. I plowed into a tree. The guy didn't even stop, just kept going."

"And you think that's related somehow to—"

"If you'll just let me finish," she said in exasperation.

"Sorry." Riley held up both hands. "By all means." He only hoped she got to the point before midnight.

"It wasn't easy, but I got the car out of the ditch and made it pretty close to the main road. I probably did even more harm to the car, but I didn't like the idea of sitting there alone in the park, especially since it was starting to get dark."

"Smart."

"I thought so. My cell phone had gone dead, so I thought I'd have a long walk ahead of me, but then the senator came by and he drove me to a phone. He even offered to wait with me, but I told him to go on. Wasn't that awfully nice of him?"

"He's supposed to serve the people, honey."

"Not as a taxi. Anyway, I called my boss from a diner. He called for a tow truck then came to pick me up and drive me back to my car. You won't believe what I found."

Numerous possibilities ran through his mind, but he said only, "What?"

"Someone had broken into it."

"You didn't lock it up?"

"Of course I did. But the driver's side window was smashed. I thought for sure my stereo, speakers and CDs would be gone."

"I gather they weren't?"

"No. The car had been ransacked, my glove box emptied, all my papers strewn around, but nothing was missing as far as I could tell."

Riley frowned. He had to admit that sounded odd. Had someone been looking for something specific? "What did the police say about it?"

"That I must have returned in time to scare the robbers off."

Possibly. But he wasn't one to always accept the most obvious explanation. "You have another theory?"

"Yes. Looking back, I think that SUV ran me off the road on purpose. I think he came back later to look for something in my car."

"If that's so, if he was really that determined, why not just follow you home?" Even saying it made Riley's protective instincts twitch. If someone *had* followed her, what might have happened? He didn't even want to contemplate such a scenario. From now on, he intended to keep a closer watch on her.

"I'm not a criminal so I can't know how a criminal's

mind works. But maybe he knew I lived in a busy complex, so going through my car wouldn't have been easy. The thing is, I can't imagine what I'd have that anyone would want, but I am really grateful that Senator Welling was there to drive me into town. If he hadn't…"

"You might have been sitting in your car, all alone, when the burglar showed up." Riley reached out and took her hand. "Could be your presence would have deterred him."

"But maybe not. He did run me off the road without much concern, so maybe he'd have just hit me over the head or something. Maybe he'd have even—"

Riley's teeth hurt from clenching his jaw. "Don't." No way in hell did he want her to cavalierly discuss deadly possibilities. They'd already occurred to him, of course, so he didn't need embellishment of his own grisly thoughts.

"Well, after everything else that's happened…"

"Such as?"

"I left work one night after finishing up some research. Phone calls mostly. It was about eight, dark outside already. Just as I started to step off the curb, a black Porsche nearly ran me down. I had to jump back fast to keep from being hit. I landed on the ground, tore my panty hose, broke two fingernails and twisted my ankle."

Anger swelled inside him. "Jesus. You could have been killed."

"I think that was the point. But the police wrote it off as a sloppy driver, not a deliberate intent to hit me. They thought it was unrelated to the other incident and they said there was nothing they could do about it since I didn't get the license plate number."

Rationally, Riley knew they were right. Without a direct witness or a way to track down the car, the police were helpless. But at the very least, they could have taken the threat to her seriously.

Only, he didn't know if he would have either. Not with so little to go on. The first violation appeared to be a bungled burglary. The second *could* have been a drunk driver or a speeding kid....

"A week after that, some bully tried to grab my purse. I held on to it—"

Riley had gotten more and more rigid as the enormity of her dilemma sank in, and now his control nearly snapped. *"You held on?"*

The dog lunged at him for raising his voice. Riley pulled Butch up to his chest with one hand cradled under his body. He bounced him as he'd often done with his nieces and nephews when they were fussy babies. Butch had no idea what to make of it. He looked confused, but he quieted. His eyes were wide, his ear perked up. He peered at Regina, then back at Riley.

"It was *my* purse, Riley. No way was I going to just give it up."

"He could have hurt you, damn it."

"He *did* hurt me."

Through stiff lips, Riley growled, "Tell me."

His tone was so gruff, she gave him an uncertain look. "He...well, he belted me. Gave me a black eye."

"Son of a bitch."

"Riley!"

The dog howled and Riley released Regina's hand to stroke the dog's back, scratch his ears. "What did the police have to say about that?"

In a strange shift of mood, Regina scooted closer to

him and stroked his shoulder. "It was weeks ago, Riley. There's no reason to get so upset now."

She attempted to soothe him much as Riley soothed the fractious dog. "I'm furious, not upset," Riley muttered, then added, "Women get upset."

"Your shoulders are all bunched and one eye is narrowed more than the other and you've got this strange tick in your jaw."

"Fury."

"All right, then don't get so furious. That won't help."

Knowing she was right, he drew a deep breath that didn't abate his anger one bit but gave him the elusion of calm. "Tell me what the cops said."

"Well, they were a little more concerned this time because after the guy hit me, my purse was dumped, only he didn't steal anything. My wallet was right there with two credit cards and about forty dollars, but he just rifled through the stuff on the ground, cursed me, and when we heard people coming, he ran off without a single thing."

Butch flopped onto his back in Riley's arms and went back to sleep. Apparently, he liked the rough rocking.

"What did the man look like?"

"I'm not sure. It was raining that day so he had on a slicker that closed up to his throat. He wore a hat and sunglasses, though there wasn't a speck of sunshine to be found. I noticed he was dark because he had five o'clock shadow and dark sideburns. His hands were tanned."

"Did the police try to follow him?"

"By the time they got there, he was long gone. They didn't know what to think until I explained about the other things that had happened. Then they wanted me to tell them about all my recent assignments." She shrugged. "But there hasn't been anything that would upset anyone. I don't write derogatory, cutting-edge pieces." She looked disgruntled with that admission. "I cover parks and new cookbooks and special-interest groups."

"So what had you written?" Riley continued rocking the dog. Butch twisted awkwardly, tucking the back of his head into Riley's neck and nuzzling closer in doggy bliss. Damn it, he was starting to like the dog.

"Let's see. I'd done the park feature...."

"No, before that. Everything started the day of the park, right? So it had to be something you'd done prior to that."

"That makes sense." She scrunched up her nose in thought. "Well, I did do an article on a professional football player arrested for a DUI, but my angle was on the time he donated to underprivileged children, something he'd been doing even before being assigned community service. And I did an interview with the author of a popular cookbook. The book was a hit, but it turned out the author had stolen some of the recipes from her mother-in-law's great-great-grandmother. But she in turn donated half her royalties to her mother-in-law's favorite charity, and they worked everything out amicably."

Riley frowned in thought. "Not exactly life-altering news, huh?"

Sounding defensive, Regina said, "I have done a few more critical pieces."

"Like?"

"About a month earlier I'd covered a dog shelter that

wasn't treating the animals right. They were crowded, dirty, underfed, and naturally I was outraged."

The mistreatment of animals would have outraged him, as well, but Regina was so softhearted, so genuine, he could imagine how emotional she'd gotten over the whole thing.

"The article I did was small, but it ended up getting a lot of attention. The shelter got shut down and heavily fined. With the help of the paper, I spearheaded a campaign to find homes for all the dogs. We eventually succeeded. I would have loved to have kept a few of them myself, but I had no hopes of getting my own home then, and a small apartment is no place for a dog."

Riley looked down at Butch. The dog peeked at him, turned his head to lick Riley's hand and stretched. Riley grinned. "Unless the dog is really small."

Regina smiled, too. "Look at him. He's already fond of you."

Hearing that special soft tone in her voice gave Riley an idea. He could get closer to her by getting closer to her dog. "He knows I respect him. But I imagine if I touched you right now, he'd go right back to bristling." Riley gave her a long, intimate look. "He's going to have to learn to share. But I'll be patient—with him and you."

Regina's lips parted. She caught her breath, then looked at his mouth.

Oh, she was begging to be kissed. Unable to resist, Riley slowly leaned toward her.

He ended up kissing the dog when Butch leaped up between them. He nipped at Riley's mouth and nose, making an awful racket.

"You ungrateful mutt." Mindful of his intentions, Riley kept his tone friendly instead of irritated. Seeing that no kissing would occur, the dog resettled himself against Riley and gave him a big-eyed innocent look.

Regina smothered a laugh. "How could anyone ever hurt an animal? I can't understand it. I don't regret what happened with the shelter, but afterward the owners showed a lot of animosity toward me. Of course, that's understandable because I started the ball rolling that eventually lost them their business. The thing is, unless they just wanted to harass me, they wouldn't make likely suspects because I don't have anything they'd want to steal."

Riley tried to let the pieces come together naturally in his mind, but he knew Regina was right. He was too personally involved. All he could think of was how she might have been hurt worse. "Is there anyone else you can think of who'd dislike you?"

"Why would anyone dislike me?"

That made him grin. "Why indeed? Any problems with the people you work with? Why did you move here?"

The careful way she masked her expression told him he'd hit a nerve. "I got along with almost everyone at work."

"*Almost* everyone?"

She folded her hands in her lap. "There was one guy who was pretty persistent in trying to get me to go out with him. The more I refused, the more hostile he got."

"You left because of him?"

"Partially. He started showing up at my place at odd hours, watching me all the time. But he wasn't a threat, just a pest. Mostly I left because I thought I might be safer here. I hate to admit to being a coward, but I got spooked. I'm not used to being hit—"

"Hell, I would hope not."

"—and when that man slugged me, that was more than enough for me. I had to wear sunglasses for a week before the bruise faded enough that I could hide it with makeup. So I quit my job, relocated here in Chester and got hired on with the local paper."

Wishing he could get his hands on not only the man who'd dared to strike her, but the weasel who'd hassled her at work, too, Riley shook his head. "And you still found yourself in trouble."

"Right. Unless, as the local police say, it's just a co-incidence. Maybe the fire was an accident."

Any time Riley thought of the damn fire, his guts cramped. "I don't think so, Red."

"You don't? Why?" And then she asked with suspicion, "Riley Moore, do you know something I don't know?"

Careful not to disturb the dog, he touched her cheek and gave her a tender smile. "I probably know lots of things you don't know, especially about dangerous situations. But specifically about the fire, no."

"Then why?"

"I dunno. It's just that the day of the fire, you were so jumpy, so nervous. Call it women's intuition, gut instinct, or just caution, you seemed to instinctively know something was about to happen."

"I did feel especially edgy. It felt like people were watching me."

"Maybe they were." After she'd left Riley that day, he couldn't shake off the picture of her nervousness. And her nervousness had become his, until he knew he wouldn't be able to relax for worrying about her.

"That sort of thing can be felt," he murmured, more to himself than her.

"That's why you were trailing me?"

"Yeah." He'd known she was meeting Ethan to complete her interview, so he'd gone along, hanging back so that no one would notice him, but close enough to keep an eye out for her. When she'd met up with Rosie first and the two of them had gone to the firework's dealership, his edginess had increased. With good reason.

"I'm glad you followed me," she said. "If you hadn't, who knows what might have happened."

The alarms had brought Ethan to the scene, only he'd thought Rosie was still inside the building. He would have gone in after her if Riley hadn't held him back. Regina and Rosie would have been safe, but Ethan would have died.

Riley shook off the awful memories, then touched the corner of Regina's mouth. It looked tender and ripe and he wanted to kiss her, but first they had to talk. "I was feeling territorial even then." He watched her eyes darken and smiled to himself. "I wish like hell I'd gotten my hands on the bastard who carried you out. He's probably the one who stole your camera."

"Likely, since I'd taken some good photos of the fire hazards. If only I'd realized how serious those hazards were, I could have saved poor Ethan a terrible scare."

"And me as well."

"You?"

"Damn right." The picture of her sitting on the curb, blood on her forehead, her eyes dazed, would stay with him for a lifetime. "I felt like I'd taken a kick to the stomach."

"You didn't look scared. Not like Ethan."

"I'd already found you, and though you were hurt, I knew you were going to be okay. Ethan thought Rosie was in the fire." And he'd been a madman, fighting to go inside after her even though it would have meant his own death. Once Rosie had shown up, having left the building on her own by an upstairs window in the back, Ethan had just collapsed. To this day, Ethan trembled when anyone mentioned the fire. Oh, he was still a fireman, still did his duty with fearless determination, but you didn't mention the fire that almost took Rosie from him.

Riley didn't ever want to be so afraid that he lost all reason and discipline. Which was why he was taking matters into his own hands. He didn't love Regina the way Ethan loved Rosie, but he liked her, he wanted her and for as long as he held a claim, he'd damn well keep her safe.

He dropped his hand. "Maybe I'm just buying into your fears, but its possible you have a good reason to be afraid. I'm not willing to put it to chance."

She pressed back against the couch cushions. "You say that like it has some hidden meaning or something."

"It does." He stared at her hard, keeping her pinned in his gaze. "Regina, I don't want you by yourself until we figure out what's going on."

It took her a second to catch his meaning, then her eyes slanted his way in speculation. "You think you should stay with me?"

"If you move from the apartment, yes."

"No."

He went on as if she hadn't voiced the denial. "Here you're surrounded by people. Help is only a few feet away and anyone could hear you through the thin walls. In a house, you'd be all alone."

Her shoulders straightened. "I'm a big girl, Riley. I'll be extra careful. But I won't—"

"You can't be careful enough. Do you intend to be home before dark every day? And what does it even matter when by your own admission, you've been attacked during the day? You can't imagine how many ways an intruder can get into your house without you even knowing."

Her slim brows pulled down.

"What if someone doesn't want to steal from you at all? What if someone just wants revenge?"

She pushed to her feet to pace away. Riley noticed her hands had curled into fists at her sides, evidence that she'd had the same worry. "Stop it. You're trying to scare me."

Riley set the dog beside him and stepped up behind her. "Bullshit. I *am* scaring you. And you know why, Red? Because you're smart enough to know I'm right." He clasped her upper arms and pulled her back against his chest. Her hair smelled sweet. *She* smelled sweet. And soft and female and delicate. She demolished his control and intentions without even trying.

Riley pressed his jaw against her temple, and in a roughened voice, said, "Will you check every room, every closet, under every bed and in every corner each night when you first go in? What will you do if you find someone, crouching in the dark, waiting for you?"

Jerking around to face him, she said again, *"Stop it."*

His hands closed over her shoulders and he brought her to her tiptoes. "The hell I will. You say the threat is real. I believe you. So don't be dumb, Regina."

"What am I supposed to do?" She was so shaken, she practically wailed, then thumped him solidly on the chest. "Hide? Stop living? I have work and friends and errands...."

He caressed her tense shoulders. "Let me help."

"By moving in?" She shook her head. "No, I won't do that. It wouldn't be—"

"Proper? Screw proper. Who's going to know besides our friends?" She started to walk away from him and Riley crushed her close. Her eyes flared. "Improper beats the hell out of dead any day."

The dog started barking, anxiously looking for a way off the couch. But he was too small to try jumping down.

"You're upsetting my dog."

"Misery loves company." He kissed her, hard at first, but when she went immobile, then soft and sweet against him, he gentled. Her hands curled against his chest, telling him she liked the kiss almost as much as he did. He caught her face, held her still while he sank his tongue in. Her heartbeat pounded against his chest, her soft moan vibrated between them.

Riley carefully pulled back. Her eyes stayed closed, her lips parted. "Listen to me, Red. I'll do everything I can to figure this out before you're due to move. I swear it. But I don't want you living alone."

Her eyelashes fluttered, lifted. Slowly, comprehension dawned and she looked beyond him, then stepped away to scoop up the dog. With her back to Riley, she went about soothing Butch. "If you're that close, you know what will happen."

"We'll sleep together." He crossed his arms over

his chest, anxious for it to happen, wondering if she'd admit it.

"Every time you touch me, I forget who I am."

"Meaning?"

"Meaning I'm not the type to get carried away with the moment, but when you're kissing me, it doesn't seem to matter."

She would be ready, more than ready, by the time he got her in bed. He'd see to it. "It's going to happen no matter what, Red. You know that."

She swallowed, then nodded. "I know." She looked none too pleased with that admission, making Riley frown.

A real gentleman would have told her not to worry about it, that he'd control himself, protect her. He wasn't that much of a gentleman, and he wanted her too much to start playing one now. "We'll go slow." As slow as he could manage, considering he'd held himself at bay for weeks already.

She walked over to the balcony doors and looked out. "I'm sorry. I don't mean to be…coy. It's just that I can't be cavalier about sex."

Her honesty was refreshing, something he hadn't expected. "You don't need to apologize to me for speaking your mind. But we're both adults, both uninvolved." When she didn't look at him, he said, "I don't mean to push you…"

Her laugh sounded strained. "That's all you do is push."

His smile caught him by surprise. "For your safety, yeah. But I'm not cavalier about sex, either. No one in their right mind is these days."

"Then I know a lot of men not in their right mind."

He wouldn't think about her with other men. It'd make him nuts. But he could be honest in return. "I can't promise not to touch you, Red, because I will."

Her shoulders lifted on a deep breath. She waited, anxious and still.

Seeing her response, Riley took two steps closer. "Is it worth your safety? Is avoiding me worth risking your life?" And because he knew she already loved her little dog, he pressed her, saying, "Is it worth risking Butch's life?"

He waited, and finally she turned. She looked sad, resigned. "No. I tried ignoring the threat. I tried to believe it was all coincidence like everyone said. I wanted to just go on with my life, keep doing what I always did, keep working." She shook her head and said in a nearly soundless whisper, "I almost got Rosie killed."

Riley knew she still felt guilty for allowing Rosie to be involved, even though everyone knew Rosie did just as she pleased. Ethan couldn't control her, so it was for certain that Regina would never sway Rosie from something she chose to do.

"I know the risks now, but the thing is, Riley, I can't just hide away. I love my job and I won't give it up. Yet, that's when a lot of things seem to happen. Out of control cars, purse snatchers…"

"I have an idea about that, too." A stupid idea, one he was sure to regret, but damn it, he had to be certain she was safe. "You wanted to interview me."

Sudden excitement lit her eyes. Both she and the dog stared at him, she with delighted surprise, Butch with mere curiosity.

After clearing his throat, Riley forged on. "Well, here's your chance. I'm on vacation for the next two weeks. While you finish up any current assignments, I'll accompany you—and no, there's no negotiating on that point, not if you want to interview me next."

"That's blackmail," she pointed out, but she didn't sound too upset about it.

"Take it or leave it."

For three heart-stopping seconds she hesitated. Her slow smile gave him warning. "I'll take it."

Already dreading it, Riley nodded. She sounded enthusiastic enough to make his stomach clench. "During the evening we'll work on your training. I want you to have at the very least a basic understanding of self-defense. While you're still in the apartment, I'll check into the things that've happened to you to see if I can turn up anything."

"But hasn't it been too long?"

"Maybe. But maybe not. Cops file all their reports, so I'll check through that and see if anything jumps out at me. Back when things first happened, they were looking at each incident with the thought that you were a hysterical woman. I'll look with the thought that you're in danger. Two very different perspectives."

She licked her lips. "It happened in Cincinnati, not Chester."

"Don't worry. I'll find what I need to get started."

Still she stood there.

Riley touched her cheek. "Try not to fret, okay? Everything will work out."

"And if you haven't found out anything when it's time for me to move?"

He'd have kissed her again, but Butch started a low rumbling, ears back, body poised to attack. The little dog had enough to get used to without worrying that

Riley was accosting his new mistress. "Then you'll continue to stay with me."

"With you? But I thought you—"

"Intended to move in with you? No. My place is already secure. And look at it this way, you can use the time to get your new home up and running." And in the interim, he'd have her—in his home, under his protection and in his bed.

The setup worked for him.

CHAPTER FOUR

BUTCH DIDN'T LIKE sleeping alone.

Regina found that out after a long night of listening to pitiful howls that finally broke her down. At two in the morning she gave up, retrieved Butch from his pen in the warmest corner of her kitchen, and carried him to bed.

He did a reconnaissance of the perimeter, sniffing every corner of her bed, her pillow, the sheets, before crawling under the covers. She watched the lump move here and there, then finally settle close to her. He dug—*endlessly.* She had no idea what he thought he was doing, but he ignored her pleas to stop and finally curled up behind her knees. She couldn't move without making him grumble.

For a four-pound dog, he was sure bossy about his comfort.

At six, when her alarm went off, Butch scampered out, yawned hugely in her face, then wanted to play. When Regina only blinked at him, he reared back on his haunches, barked and nipped her on the nose. She groaned, which he took for a sign of life and started bouncing around the covers like a tiny rabbit. He could stop and start so fast, darting this way and that, it was comical. Even half-asleep, she grinned as he raced up to her, gripped the edge of her pillowcase in his teeth, and began tugging.

"Okay, okay." It was a sorry truth, but she wasn't a morning person. She'd tried over the years to become one, only because it seemed like the thing to do. Good, honest people went to bed at a decent hour and rose early to begin their day. They didn't lie around for hours, being lazy.

Well, she was decent and honest, but she just couldn't force herself to be alert first thing. It took her at least two hours and a pot of coffee to get her head together. Before that, she didn't want to face the world. And with the way she looked in the morning, she doubted the world wanted to face her.

Moving around in the dark, she made a quick trip to the bathroom, turned on the coffeepot, which she'd prepared the night before, and put Butch out on his lead so he could potty. Because the morning was damp that late July day, he finished in a flash.

With only a dim light on over the sink, she slumped at the table in her cozy cotton jammies, nursing her first steaming mug of caffeine. Butch curled in her lap, content just to be with her—until a knock sounded on her door.

She froze.

Butch did not.

In what she now considered typical Butch frenzy, he leaped from her lap and ran hell-bent for the door. He made so much noise, she knew any thoughts of ignoring her early-morning caller were shot. Through the peephole, she spied Riley standing impatiently in her hallway, and she ducked away as if he might see her, too. Good God. What was he doing at her door so early?

"Open up, Red. I can hear Butch, so I know you're up and about."

No. A thousand times no. Still plastered to the side of the door, her heart racing, she croaked, "What do you want?"

"You," he said with a discernable smile in his voice. "But I'll settle for conversation."

Eyes closing in mortification, she shook her head. "Not at six-thirty, Riley. Go away till eight." She could be ready by eight. It'd be rushing it since she usually didn't leave for work till eight-thirty, but under the circumstances— "Not happening, Red. Now open the door." And then he tacked on, "I have a gift for Butch."

"You do?" She chanced another peek out the peephole and saw that Riley held up a stuffed Chihuahua toy. It looked almost like Butch, but bigger and not as cute. She covered her face with her hands. The man had brought her dog a present. She groaned, undecided.

Beside her, Butch continued to encourage her with barks and jumps and circles. She pressed her forehead to the door. "If I let you in, will you not look at me till I've had a chance to get down the hall?"

Riley laughed. "Why?" And then in a throaty tone, "What are you wearing, Red?"

Regina looked down at herself. Sloppy, blue-flowered cotton pajamas hung on her body. Her loose, tangled hair fell in her face. Even without a mirror, she knew that her eyes were puffy and still heavy from sleep.

"I'm waiting."

This was ridiculous. Half her neighbors would hear him if she didn't do something quick. She flipped on the entry light, turned the locks and cracked the door open. "Riley?" she said in a harsh whisper.

"Yeah?"

"You can come in, but I mean it, don't you dare even think to look at me. I'm a mess and I don't like it when people see me a mess."

"All right, honey, calm down. I promise."

She could hear the laughter in his tone. "The door is unlocked, so just give me thirty seconds to—"

Behind her, the shattering of glass disturbed the early morning quiet.

Screeching, Regina whirled around to see the devastated ruins of her patio doors. Shards of glass glittered everywhere. "Oh my God." She snatched up Butch, who had tucked in his tail and darted behind her before yapping hysterically.

Riley stormed in, moved her to the side and took in the mess in one sweeping glance.

"Close and lock this door, then call the cops." He tossed the stuffed toy dog on the couch, and sprinted across the floor, through the broken patio doors and, to her amazement, right over the balcony.

"Riley." They were only about eight feet up from the ground, but still… Regina slammed her door shut and started after him, but she was barefoot and there was glass scattered everywhere, all over her floor, some atop her furniture. Her heart hammered so hard, it hurt.

Cautiously, she stepped up onto the couch, Butch clutched in her arms. "Ohmigod, ohmigod, damn you, Riley, ohmigod…" She stepped off the other end of the couch nearest to her kitchen. Being careful to avoid any sharp shards of glass, she went to the phone and dialed 9-1-1.

In less than two minutes that seemed like a lifetime, Riley was back. This time he climbed up and over the balcony railing. Regina didn't have a chance to worry about her appearance because he barely spared her a glance. "I need a flashlight. It's still too dark out there to see and I don't want to mess up any evidence."

Skin prickling with sick dread, Regina pointed to the middle of the floor. "It was a rock."

Riley nodded. "I know, honey. Where's a flashlight?"

Flashlight? She felt shocked, disoriented. She hadn't had near enough coffee.

"Regina?"

One deep breath, and she felt marginally more in control. "In my bedroom, in the nightstand drawer."

"Stay put." His booted feet crunched over the remains of her patio door. An early-morning breeze blew the curtains in. The blackness beyond the doors seemed fathomless, sending a chill down her spine.

Belatedly, Regina remembered what else was in her nightstand drawer. *Oh no.* Her heart dropped into her stomach and she started across the floor in a rush, the glass forgotten.

Riley reappeared. Not by look or deed did he acknowledge anything he might have uncovered beyond the flashlight. He crossed to her and handed her a housecoat and slippers.

"You okay?"

Maybe. "Yes."

He cupped the side of her face, his touch gentle and reassuring. "The cops should be here any second. Tell them I'm out back. I don't want to get shot by some overeager hero."

Shot! "Riley, wait." She closed her hand around his

arm above his elbow. His muscles were bunched, thick with tension. To someone who didn't know him better, he might almost appear calm. But Regina noted the unfamiliar, killing rage in his blue eyes. He felt warm and strong and secure and she didn't want him to walk away from her.

As if he understood, he bent down to look her in the eyes and said with deadly calm, "It's okay, Red. I know what I'm doing. I want you and Butch to wait in the kitchen."

"No. Don't go out there."

Riley scrutinized her. "You should put on more coffee. The officers will appreciate it."

Coffee? That sort of made sense. At least, with her mind in a muddle, it did. "Oh. Right."

For one brief moment, his gaze moved over her, touching off a tidal wave of warmth. He paused at her mouth, her breasts, then shook his head in chagrin. "Be right back."

Butch squirmed to be let down, but she didn't dare, not with so much glass on the floor. A sort of strange numbness had set in. She blocked the kitchen off with his small pen, pulled on her robe and fuzzy slippers, and went about making more coffee by rote.

This time the knock on her door didn't startle her.

Holding Butch like a security blanket, his small warm body somehow comforting, she skirted the glass and made her way to the door again. Two officers in uniform greeted her. Young, fresh-faced and eager at the prospect of a crime, they looked the complete opposite of Riley. Regina wanted to groan.

Butch wanted to kill them both.

His rabid beast impersonation was especially realistic this time. Regina tried, but there was no shushing him, so she gave up.

At her invitation, the officers cautiously ventured inside, keeping their eyes on Butch. The first officer removed his hat, then nodded at the dog. "What is that?"

Here we go again, Regina thought. "My dog, Butch."

"What's wrong with him?"

"He doesn't like you." Regina closed the door behind them. "Would you like coffee?"

They looked at each other, then her. "Uh, sure." They had to speak loudly to be heard over Butch's furor. "Maybe after you tell us what happened here?"

"Oh." She looked behind her at the devastation. "A rock. Riley Moore is out back poking around with a flashlight. Don't shoot him."

"Riley?" The darker-haired officer lifted one brow. "Why's he here?"

"He was, uh…" Why had Riley dropped in? Oh yeah, a gift for the dog. "Visiting Butch."

"That right?" The two cops shared another look, this time of masculine comprehension.

Regina pulled herself together enough to fry them both with her censure. "Riley is a friend," she stated, emphasizing the last word. "He had just knocked on the door when the rock came crashing in."

At that moment, Riley opened the door behind them and stepped inside. His brows were down, his eyes glittering. "I thought I told you to lock this."

"I did, but then they arrived." She gestured at the officers and shrugged.

Riley glanced at both men. "Dermot, Lanny. Thanks for coming over."

The men looked like little boys next to Riley. Regina

allowed herself a moment to appreciate the differences, then said again, "Coffee?"

Riley nodded. "Thanks, babe." He kissed her full on the mouth, annihilating her previous claims of friendship. "We'll be right there."

He wanted to dismiss her? Oh no. She squared her shoulders, but it wasn't easy with Butch putting on such a show.

Almost without thought, Riley took the dog from her. "Good dog." He stroked Butch's back, found just the right spot behind his big ears, and Butch magically quieted. He kept a narrowed gaze on the officers, but the awful racket ended.

Regina turned on her heel and stalked away, muttering under her breath about pigheaded males of both the human and animal variety. From her position in the kitchen, she could hear the men talking in muted tones.

Riley waited, giving the officers a chance to look around. The one he'd called Lanny shone a flashlight over the small balcony—the balcony Riley had jumped from—and shook his head before meandering out there. He came back in and looked around the floor at the broken glass.

"Better call someone to fix that window," Dermot said. "Damn vandals."

"The work of kids, no doubt," Lanny added. "No one supervises them anymore. In my day, my mother would have taken a broom to me for a prank like this."

By the time the officers entered the kitchen, Regina had four mugs out, silverware, a crystal sugar bowl and a matching pot of creamer. "Have a seat, please," she told them.

Lanny nodded. "Thanks." Then, apparently disappointed that he couldn't do more, he said, "I'll take a report, but whoever did this is long gone."

Riley leaned back in his seat, noticeably silent. He continued to stroke Butch who kept looking up at him adoringly, turning his head to get a new spot scratched.

Dermot doctored his coffee, took a long drink, then asked, "You didn't get hurt, did you? The rock didn't hit you?"

Regina shook her head. "No. I'm fine."

Dermot shook his head. "I'm sorry, Ms....?"

"Foxworth. Regina Foxworth."

"Right. You did the right thing calling us but unfortunately, there's not much we can do other than have a squad car drive by and keep an eye on things for the rest of the night."

Same old song, Regina thought. "I understand."

"Well, I don't." Riley blew out a sigh of disgust. "Neither of you went outside to look around the complex."

Dermot frowned at him. "For what? It was a rock."

Lanny nodded. "You know how it is, Riley. We get crap like this all the time."

"No, you don't. And even if you did, that's no excuse for not being thorough."

New tension filled the air. Tones and posture abruptly changed. Lanny was the first to speak up. "Look, Riley, I know you have more training, but—"

"But nothing. I went outside. I looked—just as you should have done. Someone was outside her window for about an hour, just watching."

Regina straightened in new alarm.

"Not a group of unruly kids, but one man. He's a patient son of a bitch, too, and I personally think he was waiting for her to be awake to throw that damn rock."

With sudden clarity, Regina said, "It was right after I turned the light on." She stared at Riley. "Before that, I'd been drinking my coffee in the dark."

"He probably thought it'd shake you up more to catch you when you first woke up." Riley glanced at Regina with an expression close to satisfaction. "Didn't rattle you too much though, did it, honey?"

He sounded teasing, which she didn't understand at all. She calmly sipped her coffee and hoped only she noticed how her hands shook. "No."

Riley smiled, a secret, intimate smile. Turning back to the two men, the smile disappeared to be replaced with a scowl. "If you'd checked, you'd know Ms. Foxworth has a recent history of threatening incidents. In light of that, I don't think anything, especially a rock through her window at dawn, should be taken lightly."

Lanny didn't like the criticism. "Sounds to me like you're personally involved here."

"I am."

Regina nearly choked on her coffee. Why didn't he just take out an ad in the paper? He could tell more people that way.

"But that's irrelevant." Riley wasn't through lecturing. "What pisses me off the most is that neither of you did your job." He encompassed them both in a look.

Regina thought it might be a favorable time to intercede before Riley got too insulting. She pushed back her chair. "Good grief, Riley, have you had breakfast? Surely, a temper like that is wrought from hunger. Would you like some pancakes? Lanny, Dermot? I can put a batch together if you'd like."

Riley stared at her in disbelief. "You're not going to feed them."

"I am if they're hungry." Her chin lifted. "Pancakes would give you something to chew on besides two officers who are only trying to do their duty."

His expression darkened. "They're not doing it very well."

"It's my fault that I didn't mention the other incidents, not theirs."

"Victims get rattled and forget important details. An officer is supposed to know that and ask pertinent questions."

Regina sucked in a breath at the insult. "Are you saying I'm rattled?"

Dermot stood, interrupting the escalating argument. "So how'd you come to all these brilliant conclusions, Riley? That's what I want to know."

Almost in slow motion, his movements rigid and calculated, Riley came to his feet and handed a sleepy Butch to Regina. With his gaze on Dermot, he said, "I'll take pancakes. They'll be leaving—after I explain."

Seeing no hope for it, Regina stepped out of the line of fire.

Riley took a step closer to Dermot, which had the other man's eyes flaring a bit in alarm. "There's damn near a pack of cigarette butts below her window. Red doesn't smoke—"

"Red?"

Regina raised her hand. "He means me."

"Oh." Dermot cleared his throat, glanced at her hair. "Yeah, I guess that makes sense."

In a voice raised to regain attention, Riley continued. "—so they sure as hell aren't hers, but they were fresh, one still smoldering. You know what that means, Dermot?"

Again, he cleared his throat. "Uh, that someone was out there just a few moments ago?"

"There's also one set of prints in the ground. Big adult-size prints. There are no rocks in the apartment landscaping the size of the one now in her living room, so whoever threw it probably brought it with him, meaning this was premeditated, not just a last-minute bit of mischief."

Both officers looked dumbfounded and a little awed.

"Can you maybe get some prints off the rock?"

Riley shook his head. "To get prints, surfaces need to be smooth. Since the rock isn't, there's no point in checking it."

"So what have we got?"

"Speculation. When I stand outside, about twenty feet from the balcony, I can see right into her living room. I think he watched, and saw her light come on."

"I let the dog out before that."

Riley slued his gaze her way. "With a light?"

"Um, no."

Riley nodded in satisfaction. "You need a floodlight out there, Red. And you should never open your door in the dark."

Lanny put his hands on his hips and dropped his head forward. "Okay, so you're a big-shot crime scene tech." He looked up, eyes narrowed. "We're not."

"Learn." That one word fell like a ton of bricks, discomfiting both officers.

Silence throbbed in the kitchen, making Regina more edgy than ever. "I think I'll make those pancakes now."

"Make plenty. I'm starving." Riley didn't spare her

OFFICIAL OPINION POLL

Dear Reader,

Since you are a book enthusiast, we would like to know what you think.

Inside you will find a short Opinion Poll. Please participate in our poll by sharing your opinion on 3 subjects that are very important to all of us.

To thank you for your participation, we would like to send you **2 FREE BOOKS** and **2 FREE GIFTS!**

Please enjoy them with our compliments.

Sincerely,

Pam Powers

YOUR OPINION POLL
THANK-YOU FREE GIFTS INCLUDE:

▶ **2 ROMANCE BOOKS**
▶ **2 LOVELY SURPRISE GIFTS**

a glance as he led both officers to the front door, where he gave them the information they needed to file a report. Regina could just make out the low drone of their voices.

Now wide-awake, she mixed up pancake batter with a vengeance. She thought of everything she now had on her to-do list: clean up glass, vacuum her furniture, have the glass replaced in her door... She probably needed to call into work because she'd surely be late.

Butch sat at her heels, staring up at her, just waiting for her to sit down again so he could reclaim her lap. Whenever she glanced at him, his eyes widened hopefully and he wagged his skinny tail in encouragement. Regina shook her head. "There won't be much sitting for me today, sweetie."

Riley strode back in just as she'd pulled out a skillet and set it on the stove top. He didn't stop at the table, though, or even slow down. Startled, Regina drew back as he stalked right up to her, his long legs carrying him quickly to her. He pulled her close and without hesitation, without warning, took her mouth with a surprising hunger that completely caught her off guard.

His big hands, hot and callused, held her upper arms, straining her upward. His head was bent so that his mouth fit hers completely. His lips pressed hard, parting hers, and his tongue thrust in, deep and damp and insistent.

Regina hung in his grip, a little stunned, quickly warmed. Her heartbeat thundered in her ears. He changed position, gathering her to him with one arm tight around her waist so that his other hand could tangle in her hair, tipping her head farther back. He rubbed against her, groaned, then lifted his mouth enough for her to catch her breath.

Against her lips, he murmured, "Christ, you look good."

"Hmm?" With almost no effort, he aroused her to the point of incomprehension.

Damp, warm, openmouthed kisses were pressed to her throat, along her shoulder where the robe had opened and the loose neckline where her pajamas drooped....

Her pajamas.

"Riley!"

He held her head in his hands, brushed her cheeks with his thumbs. In a rushed voice, hoarse and low, he said, "You're beautiful."

Beautiful? Regina blinked over such an absurd comment. Her hair was a mess, more so now that he'd tunneled his fingers through it. Her eyes were sleep-heavy and she had not a single speck of makeup on. The pajamas were comfortably baggy, not in the least attractive. "I...I need to go get dressed."

Slowly, he shook his head. "No. I like you just how you are." He kissed her again before she could argue. This kiss was deeper, hotter. She was aware of so many things—the press of his strong fingers on her skull, keeping her immobile, the heat of his breath, the taste of him.

His tongue retreated, moved over her lips, then licked into her mouth again. When his hands released her head, she kept the kiss complete, unable to get enough of him. His tongue retreated, hers followed. His sank in again and she sucked at it.

She knew his hands were roving over her, not strok-

ing her breasts as he had done before, so she didn't understand what he was doing—until her robe fell open
and he pushed it aside.

Oh, but it was hard to think with Riley holding her
so close, touching her in such remarkable ways. He
smelled delicious this morning, like soap and the outdoors and like himself. He was so warm, the cotton of
his T-shirt so soft over solid muscle. His callused fingertips slipped beneath the hem of her pajama top to
trace the indentation of her waist, then higher, until he
teased just beneath her breasts. He circled, glided over
and under her nipples, not touching them but bringing
her breasts to a tingly, almost acute sensitivity. She held
her breath, wanting more, wanting everything.

In the next instant, his thumbs brushed up and over
her nipples. The touch was so electric, so anticipated,
she jolted against him, gasped, and her fingers bit into
his upper arms, closing on rock-solid muscles.

Regina didn't want him ever to stop touching her;
if anything, she wanted more and tried to tell him so
by pressing closer with a soft moan. Though he hadn't
touched her below the waist, her whole body sang with
awareness. Her thighs trembled, her belly had filled
with butterflies and a curling, undulating sensation of
ripe pleasure expanded and retreated within her.

Riley removed his hands, then drew her head to his
shoulder, rocking her a little, rubbing her back in a
soothing, calming way.

She didn't understand. "Riley?"

"I have to stop, Red. When you agree to sleep with
me, I want you to be totally clearheaded, so you won't
have regrets."

Regina didn't know what he was muttering about.

She pressed her nose into his throat and breathed in his warm male scent, filling herself up. She wanted to taste his skin, but knew that might not be wise.

Against her ear, Riley rumbled, "While you fix the pancakes, I'll clean up the glass and call someone to replace the door." His tongue touched her ear, traced the rim, dipped inside. Little shivers of excitement raced along her arms and nape and she almost melted. "After breakfast you can pack."

The fog thinned. "Pack?"

"Yeah." His hard hand drifted lower, all the way to the base of her spine. He pressed gently—and she felt his erection against her belly, long, hard.

Regina shoved back. "What do you mean, *pack?*"

As if she should have already understood, Riley held her face turned up to his so she couldn't miss his frown. His gaze bore into hers, insistent, unrelenting. "You can't stay here now."

When she still stared at him in confusion, his frown became a black scowl. "Red, someone is getting pretty bold. And if that doesn't alarm you, then look at Butch."

She glanced down at the dog. He had his tiny front paws crossed over Riley's big foot with his head resting on them. His big brown eyes stared up at her trustingly. He was so shaken, he hadn't even protested their intimacy.

"Do you really want to chance letting him outside to do his business again, knowing someone could be lurking there, that they might snatch him away or, worse, use him to upset you?"

She knew what he was saying, and her heart squeezed tight. *"No."* In a protective rush, Regina scooped him up and hugged him to her breasts. He twisted and rubbed against her, luxuriating in the human attention. She needed the comforting contact as much as her dog did.

"Look at him," Riley said, "he's still shaking."

Without removing her cheek from the dog's neck, she said, "He always shakes and you know it." She had a feeling Riley only used the dog as leverage, and still she had to admit he was right. She'd be heartsick if anything happened to him. He trusted her to keep him safe, to take care of him, and she intended to do just that.

"I have plenty of room." Riley watched her with a sort of cautious regard. "You'll be safer with me."

Regina looked past him, through the kitchen doorway. The sun was on the rise, a crimson ball that reflected like fire on every sharp, jagged shard of glass littering her once secure home. She chewed her lip in indecision, but no other option came to her. If she went with him, it wouldn't be just an agreement to share space, and she knew it. It'd be an agreement to start an affair.

Her heart pounding for an entirely different reason now, she glanced at Riley, drew a breath, and said, "All right."

Riley encompassed both her and Butch in a bear hug. Butch bit his nose.

Now that he'd gotten his way, Riley grinned like a rascal. "You really do look great in your pajamas and with your hair all loose and tangled." He fingered one long curl. "Sexy as hell."

Heat rushed up her neck to warm her face. She turned her back on Riley and set the dog down. "I didn't even realize…"

"You were rattled, just as I said."

Regina wanted to groan. She was *still* rattled. "I can't believe I sat there in front of those men…"

"They thought you looked hot, too. I wonder if they think we've been sleeping together."

She slanted him a sharp look. "You tried hard enough to give them that impression."

"No choice. With them both eyeing you, I had to stake a claim." Totally unrepentant, he kissed her ear again and squeezed her waist. "I didn't want them getting any ideas about pursuing you."

Feeling like a fool, Regina smoothed her hair and retied the belt of her robe. "I guess I ought to call work since it looks like I'll be late." She picked up the receiver.

"Go ahead." Riley's blue eyes twinkled with teasing. "While you do that, I think I'll just go put the flashlight back in your nightstand—"

Regina whipped around so fast she almost fell. She grabbed Riley by the back of the shirt. "No."

He cocked a brow. "No?"

She dropped her hands, dusting them nervously across her thighs. "That is, I'll do it." She snatched the flashlight away from him. "You should call about the door."

"Right." And then with feigned confusion, he said, "But I thought you were going to call work."

The unholy grin gave him away, and her temper ignited. "You snooped in my drawer, didn't you?"

"Snooped? Now why would I do that, Red? What are you hiding in there?"

Regina swatted at him, embarrassed, irritated. "You had no right." In a snit, she went past him, stepping over the dog's pen and marching toward her bedroom. Glass crunched beneath her slippers, but she barely noticed.

Riley was right on her heels. "The *Kama Sutra,* Red? That's a little dated, isn't it?" His teasing voice grated along her nerves. "But that other book...what was it called? Oh yeah. *Getting the Most Pleasure in Bed.* Now that's current, right?"

Stopping beside her bed, Regina pointed an imperious finger at the door. "Get out."

He didn't budge. "And no less than a dozen rubbers. Woman, what have you been planning?" He stepped closer, forcing her to back up until her legs hit the side of the mattress. "More importantly, any chance you were planning it with me?"

With sudden clarity, Regina knew he hadn't seen the photo. No, being typically male, he'd only noted the silly books and condoms. "No."

"No, what? You weren't planning anything with me?"

She shook her head, felt silly for going mute, and managed to say again, "No."

His smile turned smug. "I didn't really think so. After all, those condoms are smalls." And totally deadpan, "They'd never fit."

Regina's heart jumped into her throat. She licked suddenly dry lips. "No?"

He shook his head. "I'm just an average man, Regina."

"There's nothing average about you."

His slow smile nearly melted her heart. "Maybe you should wait until we've made love to make that judgment."

A tidal wave of awareness nearly took out her knees.

They were in her bedroom, right next to her unmade bed. Her heart gave a hard thump, then tripped into double time.

Riley stepped closer, a grin playing about his mouth. "Such a pretty blush, Red." He looked at her bed, gave a small shake of his head, and all teasing evaporated. "So tell me, Red. What have you been planning, and with whom?"

No never. Not in a million years. "The books are just...curiosity."

"Curiosity about sex?"

It wasn't easy, but she gave a cavalier shrug. "About... variety." She knew about sex. She even knew about pleasure. But things didn't always go right, no matter how she tried. With an airy wave of her hand, she explained, "I bought the books and condoms months ago, when I was engaged."

"Engaged?"

His thunderous expression surprised her. "Yes."

"You were in love with someone?"

He said that like an accusation, confusing her even more. Because he looked so red in the face, she decided to admit the truth. "No, I didn't love him. I thought I *could* love him, and I loved the idea of being married and starting a family...."

He'd grown so rigid, she rushed on to explain. "The engagement ended almost as soon as it began. I realized what a stupid move it was, and he made it plain he didn't love me and likely never would. I think he just used the engagement as a sham, a way to..."

"Get you into bed?"

It sounded so stupid, and she'd been so gullible, that she only shrugged. "The, um, condoms have never been opened. I just haven't had the nerve to throw them out. I didn't want anyone to see them in my garbage."

Slowly, Riley relaxed. His frown smoothed out, replaced by a tender expression that seemed so incongruous to the hard man he could be. "Wouldn't be proper, huh?"

"It's private, that's all."

He started to say more, but Butch gave an impatient howl from the kitchen.

Riley glanced that way, then back at her. "I'll get him." He touched her chin, lifted her face and pressed his mouth to hers for several heart-stopping moments. "You better get dressed before I forget my dubious code of honor and the fact that we have a lot to get done in the next couple of hours." He turned and went through the door.

The second he disappeared, Regina jerked the drawer open, took out the framed photograph and looked around for a good place to hide it. She'd just lifted her mattress, ready to shove it beneath, when Riley stepped back in with a wriggling Butch in his arms. He drew up short when he saw her, then his brows came down.

His gaze went from her guilty face to her hand, which she quickly stuck behind her back. "All right, Red. What are you up to now?"

CHAPTER FIVE

RILEY WATCHED AS Regina jerked the framed photo behind her back. Green eyes wide and innocent, she said, "It's nothing."

"Right." He strode forward, watched her quickly back up and move around the bed to the other side, and his suspicions grew. He set the dog on the mattress. Butch ran to Regina, came up on his hind legs and begged to be held.

Without taking her gaze off Riley, she caught the dog up one-handed. "If you'll leave, I'll get dressed."

Riley crossed his arms over his chest, not about to oblige her. "I'm damn curious, Red, what's worth hiding from me when I already saw the dirty books and rubbers."

Her jaw firmed. "They're not *dirty* books, they're educational."

"Uh-huh."

"And it's none of your business."

"Someone is trying to hurt you. Everything is my business."

Her cheeks colored. "This is…personal. Nothing that anyone else would care about."

"You don't trust me."

"Of course I do."

"Then let me see."

"Riley."

She wailed his name, making him smile. Stalking her, he started around the bed. She took one step back, then planted her feet and glared. Butch licked her chin in commiseration. Absently, she patted his back.

She was such an affectionate woman, so soft and gentle. It didn't take much to make her blush—a smile from him, a touch and her cheeks turned pink. The more he was with her the more he wanted her, and the more he wanted to know all her secrets. She'd kept parts of herself away from him, her engagement, her insecurities…but no more.

He stopped right in front of her and held out his hand.

She shook her head in exasperation. "This is stupid."

Riley waited.

Finally, with no graciousness, she slapped the picture frame into his hand. His curiosity keen, Riley turned it over, and was met with the charismatic smile on Senator Welling's face. Riley decided it must be the photo she took in the park, given the fountain beside him and the large trees behind him. Regina had written at the bottom of the photo, *Senator Xavier Welling,* along with the date of the photo.

The senator was easily in his mid-fifties. He was tall, gray-haired and aristocratic. In order to always make a good public appearance, he'd kept in shape. He had no paunch and his shoulders were still wide from his college football days.

Riley saw red. Through stiff lips, he said, "You keep a picture of the senator beside your bed?" And then with jealousy pricking his temper, he added, "Next to the goddamned *Kama Sutra?*"

Regina drew herself up. "Don't raise your voice to me."

It wasn't easy, but Riley reined in his temper. He tossed the picture onto the bed. "What the hell does it mean?"

"What does what mean?"

"Don't look so confused, Red. You've got his picture in your nightstand drawer, next to your bed, with books on sex and a load of rubbers." Hell, just saying it made him madder. "You got the hots for him?"

She gasped so hard, Butch started to howl again. She absently stroked him. "Of course not. He's a wonderful, respectable man with a wife he loves and a family he cherishes."

"Don't make me puke. He's a politician, first and foremost."

Regina went on tiptoes to poke him in the chest. "Yes, he's a politician. A wonderful senator. He's fought hard for the health and safety of children. He supports local law enforcement. He's won numerous awards and honors for leadership and—"

Riley turned his back on her. "Jesus, you're besotted."

Using her free hand, she caught the back of his shirt. "I am not," she all but shouted. "Senator Welling is an inspiration. I admire him, just as I admire his family and his aspirations and his beliefs." And then, in a smaller voice filled with vulnerability, she said, "I admire everything he stands for."

Riley turned to stare at her, something in her tone touching deep inside him. "Just what does he stand for, Regina?"

Still disgruntled, Regina chewed her lip, not looking at him. "Family. Community. Everything that's good. When you see him campaigning with his wife and kids, you just know that's how it *should* be, all of them smiling, happy, secure." She lifted her gaze to meet Riley's. "I see them together and I know it can happen, because it's right there, live, real."

Riley didn't know how real a politician's public persona might be, but he could tell Regina believed in it. When she'd talked of her family, she'd done so with very little emotion. He'd found that strange, but hadn't pondered it long, not when most of his thoughts centered on carnal activities.

Feeling like a complete bastard, Riley pulled her into his arms. Butch wiggled until he was up between their faces, making sure no kissing would occur. But Riley felt content just to hold her. At least for now.

"I'm sorry."

Against his chest, she murmured, "For what?"

"For prying. And for not understanding." Keeping one hand on Butch so he wouldn't fall, Riley stroked Regina's back. He wished he could touch her bare silky skin again, but he didn't dare. It had been a close thing in the kitchen, his control severely tested. Only the fact that he knew damn good and well she wasn't thinking straight had kept him from laying her across the kitchen table. She'd been ready, damn it, whether she wanted to admit it or not.

"I guess it's okay," she said while rubbing her cheek against him, setting him on fire again. "It's not a secret that I admire the senator and what he stands for."

"Looks can be deceiving, you know."

She shook her head. "Being a politician does not automatically make him a fraud, Riley."

"No. But the world is filled with cheats and liars,

people you'd bet on in a pinch, who turn out to be more unscrupulous than you ever could have imagined."

Leaning back, she looked at him thoughtfully. "Have you known people like that?"

He skirted that question by stating the obvious. "I'm a cop, Red. I see the worst of mankind all the time."

Her hand smoothed over his chest. She couldn't know how the innocent touch inflamed him. If she did, she wouldn't now be looking at him with so much understanding. "You deal with that element of life. But Senator Welling is just the opposite. He's part of the good team, Riley."

Riley wanted to shake her for her naiveté. He knew firsthand how difficult it was to read the people you cared about. Blind trust was never a good thing, but since he wanted it from Regina, he didn't say so.

Riley tucked a long curl behind her ear. "Can I ask you something, honey?"

She laughed.

"What?" He held her away so he could better see her face.

"You're so funny, Riley. Demanding one minute, requesting the next."

"I'm glad you're amused." He smiled, too. "So is it all right?"

"Sure. At this rate, I won't have any secrets left at all."

That'd suit him just fine. He intended to make her his, but never again would he be made the fool. Knowing everything about her would be a safeguard against unhappy surprises.

He released her and she sat on the bed. Butch circled her lap, then nudged his way beneath her housecoat so he could curl up against her stomach. She tucked him in before looking at Riley in inquiry.

Riley settled himself beside her. "Who footed the bill when your parents died?" If she'd been the only one responsible, it'd help explain her need for doing things right, to always be prepared and proper.

She appeared confused by the question. "I did what I could, but I didn't have enough money to make a huge difference in their care. What I had to give wasn't enough, so instead I spent days researching ways to get them the help they needed. It's wasn't easy. That's one of the things about Senator Welling. His health benefit programs would have done my parents a world of good."

Riley did not want to talk about the damned senator. "What about your brother? Did he help out?"

"I told you, he's just like them. I had to loan him money to buy a suit so he'd have something decent to wear to the funerals."

Damn, that meant she alone had had the burden of her parents' care. "Loan—or give?"

She shrugged, which was all the answer Riley needed. "What about your fiancé? What happened there?"

Hedging that question, she asked, "Just who is the reporter here, Riley? Me or you?"

With a straight face, Riley said, "I just wondered if he could possibly be the one bothering you now." He spoke the truth, but it wasn't the only reason he asked. Possessiveness had a lot to do with his interest, too.

"Oh. No, he didn't help with my parents. Our engagement was after their deaths. And, no, it's not him."

"How do you know for sure?"

She untangled a grouchy Butch from her lap and

pushed to her feet. "Trust me. He has no reason to hold a grudge."

Riley took the dog from her. He immediately rooted underneath Riley's shirt, circled into a small ball, and sighed himself back to sleep. Riley looked down at the lump where his flat abdomen used to be, shook his head, and put one hand over the dog. "Men see things differently than women. Maybe your take on the breakup isn't the same as his."

Regina rubbed her head. "It's not. But that has nothing to do with anything."

Her reluctance to talk about the other man couldn't have been more plain. It nettled Riley. "So who did the breaking up, you or him?"

"I did, but he didn't mind."

"How could he not mind? That doesn't make any sense. If he'd asked you to marry him—"

"He didn't want me, all right?" She threw up her hands. "There. Happy? He called me a prude and said I was unappealing. He wanted me to change myself and I can't do that, and he said that no man would want me, especially in bed, and so I *left*. End of story."

Stunned speechless, Riley watched her storm out of the room.

For long minutes after, he remained on the bed, soothing Butch who had gone a little frantic at Regina's raised voice. He'd crawled up Riley's chest, grumbling and growling, then poked his head out the neck of the shirt, just beneath Riley's chin. "Her fiancé sounds like a complete ass, doesn't he, Butch?"

Butch whined.

"I wonder, is that why she bought the books? Had she already realized that things weren't going well between them? Not that I'm sorry to hear it, because if she hadn't, she might have married him."

Butch whined a little louder.

"I agree." Riley had to take off his shirt to get Butch free. "Does she still love the guy, do you think?"

Butch had no answer.

When Riley entered the kitchen, Regina was on the phone with her editor, explaining about the glass. She didn't look at Riley, and after she hung up, she went past him to the living room.

"I won't be going in today at all. Most of the work I need to do for the rest of my assignment can be handled on the phone and typed up on my computer." She paused. "Is it okay if I bring my computer?"

Riley followed behind her, cautious of her new mood. "You can bring anything you want."

"Thank you." She pulled out a phone book from the closet and carried it back to the kitchen.

"What are you doing?"

"Looking up numbers for glass replacement. I want this fixed before the evening."

Riley followed her. "I'll take care of that."

"You said that half an hour ago."

"This time I mean it." He wrested the book out of her hands and plunked Butch into her arms. The poor dog had been passed around a lot that morning. "Go shower and pack whatever clothes you need right away. I'll call for the door replacement, take you to my place, then come back here and get your computer and any other stuff you need. All right?"

"I am not helpless."

"Far from it." He tried a smile that she didn't return.

"C'mon, Red. You look stressed and tired and I want to take care of you just a little, okay?"

She stared up at him for long moments. "I'll finish up my work on this current piece today."

The swift change of topic threw him. "Great."

"That means tomorrow, or even later tonight, I can start my interview on you."

His smile slipped a little, but he managed to hang on to it. "Okay."

"I have so many questions, it might take a few... days."

His smile felt like a grimace. "I did agree."

"Yes, you did." She handed Butch back to him. "Can you keep an eye on him while I shower and dress? Thank you."

Both Riley and Butch watched her leave yet again, her walk a little more sassy this time. Oh, she wanted payback with the interrogation, he could tell. Riley wondered how many answers he could give without telling things he never wanted to reveal? It'd be tricky, but he could handle it.

If all else failed, he'd distract her with a kiss—and more. After all, he'd given her fair warning of what to expect. And still she'd agreed.

That thought brought back his smile in full force. In the end, he'd get what he wanted most: Regina. That made the rest worthwhile.

"WELL, THIS ANSWERS one question, doesn't it?" Regina stated.

Riley had parked his truck behind her Escort in his allotted garage space, then joined her. She stood between the car and the opened door, staring at his apartment.

Unlike most women Riley knew, Regina hadn't lingered in the shower. Butch, unwilling to wait in the kitchen while Riley cleaned up the glass, had howled endlessly until Regina stuck her head out the bathroom door and asked Riley to hand him to her. Butch had curled up on a towel and slept while she quickly showered and dressed in white slacks and a sleeveless cotton sweater and sandals. With her long red hair restrained in a French braid, minimal makeup and small earrings, she looked classy and sexy combined.

A large satchel with files and notes from her current project was slung over her arm. Riley hadn't realized that she gathered so much info just for one story. And since she'd told him her current article was about the silly talent show held by a local television station in the mall, he was doubly surprised.

They'd both driven so Regina would have her car handy. Not that he wanted her out driving around alone until he figured out what was going on. But neither did he want her to feel trapped or overly dependent on him. He knew she would rebel over that and he'd lose her before he could get her used to being with him.

Butch was on a thin leash, so Riley lifted him out of the car, then took Regina's elbow to move her forward. He closed her car door. "You disappointed?"

"That you don't have your own house?" She glanced at him over her shoulder and smiled. "No, of course not." Then she asked, "But why don't you?"

Riley shook his head. Before meeting Regina, he'd thought he had enough of hearth and home to last him a lifetime. He said only, "This is easier. Less maintenance." He led her and Butch up the walkway. "I'll show you around, then unload your stuff."

All she'd brought this trip were a few changes of clothes, her bedding—because she claimed she needed her own pillow to sleep—Butch's belongings and the material for her current assignment. She'd packed up more stuff at the house and disconnected her computer, but Riley told her he'd get all of that when he returned to meet the glass repairmen. Everything else they could retrieve as needed.

Since his place was on the ground floor, it'd be more convenient for Butch. He only hoped Butch liked the big golden retriever next door, since they'd be sharing yard space. He unlocked the door and pushed it open for Regina to enter.

"Oh, Riley, this is very nice."

He watched her look around. Luckily, he was a tidy man, otherwise he couldn't imagine her reaction. She touched her hand to the arm of a brown leather sofa, glided her fingers over a marble tabletop. "Did you decorate yourself?"

"Yeah." At the time, he'd taken enjoyment in only pleasing himself, with no one else to consider. He hadn't expected ever again to want the approval of a woman. And Regina wasn't just any woman, but an immaculate one at that.

Only it looked as though Regina liked his choices. "There's only one bath, but we'll work that out." Maybe they could share the shower? He grinned, then covered that reaction by discussing the dog. "I'll hook a lead up for Butch so he can run a little more outside. Oh, and if you need me to pick up any groceries for you, just let me know. I tend to do a lot of fast food."

He tugged Butch inside and closed the door.

Butch's ears perked up with his first glimpse of the place, giving Riley warning. He leaned down to unleash the little rat. In a stern voice, his finger shaking in the dog's face, Riley said, "Now listen up, bud. No piddling on the furniture, okay?"

Rather than feeling intimidated, Butch snapped at his finger, making Riley grin. "I almost forgot, with all the excitement." He pulled the stuffed Chihuahua from his pocket and tossed it toward the middle of the room. Butch jerked about to watch the stuffed animal land, then he reared back on his haunches, did a bunny hop to where the floppy toy lay—and attacked.

Regina started laughing at his antics.

Riley had to admit it was pretty cute the way he shook the toy, threw it this way and that. For such a small dog, he made feral sounds. Then as if expecting it to follow, Butch went into flight. It was so funny to watch him run. Somehow he managed to streamline himself, laying his ears back, tucking in his tail and dashing around furniture and corners so fast he was practically a blur.

His tiny feet made a distinct patter on the wooden floor. He slid around the corner, took a second to get some traction, and was off again.

Regina watched in wonder. "He doesn't know your place yet. How can he be sure he won't run into anything?"

Riley slung his arm around her shoulders, already enjoying having her in his home. "Men have great reflexes."

She cocked a brow at him. "And women don't?"

"Some women do." He pinched her chin, tipped up

her face and kissed her mouth. "We'll be working on yours, remember?"

A knock sounded on his door. Regina pulled back in surprise, but Riley just shook his head. He opened the door and there stood Ethan, Rosie, Harris and Buck.

As usual, Rosie was pinned up against Ethan's side, and she appeared most comfortable there.

Harris, a firefighter at the same station as Ethan, looked fatigued, a good indicator that he'd recently come off his shift. Though Riley knew he'd have showered, the scent of smoke still clung to him. He pushed his black hair back with a hand and lounged against the door frame, his blue eyes tired and a little red.

Riley gave him the critical once-over. "Hell, Harris, you look like you should be in bed."

Harris yawned hugely. "Just left bed, actually." His satisfied grin said he'd just left a woman, also.

Riley grunted. "Maybe you should have tried sleeping."

"Did that—*after*. But last night was a bitch so I'm still sluggish."

Ethan nodded. "Had a pileup on the expressway. Three cars caught fire. No one died, thank God, but we worked our asses off."

Buck threw a thick, muscular arm around Harris, nearly knocking him off balance. Being the owner of a lumberyard and used to daily physical labor kept Buck in prime shape and made him the bulkier one in the group. Like Harris, Buck was single and enjoyed playing the field.

Still holding Harris, Buck pulled off a ball cap and scratched his head, further messing his brown hair. Green eyes alight with laughter, he said, "Harris never minds toiling through the night, 'cuz the ladies like to fawn all over him the next day."

"Jealous?" Harris asked.

"Naw." Then with a huge grin and a feigned yawn, he said, "I just got out of bed myself."

Riley laughed and held the door wide open. They all piled in, and Rosie was about to say "hi" when Butch flew around the corner, skidded to a halt, and went into a rampage of spitting Chihuahua fury.

Ethan tucked Rosie close. "What the hell?"

Rosie said, "Oh, it's so cute!"

Harris shrank behind Buck, pretending to cower. "Cute? What is it?"

"Whatever it is," Buck added, "it's demonic."

Riley caught Regina's scowl and laughed. "You might as well get used to hearing that, Red. It seems to be the typical response to your dog."

Buck and Harris said in unison, "Dog? You're kidding, right?"

Riley lifted Butch, who seemed to take extreme dislike to Ethan holding his wife. Most of his ire was directed at him.

"What did I do?" he asked

Rosie laughed, saying, "What haven't you done?"

"Hey." Riley held the dog eye level. "They're friends. You can relax now."

But Butch wasn't having it. Rosie dared to try to pet him and Butch practically went over Riley's shoulder in his effort to escape her. As long as he thought he had everyone cornered, he was as brave as a German shepherd, but let someone reach for him and he tucked his tail quick enough.

Regina took her dog. "He's still getting used to me and Riley. He's…shy."

Buck forced Harris to turn him loose. "Yeah? Is that what you call it?"

"I'd call it rabid," Ethan said.

Now that he was close to Regina, Butch quieted and started to lick her chin. Harris curled his lip. "That's disgusting."

"I think he's adorable."

Harris nudged Buck. "Yeah, Rosie, but you think Ethan is adorable, too, so you obviously have lousy taste."

Riley attempted to get things back on track. "Now that you're here I can explain."

Regina froze. "Explain what?"

"What's going on, of course." He knew she wouldn't like it, but he thought the extra backup wouldn't hurt. "They're friends, Red. And I want Harris and Buck to help me move some of your stuff."

Ethan sent his wife a look, then stared at Riley. "She's moving in with you?"

"Temporarily," Regina rushed to clarify.

At the same time, Riley said, "She is."

Rosie just grinned. "This is great. But what about your house?"

"As soon as it's mine, I'll—"

"As soon as it's *safe,* she'll move in there." Riley didn't want to think about her being on her own like that until he knew for certain that no one would hurt her. "Rosie, why don't you help Red make up the guest bed?" Riley suggested, and saw Harris and Buck start elbowing each other again. "And I'll get these goons to lend a hand unloading."

Rosie frowned. "Why can't Harris help her make the bed? I'd rather hear the scoop."

Harris stepped forward eagerly, eyebrows bobbing. "Oh yeah, I'll help her—"

Riley hauled him back with a hand in his collar. "I need to talk to you." Then to Rosie, "Regina can tell you what's going on."

"Yeah, well, somehow I think I'd hear a different version from you. Guys always have a different version."

Regina looked pained. "Really, I can make the bed myself and there's not that much to carry in."

Ethan grabbed his wife and kissed her. It wasn't a quick kiss or a timid one. Against her mouth, he teased, "Riley's suffering here, sweetheart. Be agreeable for once, will you?"

Dreamy eyed, Rosie said, "I'm agreeable every night."

Ethan touched her cheek and grinned. "Yes, you are."

Harris rolled his eyes. "God, will the honeymoon never end?"

In a quick mood switch, Rosie reached around her husband and shoved Harris, who fell into Buck. In a huff, she turned and grabbed Regina's arm. "Come on. Let them do the grunt work. You'll probably tell it right where Riley will only beat his chest and play Neanderthal."

That observation had Regina laughing. Butch gave the men a bark of farewell as the women disappeared around the corner.

"Okay," Ethan said, now that they were alone. "What's going on?"

"Outside. I don't want Regina to hear me."

Harris said, "Why is it the second a guy starts really caring about a woman, he complicates things?"

Buck nodded. "It becomes one big soap opera, doesn't it?"

Ethan and Riley hauled them out the door. At Regina's car, Riley said, "Someone is trying to hurt her, or scare her. I'm not sure which, and I don't know why."

Harris leaned on her fender. "No shit?"

"She okay?" Buck asked.

"Yeah. She's hanging in there. Regina is tougher than she looks."

Harris snorted, and when Riley glared at him, he held up his hands in surrender. "Hey, I wasn't casting aspersions on the lady. It's just hard to imagine anything tough about her."

Buck grinned, adding fuel to the fire. "She is a rather soft-looking woman, huh?"

Ethan rolled his eyes. "Quit baiting him, you two. He's got enough on his mind as it is."

All humor vanished when Riley said, "Someone threw a rock through her patio doors this morning." Seeing that he now had their undivided attention, he added, "And that's not all." As quickly as possible, Riley explained what had been happening.

"Could be coincidence," Ethan pointed out. "But I gather by your expression, you don't think so."

"No."

"Any ideas?" Harris asked.

"I'm going to check into her old fiancé. Things ended only a few months ago."

"Regina was engaged?" Ethan looked startled by that disclosure.

"Yeah, and there's some idiot who made a pest of himself at her old job. I'll get names from her tonight." Riley also intended to talk to Senator Welling. That might be a little more difficult to accomplish, but if Welling had seen anything the day her car was run off the road, or if he'd noticed anything suspicious at the park, Riley wanted to know about it. The senator had an appearance scheduled at a ceremony for the historical society. Should be easy enough to grab a few words with him then.

"And in the meantime?" Ethan asked.

"I don't want her alone." Which was the main reason he'd gathered his friends together. He couldn't be with her 24/7, so he'd count on them to help out. "For right now, I figured Rosie could stay here with her while we go get some of her things. Plus, I don't want repairmen in her apartment without supervision. They're due in about an hour."

"If it's not safe, then I don't want Rosie involved."

Riley sent his best friend a long look. "Would I put Rosie in any danger?"

"I wouldn't think so."

"Then relax. They're safe enough here, especially since no one knows Red is staying with me."

Ethan scrutinized Riley. "She says it's temporary."

Riley drew a breath. "For now." And then as he walked back to the apartment carrying Butch's pen and bed, he added, "But I'm working on it."

CHAPTER SIX

THE SECOND RILEY opened her apartment door, he felt the tension. With a raised hand, he shushed the men behind him and stepped silently inside. There was no noise, but the silence was thick, somehow alive. Automatically, Riley's gaze searched out every nook and corner, fast but thorough. He noted the unfamiliar shadow in the bedroom doorway. As he stared, it shifted the tiniest bit and all his senses went on alert.

He flattened his hand on Ethan's chest. In a nearly soundless voice, he ordered, "Stay here."

Ethan took exception to that with a muttered, "Like hell."

Unwilling to waste any time, Riley started into the living area. A floorboard squeaked beneath his foot, and in the next instant motion exploded around him. A crash sounded and a tall, dark man dressed all in black bolted out of the bedroom. In one fluid motion, he went through the patio doors and over the railing, much as Riley had earlier.

Without a second thought, Riley went after him.

Behind him, he heard Ethan yell, "Call the police," and then he was at the railing, cursing as Riley hit the ground. He landed in a crouch on the balls of his feet, took only a single moment to get his balance, and gave pursuit.

The man was several feet in front of him, but Riley was fast and more than a little determined. This could be the man who'd been terrorizing Regina but, either way, he'd been in her apartment where he didn't belong. Riley could easily take him apart with his bare hands— but he was a cop, and so he'd go by the law. Even if the restraint killed him.

When he'd almost reached the intruder, Riley didn't grab him with his hands. Instead, he kicked out, sweeping the man's legs out from under him.

The big man went down with a loud grunt of pain. Riley hit hard, too, jarring his bones but unmindful of any pain. He rolled and was atop the other man before the goon could regain his feet. Riley immobilized him by catching his legs with his own, then twisting the man's thick right arm up and back at a very unnatural angle. The man howled in pain. It wouldn't take much pressure to snap a bone or pull the arm from the shoulder socket, and with the way Riley felt, he was more than willing.

Another loud groan issued from his captive.

"Be still," Riley commanded, then he glanced up to see Buck and Harris standing at his side.

Buck curled his lip. "I'm not a cop, Riley. Want me to break something on him?"

The offer was so ludicrous coming from Buck—a man known for laughter, but never aggression—that Riley almost grinned. "If he moves, kick him in the teeth."

"Right." Buck planted his muscular legs apart in what appeared to be anticipation. His size twelve-and-a-half feet were encased in sturdy steel-toed boots.

Wearing a grimace, the intruder twisted to see Riley. "You're a cop?" he gritted out.

"That's right. But I'm off duty. Some uniforms will be here shortly to haul your ass downtown."

"Christ, man, you're breaking my arm."

Harris nodded. "He's right, Riley." He turned his head, contemplating the strange hold Riley had on him. "Looks like you might be breaking a leg, too."

"Don't tempt me." He nudged the guy. "What's your name?" When the man hesitated, Riley growled, "Say it, damn it. Don't make up a lie."

"Earl! My name's Earl."

"Earl what?"

Rather than answer, he groaned in agony.

"Just Earl, huh?" Approaching sirens split the air. Riley said, "Well, Earl, you want to tell me what you were doing in the apartment?"

Sweat beaded on the man's forehead. "Saw it was open. Just wanted to have a look around."

"Right. Let's try again. What were you looking for?"

"Nothing." His head dropped forward to the ground and he panted. "It's the truth, damn it."

"So you're just a regular, run-of-the-mill burglar? You weren't here earlier, tossing rocks?"

"Rocks? No."

Maintaining his hold on Earl's arm, Riley came to his feet and hauled the other man upright. Earl tried to jerk away, but only managed to cause himself more pain. "Buck, check his pockets."

Earl kicked and fought, prompting Riley to add a little more pressure. The man's back bowed with a rank curse.

Ethan showed up then. He looked far more disgruntled and angry than Riley. "What the hell are you doing, Riley?"

Buck dug in the man's pockets and produced a pack of cigarettes, loose change, and a knife. "Sorry, Riley, no wallet, no I.D."

"Shake out a cigarette."

Buck sent him a look. "It's a hell of a time to start smoking." He smacked the pack until one cigarette emerged, saying to Earl, "Nasty habit, bud. Smoking can kill you."

Earl tried to kick out at Buck and with little effort, Riley forced him to his knees.

Ethan crossed his arms over his chest. "The cops are here. Should you be abusing him that way?"

"Since he keeps fighting me, he's lucky I don't tear him to pieces."

As luck would have it, Dermot and Lanny rounded the corner. They stiffened when they caught the occupants of the scene. "Christ almighty, Riley. What the hell is going on?"

Riley forced the big man flat again, put a knee between his shoulder blades and said to Dermot, "Give me some cuffs."

Dermot rolled his eyes, but did as told. After the restraints were in place, Riley did a quick search of his captive, but found no other weapons. He released Earl into Lanny's legal hands. "Read him his rights."

"I know my job, Riley. You want to tell me what the hell we're arresting him for?"

"Sure thing. He was in Red's apartment when I showed up." Riley handed Lanny the cigarettes. "And he smokes the same brand I found on the ground below her balcony."

"Well, I'll be damned. What'd he do inside? Did he steal anything?"

Indicating the contents of his pockets, which Buck still held, Riley said, "That's all he had on him, and I don't think the blade is Red's, so it must be his own. You can add concealed weapon to illegal entry. I think we interrupted things, but I've yet to have a look around inside. You can go on. I'll be down to the station in a little while." Then Riley thought to add, "Hang on to him, okay?"

Dermot grinned. "Judge Ryder is on a fishing trip, not due back till Monday. I'd say it's a safe bet we'll have him till then."

Lanny and Dermot each took an arm while Lanny started the familiar litany on rights. They led Earl to the cruiser. Riley watched, still tensed, until the big man was folded into the backseat and the door securely closed.

Then he became aware of the silence around him. He looked at Harris, who had his brows raised, Buck who grinned and Ethan who stared at Riley so long, Riley finally said, "What?"

"You're a regular savage, Riley, you know that?"

Riley shoved his way past his friend. "Screw you, Ethan."

Ethan laughed. Buck stepped up and drew Riley to a halt so he could squeeze his biceps. "Pure steel," he crowed to his friends. "Like a real-life action hero, he is."

Harris tucked his hands beneath his chin and said in a falsetto voice, "My hero."

Grumbling under his breath, Riley jerked free and went to the balcony. Damned idiots. When he jumped up and grabbed the railing, all three of his foolish friends started joking again. Riley did his best to ignore them as he swung a leg up and pulled himself over the railing. He noticed Ethan, Harris and Buck followed suit, climbing the balcony rather than taking the long walk around the complex to the front door.

Several neighbors were out, watching the proceedings with great curiosity. Once he'd regained his feet, Riley waved down to them. "A minor break-in, folks."

They looked skeptical.

Of course, Buck was still scaling the balcony and Harris had only one leg caught awkwardly over the top rail. Riley shook his head and went inside. When Ethan started to follow, Riley warned him off. "Stay put a minute, okay? I want to have a look around. There's less chance of anything being disturbed if it's just me."

"If you need anything, give a yell."

Riley went to the bedroom first. He knew better than to tamper with evidence or disrupt a crime scene, but this wouldn't be the first time he'd ignored his conscience to do what he thought was best.

In this case, they weren't dealing with a death. More important, Red's feelings were at stake.

If anything would embarrass her, he wanted to know about it and, if possible, spare her. His intentions were altruistic—as unselfish as they'd been the first time he'd broken his own code of honor.

He saw right off that her dresser drawers had been dumped. Lacy panties and bras littered the floor in haphazard disarray, looking like a flock of fallen butterflies. Her pajamas and T-shirts had also been dumped.

Everything from her dresser top had been shoved to the floor, including hair combs, jewelry and perfume.

Items from her closet had been sloppily rearranged and her bedding pulled apart.

What really caught Riley's eye, though, were the damn rubbers tossed everywhere. Dragging a hand over his face, Riley considered the situation, but he gave in before he had time to really think it through. Rushing, he gathered up the condoms and stuffed them into his pockets. He had more than one reason for doing so.

If his friends saw them, they might think they were his and the teasing would be endless, considering the size of the damn things. In fact, he intended to dispose of them posthaste so he didn't get caught with them in his pockets. It would give him a reputation he'd never live down.

But the biggest reason was that Red would be appalled if anyone knew she had them. Obviously, they had nothing to do with whatever Earl—if that was even his real name, which Riley doubted—was looking for.

Her nightstand drawers were now empty. Riley looked around the carnage, but didn't see the photo of Welling or the damn books anywhere. Earl hadn't had them on him, and what would he want with them anyway? That had to mean that Red had taken them with her.

He didn't mind the books—hell, he'd be happy to read them with her. But the last thing he wanted in his home was Xavier Welling's smiling face. Especially since he knew Red saw the man as some sort of paragon of goodness, a damned representation of what men should be. If she expected him to measure up to a precisely staged public persona, she was sure to be let down.

Ethan said, "Everything okay, Riley?"

With the condoms out of sight, Riley called back, "Yeah. You can come in."

Ethan entered the room, followed by Harris and Buck. "Damn, someone is definitely looking for something."

Harris stared toward her underwear. Using only his pinkie, he lifted a teeny tiny thong of shimmery pale pink. "I thought redheads weren't supposed to wear pink."

Riley grabbed the garment from him and stuffed it in his pocket—with the condoms. Hell, it was hard enough for him picturing Red in the sexy bottoms. He'd be damned if he wanted Harris doing the same.

Buck propped his hands on his hips. "Do we clean this up or leave it?"

Riley shook his head. "I have a camera in my truck. I'll take some photos then we'll tidy up before Regina sees it. It'd only upset her."

Ethan crossed his arms over his chest. "All things considered, I want to give Rosie a call. We're going to be a while and I want to make sure she's okay."

"Tell her to get a list of groceries from Regina. I'll stop at the store on my way home."

Harris grinned. "Why, don't you just sound so domesticated?" He started to reach for a satin demibra, and Buck grabbed his arm, but he was laughing, too.

"Leave the unmentionables to Riley before he twists your arm behind your neck."

Riley glared at them both before heading out to his truck, but his thoughts soon left his goofy friends. He had a man in custody. He had Red in his apartment.

Things were moving right along.

REGINA HEARD the front door opening and her heart shot into her throat. Jumping to her feet, she ran to greet Riley.

With his tongue hanging out, Butch kept pace, pretending they were in a race. She knew it was idiotic, knew that Ethan said Riley was fine, but she wanted to see him for herself, to be sure.

He'd just stepped inside the door, awkwardly holding his keys in one hand while juggling grocery bags with his other. Regina halted in front of him.

Riley glanced at her in surprise. "Hey, what's wrong?"

A little embarrassed but still anxious, Regina blurted, "I was worried."

His gaze lingered on her face, his mouth curled. "About me?"

"Yes. And don't be insulted. I know you can take care of yourself."

"And you still worried?"

She nodded, which made his expression warm all the more.

Without looking away from her, Riley kicked the door shut and shifted both bags into one arm. Reaching out, he snagged her close and his mouth brushed hers. "Thanks, Red. But you don't need to fret, okay?"

She sighed. He sounded like the idea was unheard of. "You aren't invincible, Riley. And Ethan called and told Rosie what happened and—"

"And I'm fine." He gave her a squeeze. His hand started down her back toward her bottom, then he looked beyond her. His hand stopped at the base of her spine and he nodded. "Hey, Rosie. Ethan's right behind me."

"I figured as much." She sauntered forward, grinning. "So, hero, how you doing?"

Riley rolled his eyes and allowed Regina to take one of the bags. Suddenly Butch let out a demanding, yodeling howl, and when Riley looked down at him, he came up on his hind legs, dancing in excitement.

"Well, what a greeting." Riley lifted the little dog to eye level. "Met at the door by a beautiful woman and a faithful Chihuahua. What more could a man ask for?"

Regina wanted to smack him. "Riley, please tell me you didn't tackle some maniac who broke into my apartment."

He winked and, still holding Butch close, walked around her to the kitchen. She looked at Rosie, who shrugged, then she stalked after him. *"Riley."*

"Yes, dear." He was in the kitchen, Butch over his shoulder while he unloaded groceries one-handed. "Since you cooked last night, I'll do the deed tonight. Steaks on the grill or spaghetti? They're my two specialties, my only specialties really, so I bought both. Or we can go simple and just have sandwiches. What's your pleasure?"

Regina held on to her temper by a thin thread. She was in his house, and he wanted to help her. She drew a breath. "Do you or do you not have a man in custody?"

"Yeah, we do. Thing is, the bastard isn't talking. We don't even have his name yet. But, luckily, Judge Ryder is out fishing."

Regina shook her head in confusion. "So?"

"So this is a small town, not the big city. Things are done differently here. Ryder's been around forever because no one cares to run against him. Because of that, he feels comfortable taking off for days at a time when the weather looks right to catch a big bass." He winked at her. "The weather looks right."

"What does some judge fishing have to do with the guy who broke in?"

"He can't be arraigned until the judge comes back. That gives us more time to check him out. I have a gut feeling that once we turn him loose on bail, he'll disappear."

Nervousness made her voice tremble. She clasped her hands together tightly, trying to calm herself. "What are you holding him for?"

"Illegal entry and concealed weapon for starters. He ransacked your bedroom, honey, but he didn't steal anything and nothing was really damaged."

The ramifications hit her. "So he was looking for something."

"I'd say so. Whatever it is, he hadn't found it before we interrupted." Riley gave Butch an absent pat as he moved from the cabinet to the refrigerator. "The guys helped me clean up the mess."

The guys. Aware of Rosie lounging in the doorway, Regina eased closer. Her heart slammed in her chest and her palms were damp. "He, uh, trashed my bedroom?"

Riley turned toward her. After a long look, he leaned down and whispered near her ear, "Hey, it's all right, babe. I confiscated the rubbers before anyone could see."

Her relief was overwhelming. "Thank you."

His grin gave her fair warning. "Harris gathered up your panties. Sexy stuff." His gaze dipped down her body. "Makes me wonder what you're wearing right now."

Rosie cleared her throat. "It's rude to whisper in front of guests."

Riley straightened with a sigh. "Since when are *you* a guest?" He glanced at his watch in a show of impatience. "Shouldn't Ethan be here by now?"

"Trying to get rid of me?" Rosie laughed. "And here I was ready to vote for steaks."

Riley looked pained, which mirrored how Regina felt. She wanted to be alone with him, to ask him details on what had happened.

Ethan sauntered in. "Soon as I get everything out of the truck, I'm taking you home, woman."

Rosie turned to drape her arms around his neck. "Really? What for?"

It was Ethan's turn to whisper, Rosie's turn to blush. In a rush, she said, "I'll help you unload."

It was another half hour before Regina was finally able to corner Riley and get some answers.

Not once had Butch left his side. He'd followed Riley to the truck time and again, then around the apartment, watching while Riley helped to put her things away in various places. He hooked up her computer in the room he'd given her to use as an office. It was a guest bedroom, but Regina knew Riley didn't want her using the bed.

With everything now in place, they sat on the back patio so Butch could run the length of the lead Riley had stretched between two trees. Regina stared at Riley, on the edge of her seat.

"What if he'd had a gun, Riley? What if he'd pulled that knife on you?"

Sprawled out on a chaise, his ankles crossed, Riley laid a forearm over his eyes to shield them from the late-afternoon sun. "If the dumb son of a bitch had dared to pull a knife on me, I'd have..." Belatedly, he lifted his arm to take in Regina's expression of horror. His frown smoothed out. "I'd have disarmed him, honey. Okay?"

She couldn't bear the thought of him being in danger because of her. "Are you really that good?"

He sat up and swung his legs around to face her. Treating her to a somber, very direct stare, he took her hands and said, "Yeah."

He'd answered without boasting, just matter-of-factly stating what he saw as a truth. Regina shook her head at such confidence.

"Later," he told her while giving her hands a squeeze, "I'm going to show you how good I am."

Oh, the way he said that. His low tone and sensual smile left her uncertain to his meaning. Cautiously, she asked, "You are?"

"Might as well get started on your training, don't you think?"

Well heck, so *that's* how he meant it. Disappointment warred with common sense. Still, private self-defense lessons wouldn't be at all the same as what they'd done in his gym. There, he'd been all business, politely distant, and a true gentleman given the other onlookers. Here, they'd be wrapped in privacy. The thought of being alone with Riley, feeling his body over hers, touching in all the most sexual places, made her breathless. "I suppose."

"So much enthusiasm." He pulled her off her seat and into his lap—something he never would have done in his gym. She thought he might kiss her, and truthfully, she wanted him to. In the short time he'd been at her apartment and then at the station, she'd missed him. She'd worried about him, too.

Instead he said, "Tell me the name of the guy who harassed you at work, and that ass you were engaged to."

"Why?" She tried to twist around to see him, but he hugged her closer so she could barely move. The fact that she was thinking about intimacy, and he apparently wasn't, left her flustered.

"I'm going to talk to them both. And no, don't argue, Red. I won't embarrass you. You have my promise on that."

It wasn't Riley she worried about. He'd already proven to have her best interests in mind. But her ex-fiancé… "I don't know what you think they can add to the equation."

Riley shrugged. "Maybe nothing. But it can't hurt to ask them a few pertinent questions, now can it?"

Actually, it could probably hurt her pride a lot. She bit her lip, but finally nodded. Riley was a professional who knew his business inside and out. It would be ridiculous to contradict him. "The man I worked with is Carl Edmond. He's a nice enough guy, just different. Sort of intense."

"Intense how?"

"Not in a bad way. Just overzealous about everything, his work, his life—"

"And you?"

She couldn't deny that. "For a while, maybe. He fixated on me. He told me he loved me, but I knew that wasn't true. His courtship became a bother before he wised up, but he was never threatening."

Riley didn't seem convinced. "And the other guy?"

Regina hated to talk about him. She couldn't mention his name without memories swamping her, leaving her hollowed out with humiliation.

But this time, seated on Riley's lap, held in his arms, it was easier. "His name is Luther Finley." She closed her eyes and prayed Luther wouldn't reveal anything of their private past to Riley. Not that Luther considered anything private. She'd found that out too late. "I assume Carl still works at the paper. He loves his job a lot. And Luther should be in the insurance building across the street. He's a salesman." She drew a breath. "Want me to write the names down for you?"

"Carl Edmond and Luther Finley. I won't forget." Riley rubbed his big hand up her arm, then down again. He was silent, introspective, and yet he kept touching her as if he couldn't help himself.

When his thoughts finally turned from the men, Regina felt the shift in his mood and she wanted to rejoice. She tipped up her face—and Riley accommodated her by capturing her mouth for a long, deep kiss. She felt the drumming of his heart, tasted the damp warmth of his mouth, and didn't want him ever to stop.

With his mouth still touching hers, he murmured, "Damn, you taste good."

He tasted better than good. Delicious. Regina pressed closer to slip her tongue into his mouth, deepening the kiss again and making Riley groan in response.

The warm sun beat down on them, cooled only by the gentle breeze. Riley's strength wrapped around her, giving the illusion that nothing bad could ever happen. From his wide chest and thick shoulders to his flat abdomen and strong thighs, he was all male. Being with him, alone each night, would make it nearly impossible to keep any emotional distance.

Had it been only a day ago that she thought she needed to know him better before becoming involved?

She knew the truth now. Already she was way too involved, and knowing him better only made it worse. Riley believed in her when no one else did. He put himself in danger for her. By his own admission and by the evidence of his actions, he was more than capable of handling any threatening situation. On every level, he fascinated her.

She was already half in love with him.

Riley's hand moved up alongside her face. His big thumb stroked her cheekbone as he lifted his mouth. "I want to ask you something, Red."

Regina felt herself floating. She smiled. "Hmm?"

"Why did you bring the books and photo here?"

Her sensual haze lifted. She opened her eyes to see Riley watching her, his expression probing, filled with command. Because their noses practically touched, it was a rather intimidating stare.

"C'mon, Red, tell me." She started to straighten, but he shook his head. "No, I like you like this. I enjoy holding you."

"Oh." She shifted a little to get more comfortable, felt his erection, heard his low groan and immediately stilled. No one had ever touched her as much as Riley did. Not even her fiancé had wanted to hold her this way. "I brought the books because I thought, well, we are going to be staying here together. I'm not an idiot. I realize what we'll likely do before too long."

The heat in his blue eyes darkened. "Today." His kiss was soft, gentle. "It's going to happen today."

Such a sensual promise shattered all other thought. She could only stare at him.

"But, honey, you don't need a book."

Brought back to the reality of the moment, she winced and gave an awful admission. "I think…maybe I do."

Without seeming to move, he gathered her closer to his body. He glanced out into the yard at Butch, saw he was sprawled out in the sweet grass in a spot of bright sunshine. Then he looked to make certain they were well hidden between the sections of privacy fence that lined his small patio.

His gaze came back to her, resting first on her eyes, then her mouth. "How can you need a book when everything you do makes me hot? You dress up all classy and it makes me think about stripping you naked. I catch you in worn pajamas and I want to feel how soft and warm you are under them. You cook dinner and I obsess about the way your bottom sways while you stir the food."

She'd been listening with fascinated wonder until the last, then a startled laugh broke free. "You do not."

"I do." And in a growl he added, "Your backside has played prominently in all my most recent fantasies." He punctuated that statement by grasping her firmly in both hands, giving her behind an affectionate, caressing squeeze. "Damn. I can't wait to get you naked so I can explore it in more detail."

Her face flamed. "Riley."

"Regina." His smile touched her heart. "I especially like the charming way you blush. Hell, everything about you makes me hot. Believe me, honey, getting you into bed is the objective. Once we're there, it doesn't matter what you do. I won't be complaining."

Hearing him say it made her almost believe. Had

she allowed Luther's spiteful comments to influence her too much? It had been such a difficult time, such a humiliation.

But Riley wouldn't lie to her, she knew. He was better than that. "All right, I'll forget about the books if you promise to tell me what you like."

He drew her marginally closer. "I like you."

"You know what I mean."

He pressed his face into her neck and gave a gruff laugh. "The way you keep talking about this, like it's going to happen any second now, has me close to exploding."

Regina thought it *was* going to happen at any moment. She frowned at him, but before she could tell him that she wanted him now, he said, "There're a few things I want to clear up before we get sidetracked."

Sidetracked? Is that what he called making love with her? Feeling put out by his blasted patience, she said, "Like what?"

He leaned away. Some of the teasing laughter in his eyes darkened to a more serious emotion. "The photo. And why the hell you brought it along."

CHAPTER SEVEN

BLESS BUTCH'S LITTLE HEART. He chose that moment to
interrupt with a loud spate of barking. Regina sat up to
see that a rather hefty golden retriever had come over
to check him out. Regina started to jump up in alarm,
but Riley stayed her with a hand on her arm.

"That's Blaze. She's a sweet dog, honey. She won't
hurt him."

Regina doubted that after she saw Butch try to sprin-
kle the gorgeous creature's nose. Yet rather than snap at
him, Blaze lunged back playfully, shook her head, and
ran the length of his lead so that Butch could chase her.

He went so fast trying to keep up, he tripped over
his own nose and managed a complete somersault without stopping. When he ran out of rope, he yelped, and
Blaze trotted back to him.

Regina laughed. "I think Butch is in love."

Riley sat up behind her, his arms looped around her
waist. "Poor bastard. I wonder if she'll keep pictures of
other dogs around just to make him nuts."

Regina turned sharply to stare at him. Was he jealous over the picture? But no, that would be too absurd.
Senator Welling represented strong values, not sexual
allure. Surely, Riley understood that.

Riley lifted her away and came to his feet. The dogs
were still playing, making a terrible racket that didn't

bother Regina at all. She couldn't keep her eyes off Riley as he stretched, then looked up at the blazing sun.

In the next instant he reached for the hem of his shirt and pulled it off over his head.

Regina didn't so much as blink. His upper body was gorgeous. Dark hair liberally covered his well-defined chest. Sleek, prominent muscles in his shoulders bunched and moved as he haphazardly folded the shirt and laid it over the back of her chair. In unselfconscious masculine display, he dragged one hand through his chest hair, scratching a little, then flexed his shoulder and rotated his head.

Regina's mouth went dry. In something of a rasp, she asked, "What are you doing?"

"It's warm out here." He glanced down at her. "And I'm a little stiff from jumping off your damn balcony so many times." So saying, he turned to head inside and Regina caught sight of a bruise on his ribs.

"Riley." She was out of her chair in a flash, catching his arm and holding him still. "What happened?"

He looked down at the darkening flesh she indicated. "Nothing. That must be where I hit the ground when I tripped him. I had no idea there were so many little stones everywhere."

Wishing she could soothe him, even heal him, her fingertips grazed over his warm skin. "I'm sorry."

His gaze stayed on her face, piercing and bright. "No problem, Red." He unsnapped his slacks.

Regina stepped back in a rush.

"I'm going to go change before we have our little chat about that picture. Be back in a second."

Change? As in, change into *what?* Less clothes? It was bad enough when he was at the gym wearing shorts, T-shirt, socks and athletic shoes. But at the gym, there was always a crowd around, plenty of people to keep the situation less intimate.

Here, there was no one. And she just knew if Riley started flaunting himself, she'd end up the aggressor.

He was only gone a minute, but it was long enough for Regina to give herself a hot flash, thinking of the night to come.

"You getting hungry, Red?"

She jerked around, then took an automatic step toward him. Good Lord, the man oozed sex appeal. He wore gray low-slung drawstring shorts, and nothing else. She realized she'd never seen his feet before. They were big, sprinkled with golden-brown hair, narrow, and as sexy as the rest of him. Right now, braced apart as they were, he seemed to have planted himself firmly against opposition. Hers?

Not likely. Not when everything about him appealed to her.

Slowly, Regina allowed her attention to climb upward, taking in every inch of his body. Muscular, very hairy calves, nice knees. *Incredible* thighs.

Her heart raced. She already knew firsthand how strong his thighs were. She'd watched Riley grappling with some very big bruisers at his gym and he always dominated. Swallowing, she looked higher still and saw the hem of his shorts, hanging to midthigh.

A little higher and she saw… Oh my. Regina blew out a breath that sounded part whistle, part exclamation, and not in the least ladylike. Under normal circumstances, she would have been appalled at herself. But the soft cotton molded to his sex. He was right, small condoms would never fit him.

Breathing became more difficult. As an intelligent, educated and modern woman, and as one who had recently read some informed books on the subject, she knew size didn't matter. That hadn't been her problem with Luther at all.

So why did it feel like a volcano of heat had exploded inside her?

As she stared at him, unable to draw her gaze away, something twitched. Her brows lifted. Fascinated, she watched as Riley became semierect. She put a hand to her throat.

Riley, blast him, never moved.

Deciding it might be safer to continue on with her visual journey rather than keep staring at him *there,* Regina looked at his hard abdomen. That didn't help one iota. The hair around his navel and the silky trail below it appeared soft, tempting her to touch it. She wanted to so badly, but would that be crossing the line?

At the moment, did she care? How could any woman remain rational when faced with such provocation?

Almost from the start, she'd wanted Riley. Every day the feeling grew stronger. Other than her acute sense of caution and propriety, there were no real reasons for waiting.

She moved toward him.

Riley made a gruff sound of expectation.

Savoring the moment, she put her hands on his sides, luxuriating in the feel of hot smooth skin drawn taut over firm muscle. Experimentally, Regina caressed him, her thumbs inward to trace over the sleek muscles slanting toward his groin.

She looked at his face. He was rigid, flushed, waiting. "I want to touch you, Riley."

"Do."

One simple word that somehow sounded so provocative. When she looked again, she saw that he now had a full erection. *Very* full. Just from her touching his waist? Intrigued, she asked, "You like this?"

"Yeah." He drawled out the word, husky and deep.

Emboldened, she slid her hands around his back near the very bottom of his spine, close to his sexy muscled tush. The position brought her closer to his chest and she inhaled deeply. "You smell so good, Riley."

He leaned forward, pressed his mouth to her temple, and whispered, "Is that really where you want to touch me, Red?"

Her nose brushed his soft chest hair when she shook her head. She liked that, so she did it again. "No."

"I didn't think so."

Deciding to try pure honestly, she said, "We're outside...."

"No one can see us."

"But still..."

"I'm a man, not a schoolboy. I can control myself. Nothing happens unless you say so. Feel free to touch all you want and to stop when you want."

Her heart expanded. Such an incredibly generous offer.

Such an incredibly generous man.

She tipped her face up. "Will you kiss me while I do it?"

His expression hardened and his voice went low and rough. "My pleasure, baby."

This kiss felt different. Regina hadn't realized he'd been holding back, that there were so many nuances to kissing until that moment when she felt all his carnal intent in the way he devoured her mouth. It was an eating kiss, hot and hard and overwhelming. He would make love to her now—she understood that and reveled in the reality.

Again and again, his tongue sank past her parted lips and into her mouth, stroking seductively. She felt consumed. That was enough of a distraction that Riley had to nudge himself forward into her belly to remind her of what she wanted, of what *he* wanted.

Bringing her hands around, she first toyed with his navel. His abdomen had grown rigid, the muscles clearly defined, growing more so as she touched him until he felt like granite with no give to his flesh at all. The hair there was just as silky as she'd imagined.

Breathing hard, her awareness suspended, she encountered the waistband of his shorts, the ultrasoft cotton material and finally the long, solid length of his penis.

They both groaned.

Riley's fingers tightened and he lifted his mouth away to gulp for air. Keeping his forehead against hers, he encouraged her by saying, "That's it. Damn, Red…" And he groaned again, harsh and broken.

Regina could have spent an hour just exploring him. On so many levels, he fascinated her, the freedom he allowed, his open response. Her fingertips trailed up his length, measuring him, then back down again—and she felt the shuddering response of his body.

Driven by curiosity, she cupped beneath his shaft, cradling his heavy testicles in her palm and heard him hiss in a breath.

"Easy." His long fingers gripped her upper arms.

"Like this?"

"Yeah." His grip loosened, caressed, encouraged.

They spoke in muted whispers, hers awed, his raw with arousal.

Suddenly he kissed her again, so ravenously that she forgot what she was doing and her hands left him to grasp his neck, holding tight. Strong arms enclosed her, stealing her breath. Her lips were swollen, her head spinning, when Riley again cupped her face to place sweet little pecks on her chin, her cheeks, her forehead.

"You know what I think, Red?"

Overwhelmed, she whispered, "What?"

"That turnabout is fair play."

Her stomach jumped and her heart began a wild race. When she got her eyes open, Riley was smiling at her.

"You'll love having me touch you, Red. I promise. But for right now, we should take this indoors before things get out of hand and neither one of us makes a clearheaded decision."

Her head would never be clear again.

Riley nodded in the direction of the yard. "Butch fell asleep with his new lady friend."

A safer topic if ever there was one. Regina turned and saw that Blaze had stretched out on her side in the thick grass. Her golden fur looked beautiful with the sun glinting off it. Butch was curled up on her neck, his whole head practically in her ear. They made such an adorable picture, Regina's heart nearly melted and stupidly, tears filled her eyes.

"Tonight," Riley whispered to her, "I want to sleep with you curled that close." He didn't give her a chance to reply to that, not that she had a reply anyway. He picked her up and started into the house.

"Butch..."

"Will enjoy his freedom in the yard. I'll leave the window open. Don't fret, honey. We'll hear him if he needs us." Riley walked right past the room he'd given to her and into his own bedroom.

When he reached the bed, he went down with her in his arms. She'd known of his strength, but still he amazed her. He treated her weight as negligible, arranging her as easily as he would a pillow. Straightening away, balanced on one arm, he said, "You're wearing entirely too many clothes, Red. What'd you say we take them all off?" And before she could find her voice, he already had her sleeveless sweater up and over her head.

RILEY KNEW if he gave her too much time to consider things, she'd decide it wasn't proper to be having sex with him in the middle of the afternoon with the window open. He was done giving her time. She now felt comfortable touching him sexually, and he knew, even if she didn't, that they had a future together.

The rest would fall into place.

The second her sweater cleared her head, he reached for the clasp to her bra. He heard her gasping breaths, felt the urgent bite of her nails in his upper arms.

The bra, bless her feminine little heart, was white lace and so damn sexy he could have spent an hour just appreciating the way it decorated her small breasts. Instead, he flicked the front clasp open, pulled the thin cups apart, and visually sated himself.

"Beautiful."

Regina made a sound of startled embarrassment and covered herself with her hands.

Riley forced his gaze from her white breasts to her

face. "Harris was wrong. Pink and red go real nice together."

Her embarrassment faded behind confusion. "What are you talking about?"

A long curl of titian hair had come loose, and Riley used it like a feather to tease the side of her breast. "Red hair and pink nipples. It's a sexy combination."

"Oh." More color exploded in her cheeks. "But what does Harris have to do with—"

No way would Riley tell her about Harris picking up her pink panties. "And this pretty blush." He put his mouth to her cheek and felt the heat of her flush. "You're beautiful, Regina, and I don't want you to be embarrassed with me."

He gently caught her wrists, aware of the fragile bones, how small she felt in his big hands. Drawing her arms up, he pressed her hands firmly to the mattress at either side of her head. He released her and her breasts shivered with her nervous, jerky breaths.

"But I—"

Her protest died on a gasp when Riley leaned down and took one soft, plump nipple into his mouth. Regina's back arched and her fingers threaded through his hair.

Holding her shoulders down on the bed, he sucked gently, keeping the pressure light, using his tongue to tease her nipple into a stiff little point. When he lifted his head, Regina had her eyes squeezed shut, her bottom lip caught in her teeth and her body held tight.

"You like that, honey?"

Without opening her eyes, she bobbed her head.

Riley smiled, then looked at her body. Her upper torso was so slim, her rib cage narrow and her breasts pert. He skimmed his palm down her side, then inward to the clasp of her slacks. "I want you naked. I want to see all of you."

Her eyes flew open.

"Once you're naked, I can get naked and think how good that's going to feel."

Her lips parted. "Yes."

Gently, he pried her fingers from his hair and again raised her arms over her head. "I love seeing you like this, Red, stretched out on my bed." He studied her from top to toes, then kissed her belly. "Now don't move."

She agreed by curling her fingers into the bedding, holding on tight.

Her sandals slipped off easily enough, but Riley took the time to kiss each arch, then each ankle. There was one spot just behind the ankle bone that when pinched, could cause agonizing pain, maybe even paralyze the limb. In the same regard, a featherlight touch sent thousands of acute nerve endings on alert. Riley tickled with his tongue, soothed with soft kisses.

She had sexy legs, long and sleek. Her casual white slacks unbuttoned with ease, and building the anticipation, he slowly drew down the zipper. Her belly hollowed out with her sharply indrawn breath.

Riley spread his fingers wide over her hips and dragged the pants down to her knees. Her panties were the same lace as her bra, showing the springy auburn curls over her mound. He wanted her so badly he hurt, but he didn't want to rush her, he didn't want her to start searching for her damn books.

Using one fingertip, Riley traced the triangle of pubic hair. He couldn't wait to taste her, to have her completely naked and open....

"Riley?"

"Yeah?"

A long heavy silence filled the air before she said, "I don't think I can take all this waiting. My patience isn't as strong as yours."

Riley looked up at her face. Her hands were fisted, her pupils dilated, lips parted.

"Just a little longer."

Her pants tangled around her ankles with her trying to kick them off and Riley had to finish that chore for her. Her panties came off next, and then she was beautifully bare.

Her aroused scent filled his head. He kissed her belly, each hipbone, an inner thigh. Alternately, he made the kisses gentle, then rough, sometimes laving with his tongue, sometimes nipping with his teeth. Regina squirmed and gasped, on edge, unsure what the next touch would bring. He could feel the urgency pounding through her.

Parting her legs, he licked the joint of her thigh and groin, where her skin was ultrasmooth and delicate.

"Riley, please…"

Regardless of what she said, she couldn't be ready yet. His mouth open and his kisses deliberately damp, Riley made his way back up her body. She grabbed him, kissing him hard, while his hands covered both her breasts. Her nipples were tight now, her breasts swollen. He caught her nipples and rolled, squeezed, tugged.

She pulled her mouth away. "Riley."

"Shh." He kissed her again, silencing her protests while continuing to torment her nipples. The more aroused she got, the more she'd enjoy his caresses. Her legs shifted restlessly, moving alongside his until he stilled them with one of his own. Caught under him, Regina could barely move, and that suited Riley just fine.

Keeping her legs trapped, he leaned up to look at her face. "I want you as ready as I am, Red."

"I am," she all but wailed.

"No." Smiling, he dragged his callused fingertips over her ribs, her belly and finally between her thighs. The crisp curls were damp, her lips puffy, sleek with moisture. His breath caught. "Well now, maybe you are." He pressed his middle finger inside, just past her swollen flesh, no deeper. She was most sensitive here, at her opening, so he used that knowledge to circle, dip, circle again. He relished her broken moan, the way her body tried to move with him.

"I should… I should be doing something."

"What is it you want to do?"

"Touch you."

His control nearly slipped. "No, not yet. I'm on the ragged edge as it is."

Her eyes opened and her head lifted off the pillow to shout into his face, "Then quit playing around!"

Riley almost laughed. Regina amused him so much, even at a time when laughter should have been eons away. "All right. Tell me how you like this."

Her head dropped back with a groan as he began moving his finger deeply in and out, making her wetter still. As he did so, he kissed his way down her body. The closer he got to her sex, the more she stiffened.

"Riley?"

"Hush." He nudged her thighs farther apart, took a moment to enjoy her scent, breathing deep, then with a groan, he covered her with his mouth.

She gave a small cry, arching hard.

At the first flick of his tongue, her body clamped down on his finger. He licked, stroked, and finally, catching her small clitoris carefully with his teeth, he suckled.

Her body strained away from him, but Riley held her hips, keeping her still. He loved the feel of her voluptuous bottom in his hands, the taste of her on his tongue, the hot, wild sounds she made. As her excitement peaked, he worked in another finger, stretching her, filling her. She lifted up to meet his mouth, grinding against him, so close.

When he knew she was ready to come, he sat up and snagged a condom from the nightstand. Regina cried out in protest at the delay, and the second he got the protection taken care of, she opened her arms to him.

Riley settled between her wide-open thighs. Wanting every possible connection, he held her face to kiss her and nudged his way inside. She was tight, but so wet he knew he wouldn't hurt her. With one hard thrust, he entered her completely and Regina lifted her legs to wrap around his waist. He found a rhythm that quickly had them both straining toward a climax.

Her mouth devoured his, biting his bottom lip, sucking on his tongue. He loved it.

He loved *her*. If only he could make her understand that.

Sweating, his heart thundering in his chest, he slid one hand under her behind to tilt her hips up so he could enter her more deeply. That was all it took. She started coming with broken groans and mewling cries and that pushed Riley right over the edge. He could feel the throbbing clench and release of her body on his cock, the frantic bite of her nails on his shoulders, the way she shuddered and writhed under him.

He pressed his face into her neck and growled out her name. Regina wasn't quite so restrained. She screamed.

Two seconds after Riley's body went utterly limp and he gave Regina his weight, Butch began barking hysterically.

He felt Regina stiffen, but he patted her hip and made the manly offering. "I'll go get him."

Her hands slid off his back to land limply on the bed. "Thanks."

Riley forced himself to his elbows to see her face. Her eyes were closed, her French braid ruined, her makeup smudged. She was sweaty, just as he'd predicted.

And, thank God, she was finally his.

RILEY ATTEMPTED to wake her with a kiss to her forehead. Regina moaned, rolled to the side and slept on.

They'd spent the night making love and apparently, Regina wasn't used to such excesses. Truthfully, neither was he.

It had surprised him how often he'd wanted her. Watching her eat a simple dinner in her robe, seeing her coddle the silly little dog, catching her secret smiles and sudden blushes, had all provoked him. He hadn't been able to keep his hands off her.

And she hadn't minded in the least.

It'd been tricky, getting Butch to leave the room without kicking up a fuss. Riley figured he'd need to stock up on toys and tasty chews to distract the dog.

After her fourth release, she'd conked out and hadn't really come to since. Once he'd realized she was done for, he'd worked her pajamas back onto her then let Butch in the room. She hadn't protested when the dog burrowed under the covers, or when Riley had pulled her close and held her all night long.

She hadn't even awakened.

It drove home to Riley just how exhausted she'd been, and the toll her worries must have taken on her.

He hoped his presence would ease those worries, because, from now on, she'd damn well be with him. Beyond that, he didn't know if his lauded control extended to sleeping chastely each night, even if they'd made love prior to going to bed.

He hated to disturb her now, but he didn't want to leave for the day without saying goodbye. Butch seemed just as determined to keep him from doing so.

He and the dog had been up for an hour and more than once Butch had whined at her door, apparently wanting Regina to join them. Now that he was back in the bed with her, he dashed from Regina's feet to her head and back again, trying to protect all of her—from Riley.

Riley lifted the miniscule dog. "I may have gone overboard last night, bud, but I don't accost women in their sleep."

Regina's eyes fluttered open. "Riley?"

At the sound of her soft, sleepy voice, some insidious warmth expanded in his chest. "After last night, were you really expecting another man to wake you up?"

He saw confusion flit over her face, then realization. She snatched the sheet over her head. "What in the world are you doing in here?"

He sat on the bed beside her, causing a dip in the

mattress. Her rump rolled into his hip. "I slept here. It's my bed, remember?"

She groaned.

"And because Butch wanted under the covers, I put your pajamas back on you, so you don't need to hide."

"It's not that," she mumbled from under the covers.

Ah, Riley thought, appearances again. Silly woman. "Do you have any idea how sexy you look all rumpled and warm?"

She went very still. "I do?"

"Yeah. Makes me want to strip naked and get back into bed with you." He gave a grievous sigh. "But unfortunately I have some stuff to do, so I only wanted to wake you so I could say goodbye."

One slender hand emerged from the blankets, shooing him away. "I'll be out in a second."

Smiling, Riley patted her hip and stood. As an enticement, he said, "I have coffee ready and waiting."

She made a rumbling sound of appreciation. "I'll be right there."

Ten minutes later she emerged with her hair brushed and pulled back in a ponytail, wearing a casual green sundress. Her eyes were still puffy and there was a crease in her cheek probably formed from a pillowcase.

Riley wanted to consume her. Again. Last night hadn't even taken the edge off his hunger. He didn't think a hundred years could do that.

As he watched, she made her way unsteadily toward the table. "Riley? I suppose I should admit that I'm not at my best in the morning." She ended that with an enormous and inelegant yawn, giving proof to her statement.

"Coffee will help. You sit and I'll pour it for you."

She plopped down in the chair. "Thank you."

The dog made a beeline for Regina. She roused herself enough to lift him into her lap and treat him to several kisses to his round head.

Riley could have used a few of those kisses. Not that he was jealous of the attention she gave Butch, and not that he didn't understand how sluggish she felt. But this was the proverbial morning after and she'd barely looked at him.

Then he decided *what the hell.*

He handed her a mug of coffee, but forestalled her from tasting it by leaning down and taking her mouth in a warm morning kiss. "Now that," Riley said as he straightened, "is the *proper* way to say hello after a night of satisfying debauchery."

Regina gave him a bemused look, snatched up her cup and swilled her coffee. There was no other word for it. In two long gulps, her mug was empty. Enjoying this side of her, Riley fixed her another cup then seated himself across from her.

"You do remember last night, don't you?"

Her eyes darted away from his. "Of course I do. No woman in her right mind would forget a night with you. Especially not a night like that."

"Thanks. I wanted verification, given the way you passed out on me."

She groaned and covered her face with one hand. "I'm sorry."

Riley reached across the table and took her slender wrist. Her skin was warm, smooth. "I'm not. You needed the sleep."

"That's no excuse for rudeness."

Riley nearly choked on his laugh. "You were not

rude, I was excessive. And believe me, I have no complaints."

"But..."

"*None,* Red. Okay?"

Her expression softened. "I don't have any complaints either. In fact, I think I owe you a few compliments."

Riley grinned with her. "You can give them to me tonight."

"Why tonight?" She looked more awake now and somewhat interested. "I thought maybe we could..."

He groaned. "Don't tempt me, Red. Nothing would please me more than hauling your sexy butt back to bed. But I'll be gone till this afternoon."

Her disappointment was plain to see, filling Riley with satisfaction. "I thought you were on vacation."

"I am, but I want to talk to your two swains, Carl and Luther, then stop by the station and see how things are going with our intruder."

Her brows pulled down. "I'm not at all sure I like this idea."

"Why?"

"Don't look so suspicious, Riley. I'm not hiding anything important."

That clarification *important* rang like a bell in his head. "So you're hiding unimportant stuff?"

"No! And don't twist my words. It's just that I'm sure neither Carl nor Luther has anything to do with my trouble."

"With this type of continued harassment, it's almost always someone you know, and more often than that, it's someone you've been romantically involved with." She quit her protests to groan instead. Riley laced his fingers in hers. "Now, don't take this the wrong way, but I'd like you to promise me you won't take off anywhere while I'm gone."

She rubbed her eyes tiredly. "I have nowhere to go. In fact," she said, giving him a direct look, "I thought I'd finish up my article on the talent show. Once that's done, I can start on your interview."

He didn't want to talk about the damn interview right now. While he intended to discover everything he could about Regina, he detested the thought of her prying into his past. He came to his feet and stepped around the table to reach her. Caging her in with one hand on the seat and the other on the back of her chair, Riley said, "We've got a lot to do today, sweetheart."

She stared at his mouth. "We do?"

He nodded. "We're going to start on your private lessons today, remember?"

"Oh."

Seeing her disappointment almost had him laughing out loud. Aware of Butch's low growls, he touched her nose. "I'll make sure you enjoy them, okay?"

Her eyes darkened. "Okay."

"Tonight is the ceremony at the Historical Society. They're honoring Senator Welling." He watched her face and added, "I thought maybe we could go."

Excitement brightened her eyes and added a smile. "You mean it?"

Now he was jealous. Welling represented her ideal man, and for most, his stature was as unattainable as the moon. "It won't be a social call, honey. I want a chance to talk to your senator, and this seems like it might be the best opportunity."

Her excitement remained plain to see. "He's not just my senator, and Riley, you'll like him a lot, I know it."

Riley would have liked the guy more if Regina weren't so infatuated with him. "If he cooperates with me, I'll have no complaints."

"I really don't think he'll have anything to share, but it'll be good to see him again."

Because he didn't want to hear her talk about Welling, Riley kissed her quick and hard. He felt Butch nipping at his chin, his ear, doing all he could to scare Riley off. Riley drew back to stare at the little dog. "Where's your toy?"

Butch's ears shot up. He maneuvered down Regina's leg to the floor and took off at a dead run for the hallway. He returned with the stuffed Chihuahua in his mouth and dropped it at Riley's feet.

Riley laughed. "Smart dog. All right, I can play for just a few minutes, but that's all." And to Regina he added, "Finish up your coffee. There's cereal in the cabinet, fruit in the fridge. Help yourself, okay?"

Her expression was tender when she nodded. "Thanks."

Ten minutes later, Riley was on the floor, the stuffed toy caught in his teeth while he and Butch indulged in a feigned tug of war. Butch gave it his all, jerking and growling in his attempt to tear the toy away from Riley. Riley growled back, a stuffed tail and leg caught in his mouth.

Regina laughed. "You're both nuts."

Riley straightened. "Now he knows how to grapple. Did you see his triceps? Or would they be triceps, considering dogs don't have arms?" Riley shook his head. "Either way, he's buff and built like a lean bulldog."

Butch took off in a flash, dragging the toy, but when Riley didn't pursue him he returned only to smack Riley's ankle with it. "No," he told Butch. "I gotta go. Get Regina to play."

Butch dutifully dragged the toy to Regina. She laughed. "Gee, thanks."

Riley tipped up her chin to give her a long, thorough kiss. "If you need anything while I'm gone, just call me on my cell phone."

He knew he had to leave before he decided not to go at all. Today he was going to get some answers. The sooner the better. Then he'd come home to Regina.

Soon he'd have everything worked out.

CHAPTER EIGHT

THE SECOND RILEY was out the door, Regina made plans. She called Rosie at work first to find out Ethan's and Harris's schedules. She didn't want to call either of their homes if there was a chance she'd wake them. As firefighters, their hours varied. Regina told her they were both on second shift that week, and that Ethan, at least, should be up and about.

She called him and made an appointment for him to visit her at Riley's house. Next, she called Buck and left him a message since he didn't pick up.

Finally she chanced a call to Harris. A woman answered, temporarily throwing Regina off. "Um, is Harris around?"

"Who is this?" the woman asked with heavy suspicion.

Regina was about to reply when she heard some grumbling in the background, then Harris's voice on the phone. "Hello?"

"It's Regina. I'm so sorry I'm interrupting."

"No, you're not." That statement caused another ruckus in the background. Harris covered the phone, did some grousing, then came back to ask, "What's up? Everything okay?"

"Oh, yes. I just... I'm going to be doing an interview on Riley and since he's gone for most of the af-

ternoon and he doesn't want me to leave his apartment,
I figured I could start by talking to his closest friends.
Ethan's coming over in a few minutes, and I hoped, if
you weren't too busy, maybe you could come by after
him."

She heard the amusement in Harris's voice when
he asked, "Does Riley know you're inviting us over?"

"No, why?"

Now he laughed outright. "No reason. None at all.
And yes, I'd love to come over. Hell, I wouldn't miss
this for the world. Want me to pick up Buck and drag
him along? You can kill two birds with one stone."

"I already called him. He's working."

"He's the boss. If he can't take off for a few hours,
who can?"

Regina laughed. "No, that's okay. I'd rather talk to
each of you one on one."

Harris snickered. "Really? All right then." He
laughed again. "This is going to be fun." He hung up
before Regina could ask him what he meant.

RILEY MADE IT to Cincinnati in a little less than an hour.
It was easy enough to find the newspaper building. He
thought about going in to talk to Carl first, but changed
his mind and parked in the lot for the insurance company. At the lobby desk, he asked about seeing Luther,
and was told to go to the fourth floor.

On the elevator ride up, Riley thought about what
he'd say. He realized he wanted Regina's ex-beau to be
guilty, just for the satisfaction of cleaning the guy out of
her past. If she did have any residual feelings for him,
finding out he was the one harassing her, with noth-

ing but hurt feelings to motivate him, ought to take care of it.

There was no one at the receptionist's desk. Riley glanced at his wristwatch, saw it was lunchtime and waited only a moment before mentally saying, *To hell with it.* He strode to Luther's door, raised his hand to knock—and got a whiff of sickeningly sweet smoke. Pot.

What the hell?

He tried the door, but it was locked. After knocking sharply, he called out, "Luther Finley?"

There was a lot of shuffling movement behind the door before it finally opened. A man close to Riley's height, with straight black hair and shrewd blue eyes, stood there. His suit was immaculate, expensive and in good taste.

He made a great appearance. Shit. First the senator, and now this clown. If Regina was drawn to *GQ* men, Riley didn't stand a chance.

"Yeah? Who are you? What do you want?"

So this was the man Regina had bought sex books for? This was the man she'd hoped to please in bed?

Riley wanted to punch him in the nose. The urge to do so made it difficult to breathe. Ruthlessly, Riley brought himself under control. He would not behave like a Yeti. He would not prove himself to be a jealous fool.

Looking beyond Luther, Riley saw an open window, a desk drawer slightly ajar. Perfect. If he couldn't hit him, he could at least have the upper hand. There must be a fairy godmother sitting on his shoulder, to be given this advantage.

"Can I help you?" Luther said with strained impatience.

"You Luther Finley?" At the other man's nod, Riley flashed a badge. "I'm Riley Moore, with the Chester Police Department. I need a moment of your time."

Luther's eyes opened wide and he reeled back two steps. "The police? What the hell did I do?"

"I want to ask you about an acquaintance of yours. Understand, Mr. Finley, this is an informal visit and you're not in any trouble. Yet. I'd just like some information."

Riley saw the moment the man relaxed, wrongfully assuming he'd ignore the pot. "Yeah? About who?"

"Regina Foxworth. She seems to have gotten herself into a bit of trouble."

The look of curiosity faded beneath a smarmy smile. "Regina is in trouble?" He actually laughed. "Yeah, sure. Come on in and pull up a chair. I'm glad to help."

And Riley thought to himself, *I just bet you are.*

REGINA HANDED ETHAN A TALL, icy glass of cola. "Now, tell me what you know about Riley."

Ethan looked more wary by the second. He glanced around the obviously empty apartment and said yet again, "I'm not sure this is a good idea, Regina."

"No, it's okay. Riley gave me permission to interview him. And he didn't want me to leave the apartment, so this is a good compromise. He won't mind."

"Uh-huh." Ethan sipped his drink, still undecided. "What exactly do you want to know?"

Regina studied Ethan while she considered what to ask him first. He was a very attractive man with his dark blond hair and deep, intelligent brown eyes. As a firefighter he was, by necessity, built almost as handsomely as Riley. But she'd never had any interest in

Ethan. No, she'd seen Riley and been lost. She'd fought her reaction to him, but fighting did her no good. Last night had proven that.

She sighed. "Has Riley had any recent romantic involvement?"

Ethan choked, stared at her, and choked some more. She got up to thwack him on the back, but Butch didn't like that and started to howl. For some unknown reason, he'd taken a real dislike to Ethan.

Gasping and wheezing, Ethan waved her away. Regina resettled herself, allowing Butch to skulk back into her lap with a surly look thrown toward Ethan.

"Well?"

"What does that have to do with your interview?"

In the primmest tone she could muster, Regina lied, "His social habits will be of interest to everyone reading the article. They'll want to know about *him,* not just his work."

Ethan didn't look convinced. He drew a deep breath, cast her another suspicious look, and finally murmured, "He dates. Not seriously, not often."

"Really?" Now that was interesting, considering the amount of energy Buck and Harris apparently put into tomcatting around. And from all accounts, Ethan had been worse before Rosie brought him to his senses. "So he's selective?"

Ethan frowned over that. "I have no idea. It's just that Riley is…different. He's not like most guys I know. He thinks differently and he sees the world differently."

"He's dangerous."

Slowly, Ethan nodded. "I suppose you could say that, but only to someone on the wrong side of the law. To most people he's an advocate, a defender. Riley uses all his skill to help protect people." Ethan settled back in his seat, a little more at ease. "If you could have seen how he took that guy down—the one he found in your apartment—it was something else. Riley didn't look winded, didn't look like he'd used much effort, and he didn't look like he had a speck of emotion in him. Cold, swift and effective. One second the guy was running and the next he was completely immobilized by Riley. It was both awesome and a little unsettling." Then, more to himself than to Regina, Ethan murmured, "It still amazes me that he left the SWAT team to come here."

"Why did he? Do you have any idea?"

"Not a clue. Riley only lets people in so far. I'd trust him with my life and I know he's one of the best men around. But his past is off-limits. Not once in the five years I've known him has he given so much as a single clue."

Disappointed, Regina let out a long breath. Trying not to be too obvious, she asked, "Who has he been seeing most recently?"

Ethan rolled his eyes. "You."

"No, I mean before I moved in here."

"You."

"But we didn't…"

"Date? Doesn't matter." Ethan gave her a warm smile. "I remember we were all at Rosie's for dinner the day after we first met you. Riley talked about you—"

"Saying what?"

Ethan shrugged. "It wasn't what he said so much as how he said it. We all knew right then that he was interested. And the day of the fire…"

Ethan grew silent, stiff. He couldn't talk about that awful day without looking a little green. He closed his eyes, took two shallow breaths, and swallowed. "As distracted as I was that day with Rosie, I noticed how Riley staked a claim."

Regina pulled back. "He did *what?*"

Grinning, Ethan nodded. "He laid claim to you."

Flushing a little with umbrage—and with pleasure—Regina said, "But that's ridiculous."

"What did you think it meant when he picked you up and didn't put you down?"

"My head was bleeding. I was dazed."

"And unable to walk?" Ethan snorted. "He held you because he wanted to and because he decided you were his. Any guy within seeing distance knew it, and because Riley is who he is, they paid heed."

"But he hasn't asked me out or in any way acted interested." Ethan raised a brow and she quickly amended, "Until recently, I mean."

"Baloney. He's tried to teach you how to defend yourself and he's been following you around, keeping an eye on you, making your welfare his business. And he stares at you, Regina. Cracks Harris and Buck up, just to watch the way he watches you." Ethan smiled at that. So did Regina. "Riley's not one to spill his guts, but if I had to guess, I'd say you are a major distraction."

And then what? "You really think so?" She hated sounding so hopeful, but if Riley cared a little for her, if what he felt was more than just sexual…well, that would change everything.

"I know so." Ethan glanced at his watch, then stood. "Sorry to rush off, but Rosie has a few hours free." His grin told Regina all she needed to know. They loved each other so much. She wanted what they had, the closeness, the caring.

If she could have that with Riley, it'd be more than she'd ever dared to hope for.

RILEY PACED around the desk to the open window. "So you and Regina were engaged?"

Luther snorted. "Is that what she told you?"

Stiffening, Riley kept his back to the other man and asked softly, "Are you saying she lied?"

He snickered. "No. She *thought* we were engaged. But you know how it is. Regina's one of those women who has to have everything right and proper. She'd never have let me in her bed without a ring on her finger."

The clawing need to break the bastard's nose nearly choked Riley. "I see. So *you* lied?"

"I told her what she needed to hear. If you've met her, then you'll understand. She's so ladylike on the outside, I thought maybe she'd be a wildcat in bed. That made the deception worthwhile, or so I thought. But she was still stiff as a broom. No satisfaction at all. It was like sleeping with a damn board." He gave a hoarse laugh. "What the hell does this have to do with the trouble she's in?"

Riley turned to Luther with a cold smile. "Someone is bothering her. Damaging her property, scaring her. I'm trying to figure out who."

Luther shot to his feet. "You're accusing *me?*"

"Just gathering the facts—though it certainly sounds like you have a store of animosity for her."

"No. Hell no. You can stop gathering right now. When we split, I said good riddance to the little prude."

"No regrets, huh?"

Luther grunted. "Hardly." He took two incautious

steps toward Riley. "You know what that twit had the nerve to do?"

Riley cocked a brow, but Luther didn't wait for him to reply. "She bought some goddamned books on sex, and she actually wanted to talk to me about them. She acted like I held part of the responsibility for her lack of enjoyment in the sack. I told her it was damned tough to satisfy a cold fish. She got pissed, and whenever she got that way, she got all stiff and righteous with her haughty little nose in the air."

Riley's smile hurt. "Yes, I know what you mean."

"You've seen it, haven't you?" Again, Luther didn't wait for a reply. He nodded, then chuckled. "Well, I was sick and tired of her acting superior so I told her it'd help if she'd try a little harder to get my interest. She's so damn skinny, I suggested a boob job." Here he laughed outright, even slapping his knee.

Riley churned with anger, but not by so much as the flicker of an eyelash did he let Luther know. "She's slight, but I haven't noticed her lacking at all."

"Then you haven't seen her naked. She's got a nice ass, but the upstairs leaves a lot to be desired."

Riley went mute with rage. It was bad enough that Regina's childhood had instilled in her a need to make a good impression, but then to have this jerk tear her down and make her think her best wasn't good enough....

Luther's grin lingered. "Man, she hit the roof. She got all red-faced and told me she wouldn't marry a man who didn't want her as she is."

Satisfaction swelled inside Riley. *Bravo, sweetheart,* he silently congratulated her. Then through his teeth, he asked, "That ended the engagement?"

"Blew it to smithereens, which was more than fine

by me. She tossed my ring back at me, walked away
and I haven't seen her since. I haven't *wanted* to see
her since." He leaned back on his desk and crossed his
arms. "You know what? I bet she rubbed some other
poor bastard the wrong way and he's retaliating. It'd
serve the little witch right to get hassled a bit. Maybe
it'll get her to loosen up and live a little."

Riley figured Regina would loosen up when the right
man loved her, namely him. With trust would come
complete comfort. But until then, he couldn't let Luther
get away with insulting her.

He rubbed his chin thoughtfully, then moved forward
half a step. Very calmly, giving Luther no warning, he
said, "Let me explain something to you." Without haste,
he reached for Luther's upper arm, clasped him in his
right hand, easily found a pressure point, and applied
the right grip to make the man's knees buckle and to
force a short screech of pain from him.

Eyes wide with fear and teeth gritted in pain, Luther
literally hung in Riley's one-handed grip.

Without compassion, Riley watched him writhe in
agony. In a voice more deadly because of its softness, he
said, "Regina Foxworth is mine. Eventually I'll marry
her. Anyone who insults her insults me."

Luther let out a long broken groan. "You didn't tell
me that. Hey, I'm sorry!"

Riley shook his head. "No, not good enough. You
see, how do I know that you won't go spreading these
nasty rumors about her to other people? I think I should
impress on you exactly what I'll do if I ever hear of you
even mentioning her name again."

Luther gasped. "Please…"

Riley released him.

Slowly, holding his numb arm, Luther straightened. His face was pale with lingering agony.

Legs braced apart, hands on his hips, Riley said, "You have a lot more pressure points, Luther, places that when manipulated just right, can cause pain you can't even imagine. How many do I need to demonstrate before you fully understand?"

"One's enough. I swear."

Riley said, "I don't know…"

Luther rushed behind his desk, which gave him a false sense of safety. His arm hanging limp and useless, he managed to stand more or less upright. "You better get out of here," he groused in a shaky voice. "You're a policeman. You can't do this to me. I'll report you—"

Riley pulled open his desk drawer. "Yeah? Well, I can haul you in for smoking dope on the job." He lifted out a joint, along with a small bag of marijuana. "What do you think your supervisors will say to that?"

Luther's eyes went wide.

"I'll only say this once, Luther, so pay attention. Stay away from Regina, keep your foul mouth shut, and what you do on the job is your business. I really couldn't care less."

Luther slumped, but then another voice intruded from the doorway. "I care."

Riley looked up to see a slender woman in her mid-thirties, dressed much as Regina often did in business-casual wear, staring at Luther with hatred.

"You're the receptionist?" Riley asked.

Her chin went up another notch. "And I was his fiancée." She pulled off a miniscule diamond ring and pinged it off Luther's forehead. "Not anymore."

Luther groaned.

Riley went around the desk to the woman. "You overheard?"

"Yes. All of it. I came back to my desk a few minutes ago and I eavesdropped."

Riley felt a little uncomfortable. "I should apologize…"

"No. He's a pig and I'm sorry if he hurt your girlfriend at all."

"He hasn't. Regina is too smart to be hurt by him." At least, Riley hoped that was true. He'd find out for sure tonight—*after* he got her naked and let her know in no uncertain terms that he thought her utterly beautiful. Anything she didn't have, she didn't need.

The receptionist's shoulders went back. "What you did to him…the way you barely touched him yet he started whining in pain. How did that work?"

"Why?"

"I think it might be a useful thing to know."

Grinning, Riley fished a business card out of his wallet and handed it to her. "If you ever get over to Chester, stop into my gym and I'll teach you."

"Thank you."

As he left the insurance building, Riley admitted to himself that it probably wasn't Luther bothering Regina now. He'd watched the man's every expression and had seen only weakness, conceit and lewd innuendo. No real deception. Riley would keep an eye on him, but he doubted anything would turn up.

Once outside, he stopped on the sidewalk to stare at the newspaper building across the street.

One down, two to go.

REGINA GRINNED at the determined way Buck tried to
make friends with Butch. Buck looked like a felled titan
in his black T-shirt and worn jeans, stretched out on the
floor on his stomach, his chin on his crossed hands,
meeting the dog at eye level.

Butch didn't cooperate.

No matter how softly Buck spoke to him or how
he cajoled, the dog continued to give a low, vibrating
growl of warning.

Buck glanced up at Regina, his green eyes alight with
mischief. "You sure this damn dog isn't part badger?"

"I don't understand it. He's always so sweet to me."

Buck came to his feet, ruffled Regina's hair fondly
and said, "Well now, honey, you're very easy to be sweet
to."

Half-embarrassed by that odd praise, Regina gave an
uncertain smile. "Um, thank you. If you'd like to take
a seat, I can get you something to drink."

"No, thanks. Let's get right to it. You want the scoop
on Riley, right?"

"Well, yes." But she rushed to explain, "I'm doing
an interview on him."

"Uh-huh." Buck stretched out his massive arms along
the back of the sofa and grinned. "He's hung up on you
big-time. Never thought to see the mighty Riley with
a weakness, but damn if he isn't acting smitten. It's
downright fun to watch."

Regina blinked, then blinked some more. "Oh, but
I didn't mean to—"

"What? Find out how he feels about you? 'Course
you did." Buck continued to grin. "I don't mind. Riley's
tough, no way around that. But any man who guards
his past that closely has a few serious wounds. I'd like

to see him happy and I happen to think you can accomplish that. So whatever I can do to nudge things along, count me in."

Such an awesome outpouring, from *Buck* no less, left Regina momentarily distracted and without a single coherent thought in her head. "Uh…"

"I think some woman did him wrong, don't you?"

Regina stared. "Well, I…"

"That'd make sense, huh? If it was a guy, Riley would have just kicked his ass, not quit his job and moved away. And now here you are, putting him into a possessive lather, helping him to focus on better things. I'm glad you moved in with him. Ought to keep him occupied." He winked.

Regina went hot to the roots of her red hair.

"So." Buck slapped enormous hands on his thick thighs. "Is that all you wanted?"

She cleared her throat twice and attempted to get control of the situation. "I, uh, had hoped to learn more about Riley's job, what he does, his training…."

Shaking his head, Buck came to his feet. "Sorry. I don't know anything about that. He used to be SWAT, but left the city to come here. Since Chester has no need of a SWAT team, Riley fell back on his old training of CSI. That's the beginning and end of what I know." Then he frowned. "Well, one other thing."

"Yes?"

He pushed up his T-shirt sleeve over a massive, bulging shoulder and flexed his arm to show off a seriously impressive biceps muscle. "See that?"

"Yes." Regina knew she wouldn't be able to circle that muscle even if she used both hands. "It'd be rather hard to miss."

Buck nodded. "I'm strong. I do a lot of physical work, day in and day out at the lumberyard. Men walk a wide path around me if I'm annoyed. But I don't have a single doubt in my mind that Riley, scrawny as he is, would make mincemeat out of me if he ever had a notion to."

He smiled as he made that claim, especially the ridiculous part about Riley being scrawny. Compared to Buck, he was certainly leaner, but scrawny? Nope, not by anyone's standards.

Buck tugged his sleeve back down and nodded. "That's some serious training that goes beyond what you're taught for a job, even if that job is SWAT. It's a lifestyle, a personality, an inherent part of the man. Riley's like a warrior born in the wrong century. He'd die to protect those people he cares about, and he'd expect loyalty in return."

Was this Buck's idea of a warning for his friend? Regina didn't know for sure, but she touched the arm he'd just bared and offered a smile. "I would never do anything to hurt him."

Buck patted her hand. "I know. That's why I think you're perfect for him."

He started for the door, and both Regina and Butch followed. "You know, Buck, I'm a little surprised. You're usually so quiet."

"Naw. It's just that with Harris around, who can get a word in edgewise?" He laughed, opened the door, and there stood Harris with his hand raised to knock. "Well, speak of the devil."

RILEY EYED the tall, thin fellow with the wire-rimmed glasses and neatly combed blond hair. He wore a suit, complete with a tie and jacket. Everyone else in the room had removed their coats and rolled up their shirt-sleeves, loosened their ties. Not Carl Edmond.

The outward attention to detail had probably appealed to Regina, even if the man hadn't.

Bent close to the keyboard, a slight frown on his brow, Carl typed industriously at the computer. Riley snagged a chair and pulled it up close. Carl was so absorbed in his task, he didn't notice Riley until he sat down.

Shifting around, first startled, then polite, Carl asked, "May I help you?"

"Carl Edmond, right?"

"That's correct."

He didn't look alarmed, only curious. He didn't look like a predator, either, but Riley had learned long ago that even the most innocent expression could hide deceit. It was a lesson he'd never forgotten. After discreetly flashing his badge, Riley said, "I'm here informally, just to ask a few questions if you're willing."

Looking around the crowded room with a slight blush, Carl said, "Perhaps we should go someplace more private?"

"Sure."

Riley allowed himself to be led into an employee lounge. There was no one else present. Carl glanced at him. "Would you like some coffee?"

"Please." He was so courteous, Riley wondered that Regina hadn't been taken with him. He reminded Riley of a masculine version of Regina. Carl set a steaming cup of coffee in front of Riley, along with a small square napkin.

With those courtesies taken care of, Riley said, "You know Regina Foxworth."

Carl had just started to sip his coffee, but he stopped, face alight with pleasure. "Yes, yes I do." And then with sudden concern, he added, "She's all right, isn't she?"

"She's fine. But someone has made her a target." Riley explained the things that had happened, all the while watching Carl Edmond for the slightest flicker of guilt.

There was none.

"But this is terrible. Regina is… Well, she's a gentle, beautiful person. I don't mean her looks…well, her looks, too. But she's one of the kindest women I know. I owe her a lot. If there's any way I can help you to find this evil person…"

Riley leaned back in exasperation. Carl had a touch of melodrama. "Why do you say you owe her?"

The man actually blushed. "Well, it's a long story, and I really hate to admit it, but I fancied myself in love with her. I'm afraid I made a real nuisance of myself, too, following her around like a lovesick pup." Here he shook his head and chuckled. "But Regina remained kind. She sat me down, explained that she only cared about me as a friend, and then she suggested that I wise up and pay more notice to the bagel girl."

"The bagel girl?"

"She delivers fresh bagels to this room twice a day. I didn't understand at first, but I did as Regina suggested." He held up a hand, showing off the gold wedding band. "Thanks to her, I'm now married to Carolyn. It was love at first sight, at least for me."

Riley ran a hand through his hair. "Great. Congratulations." And another dead end. If the new wedding hadn't been enough, Carl's obvious happiness would have swayed Riley. He pulled out a card and pushed it across the table toward Carl. "If you think of anyone who might want to hassle Regina, would you give me a call?"

"I'd be glad to." When Riley stood, Carl reached out and caught his arm. "Mr. Moore? Please. Take good care of her, okay? She's a very, very special person."

Riley nodded. "You have my word."

CHAPTER NINE

HE HEARD THE RAUCOUS NOISE even before he finished unlocking the door. Music, laughter, playful barking.

Brows drawn, Riley turned the knob and silently pushed the door open. No one noticed him.

Regina sat cross-legged on the floor, her back to the sofa where Harris lounged on his side, his head propped up on a fist. Butch ran up Red's body, over her shoulder, along Harris's length, then back down over Regina.

Her shoulders were touching his stomach.

Harris's nose was practically in her ear.

Riley closed the door with a resounding click that seemed more effective than a hard slam. Butch jerked up. His small furry face went blank with surprise, then lit up with blinding pleasure. Yapping with berserk glee, he tumbled off Harris, rolled over Regina and came charging toward Riley. Ears bouncing and little paws moving with lightning speed, he reached Riley and slid to a halt.

"Well, hello to you, too, squirt." Riley lifted him up and got his face thoroughly bathed with a warm doggy tongue. All the while he stared at Harris.

Slowly, his mouth twisted as if to hide a grin, Harris straightened. "Hey, Riley."

Riley continued to stare.

Regina scurried to the stereo and turned it off. Hands

behind her back, she smiled shyly at Riley. *Shyly?* Now what was she up to?

She hesitated a second, then with only a bit less enthusiasm than Butch had shown, she came to him, went on tiptoe and kissed him. Not a polite welcome peck. Nope. She cupped his face and moved her soft sweet lips over his until Riley forgot that Harris was behind her. He snagged an arm around her waist, hauled her up against him, and pressed his tongue past her parted lips. When she went limp against him, Riley reluctantly ended the kiss.

"You're home," she said in a breathless whisper.

"Earlier than you expected?"

Harris chuckled. "Gee, Riley, is that a gun in your pocket or are you glad to see...Regina?"

Regina gasped, her thoughts plain on her face, but Riley relieved her mind by saying, "It's a chew toy for the dog."

Regina looked down at his lap and blinked at the ludicrously large bulge there. "Oh."

Harris cleared his throat. "I think I'll take this as my cue to get lost."

He had the nerve to stop at Regina's side, kiss her cheek, and then wink at Riley. When Riley narrowed his eyes, Harris laughed and held up both hands. "Don't hurt me, Riley, okay?"

Riley rolled his eyes. "What are you doing here?"

"Ah, well, I'm just one in a long line of guys who've trooped through your door today."

Regina elbowed him hard. Riley took her arm and pulled her to his side so she wouldn't hurt herself poking at Harris. Regina was red in the face, Butch was squirming to be petted and Harris was trying to sidle out the door.

Riley opened it for him. "Later, Harris."

"Right." With a fast salute, Harris took off.

Riley closed and locked the door, then, ignoring Regina for the moment, headed to the couch with Butch. "So, my man, you missed me?" He seated himself and Butch immediately climbed up on his chest to sniff his face. He barked, bit Riley's chin and then tried to dig underneath his shirt.

Laughing, Riley set him aside. "Anxious for your gift, huh?"

Regina inched over to the couch. She smiled. "You're spoiling him, Riley."

"I thought it might keep him occupied while I carried you off to bed."

He heard her gasp, but didn't comment on it. He was so wired, so damned...*needy* after talking to the other men, he knew if he didn't have her soon, he'd explode. He pulled a large rawhide bone out of his pocket. Butch's eyes widened and his ears came forward in an alert pose.

Setting the bone on the floor, Riley asked, "Think you can handle that?"

The dog ran down Riley's leg and circled the bone, examining it from every angle, making both Regina and Riley laugh.

"It's bigger than he is."

Butch got one corner in his mouth and started backing up with the bone until he was completely hidden beneath a side table.

"That ought to keep him busy." Riley stood and turned toward Regina. "Now for you."

Regina chewed her lower lip. "Yes?"

"I missed you."

Her smile quivered the tiniest bit. "I missed you, too."

Riley slipped his arms around her waist. Staring down at her, he said, "I was going to go really slow, Red. I was going to start by teaching you a few self-defense moves, because that's important. Then I was going to carry you to bed."

"You've been teaching me self-defense moves for a while now," she reminded him.

"Not alone. Not in private where I can mix the lessons with kissing and touching."

"You've changed your mind about teaching me?"

"No, I just don't think I can wait. We'll work on your lessons afterward."

Her smile was sweet, sensual and teasing. "I'm glad. I've been thinking about you all day, too. I don't want to wait."

She caught her breath when Riley lifted her into his arms. He strode into his bedroom, pushed the door quietly shut with his foot, and sat on the edge of the mattress with her in his lap. "How could you have been thinking about me when you had Harris here entertaining you?"

She pushed his jacket off his shoulders. Riley helped, moving his arms until the coat fell to the bed. Next she began undoing his buttons. "We talked about you."

"You did?" He didn't like the sound of that, but with her small cool hands now on his chest, he found it hard to concentrate.

"Yes." She bent and kissed his throat. "I wanted to start your interview by talking to your friends."

Riley stiffened, but she caught his neck and quickly kissed him, scattering his thoughts.

"They respect you a lot, Riley."

"They?"

"Ethan, Buck and Harris."

His groan was due partly to dismay, partly to the way she removed his shirt and rained tiny kisses across his chest. "Hell, Red, you had all three of them here?"

"Mmm. They don't know any more about you than I do." She pushed him flat to the mattress, straddled his thighs and started on his belt buckle.

Riley settled his hands on her waist, charmed with her seduction, and so turned on he wanted her under him right this instant. "You know everything about me that you need to know."

She glanced up to give him a chastising smile. "No, I don't. But I can be patient. I've decided not to do the interview until you're comfortable talking to me about your past."

"Red…"

"Raise your hips." She had his slacks undone, so Riley did as ordered. She quickly skimmed them, along with his boxers, down his legs. She paused to tug off his shoes and socks, and then he was naked.

Regina let out a breath. "You are such a gorgeous man, Riley Moore."

"I'm glad you think so. Now come here."

"Just a second." She stood beside the bed and stared down at him. "You spoke with Luther?"

"Yeah. I spoke to him." *And I made him very sorry he ever hurt you.*

Regina nodded. She bent to pull off her sandals. "He, ah, told you about our breakup, didn't he?"

Rolling to his side so he could see her better, Riley propped himself up on one elbow. "He explained that he was an obnoxious, blind ass who doesn't deserve you."

Her lips curled in a disbelieving smile. "Never in a million years would Luther say something like that."

"No, but that's the gist of it." Riley watched her fidget with the straps of her sundress. Would she be daring enough to lose the dress? He hoped so. "Whether he realized it or not, whether you realize it or not, you're an incredibly sexy woman, Red." With a grin, he added, "I sure as hell realized it the second I saw you."

He heard her inhale deeply. "Thank you." She reached for the hem and tugged her dress up and over her head. After tossing it aside, she pushed her panties down and stepped out of them. She straightened and waited.

It was the oddest feeling, Riley thought, shaking with lust while choking with tenderness. He'd never experienced it before, but then, as he'd just told her, he'd known from the beginning that she'd be different.

He reached for her and toppled her across his chest. He rolled, putting her beneath him, and cupped one satiny breast. "You're perfect."

"I'm—"

"Perfect." He looked up into her eyes. "I understand about hurt, Regina. People say and do things that, if we let them, can hurt us deep inside and linger for too damn many days and nights."

Her expression froze. "Someone hurt you?"

Riley decided then and there that he'd tell her. He wanted her trust, so perhaps he had to give it first. He wasn't a polished man and he didn't have the persona of the senator, but he could be honest. "My wife."

She went rigid beneath him. "You were married?"

"Yeah." Her naked body distracted him and he said in a growl, "Luther is an idiot. I wouldn't change a single thing about you." He bent and took a nipple into his mouth.

"Riley, wait…" she said on a groan.

"Can't." He gently sucked while pressing his hand between her thighs. She was warm and soft, her springy curls already damp.

Regina waylaid him by catching his wrist. "Riley? There's something I always wanted to try."

Breathing hard, Riley forced himself to stop. It wasn't easy when he ached with the need for release. "What?"

"This." He let her push him to his back. Her breasts were against his chest, one of her legs between his. Her hair hung loose, silky soft and tousled. "Don't move."

He considered that a tall order considering the gorgeous view of her backside that she presented while twisting around to rummage in his nightstand for a condom.

Riley said, "In a hurry?"

"Yes. Tell me if I put this on you wrong." She opened the small packet and bent close to his groin, intent on her task. He could feel her breath and it made him moan. She blinked at him in surprise. "I haven't even touched you yet."

"I know." It was a miracle he could string those two words together. Her hair tickled across his abdomen, his thighs.

She looked down at his cock and smiled. In the next instant, she had him in her small, soft hand, gently squeezing. "Is this what you want?"

His groan mixed with a laugh. "I want you any way I can have you."

"Would you like me to kiss you?"

His vision narrowed; every muscle in his body clenched. He said, "Yes," although he doubted she meant what he wanted her to mean. His body arched in delicious pleasure. "Oh God."

Her mouth was warm, damp, her tongue curious. Riley caught her head in his big hands and guided her, urging her to swallow more of him, raising his hips to help her with that.

Her small sound of wonder vibrated along his shaft, and his fingers clenched. He'd dreamed about this, about the prim Regina Foxworth giving him head—and enjoying it. The reality beat the fantasy all to hell and back.

For several minutes she drove him crazy, tasting, teasing, humming again. Finally, she lifted away and Riley's heart swelled at the evidence of her excitement. Her green eyes glowed with heat, her cheeks were flushed. "You taste good, Riley," she said in wonder.

Riley curled a hand around her thigh. He needed to come. He needed to be inside her. "So do you."

They stared at each other for a long moment before Regina bent to press one last innocent kiss to the head of his erection. Riley watched her straddle his thighs, saw her frown as she carefully rolled the condom on.

He checked it with her fascinated gaze never wavering, then pulled her over him. "Now what, babe?"

"Now I want to do it like this, with me on top."

"Yeah?" He gave her a crooked smile that almost hurt, he was so turned on. "I like that idea. That means I can see and touch all of you."

Her eyes darkened. "Yes." She lifted up, guided his cock to her opening, and slowly began sinking onto him. Riley held her thighs. She braced her hands on his chest.

It was incredible…seeing her face, watching her expressive eyes and the telling way her lips parted and her breasts rose with each deepened breath. "A little more," he urged, and her eyes closed as she wiggled, seating herself fully upon him.

Neither of them moved. Riley gasped for air, Regina's body clenched and relaxed around him.

"I can feel you throbbing."

He groaned and couldn't stop the lifting of his hips. Through his teeth, he growled, "I'm a nanosecond away from coming."

"Really?" She smiled down at him, then lifted.

"Really." She dropped and he said, "Regina…"

"I like this. Do you?"

Groaning again, he cupped her breasts, brushed her nipples with his thumbs, then caught them both in his fingers, lightly pinching, tugging. Her back arched, driving him even deeper.

He knew he wouldn't last so he moved one hand between her legs, gliding his middle finger along her swollen lips, taut around him, then up to her turgid clitoris. "Move, honey. Ride me."

Her fingers splayed over his chest and she began to rise and fall, faster and faster. He loved the small sounds she made, the way her face contorted with her concentration, her pleasure. Riley kept his fingers just where she needed them, treating her to a constant friction that worked with her own movements. Soon she was in the same shape as him, shaking, on the verge of exploding.

He brought his knees up to support her back and re-

turned her thrusts, lifting her knees from the bed as he
drove into her. With a startled cry, she collapsed against
him. Her mouth opened on his shoulder, her teeth coming down in a tantalizing love bite.

The small pain pushed him over the edge. Riley lost
control. He gripped her ass and pounded into her, groaning harshly with his own unending climax, the crushing waves of pleasure going on and on....

He wasn't sure how much time passed when he became aware of Butch jumping beside the bed, demanding attention. Regina was a soft sweaty weight over
his heart.

"Hey?" He moved fistfuls of her hair aside, kissed
her ear. "You okay?"

"Mmmrrmf."

Riley managed a grin. "What's that?"

"I'm fine," she said against his neck, wiggling lazily.
"Better than fine. I feel extraordinary."

He stroked her behind. "Yes, you do."

Her giggle was one of the sweetest sounds he'd ever
heard. She was totally relaxed with him. Soon, she'd
love him—as much as he loved her.

"We have three problems. We're both sweaty and
sticking together. The condom's going to become useless in about two seconds if we don't separate. And
Butch is none too pleased to be ignored."

Regina pressed her face into his chest. "You smell
good sweaty." Lifting up to see him, she asked, "Do I?"

Damn, but she wrenched at his heart. "Good enough
to eat."

She smiled and blushed, then turned her attention to
Butch. "You have to wait, sweetie. Give me a second
to regain feeling in my legs, and I'll get up and play."

"That dog is worse than an infant."

"How would you know? Ever had an infant?" It was just an offhand remark, not really serious.

"No." Riley rolled her to his side, filling his hand with her hair so he could see her face. "I wanted a baby though."

That bald admission, especially after lovemaking, got her attention. "You did?"

"Yeah." He kissed her, then sat up in the bed. "Stay put. I'll be right back." He headed to the bathroom to dispose of the condom. It also gave him a moment to gather his thoughts and figure out how to say what he wanted her to know, to understand.

When he returned, she was sitting up against the headboard, wearing his shirt and holding Butch. The dog took one look at Riley and tried to keep him out of the bed with his pseudo-attacks.

"You mangy little mutt, I'm the one who brought you the bone, remember?"

At the mention of the enormous chew, Butch's ears perked up and he went to the edge of the bed, whining to be let down. With a sigh, Regina lowered him to the floor. He ran out the bedroom door in a flash.

Riley found his boxers, pulled them on, and sat on the bed at her side. "You look good in my shirt."

She laughed, making a halfhearted effort to smooth her wild hair. "You know what I think? I think you just like giving compliments."

"Only to people who deserve them." He fingered the collar of the shirt, then undid the button between her breasts. He didn't know if he'd ever get enough of her—

Something solid and damp landed on his foot. Butch

had dragged the colossal chew bone over to him, and was now jumping at the side of the bed again.

"Oh no. I don't want that thing in my bed."

A barked argument ensued. When Riley held firm, Butch got hold of the very edge of the bone and tried to stand up against the bed. He couldn't. He looked ridiculous with his mouth full and he made an odd snorting noise during his struggle. Riley couldn't help but laugh. "All right, you pathetic little beggar. You win. But keep it down at the foot of the bed."

He lifted both dog and bone, then laughed again when Butch did his best to hide the gigantic thing under the covers. Riley helped by lifting the blankets for him, then caught Regina's sweet indulgent expression. "What?"

She reached out and touched his jaw. "When I first met you, I knew you were very capable and strong. That's as noticeable as your blue eyes, and I told myself that I needed to get closer to you to learn some self-defense."

"Which you've yet to do."

She ignored that. "Then after a while I decided you were a terrific friend, too. You're so at ease with the guys and with Rosie. I wanted so badly to be a part of that."

"And you are."

"Yes." She touched his mouth, tracing his lower lip with her fingertips. "After I brought Butch home, I got to see how gentle you are. That was such a turn-on, Riley." Her smile trembled. "Now, seeing your patience and generosity, it occurs to me that you'd also make a wonderful father." She laughed. "Although you'd probably spoil your kids rotten."

Riley turned his head and kissed her palm. She was getting into some pretty deep stuff here. So far, she'd admitted to liking and admiring him. He wanted more. He wanted her love.

"I think we can spend a few minutes talking before we need to get dressed for the ceremony."

"I'd like to talk about…things."

"Yeah?" He moved into bed beside her, put his arm around her and tugged her into his side. "I haven't wanted to really talk to a woman in a long time."

"You prefer to just rush her into bed?"

He shrugged. "I haven't been a saint, but I haven't been sexually attracted to that many women either. Now here you are, and I want to talk to you and be inside you at the same time. It's damn strange."

"Gee, thanks."

Riley hugged her. "You go first then."

He felt her nod before she said, "I always knew it wasn't me."

Riley just held her, waiting.

"I've never been ashamed of my build or thought I was lacking. I'm just me and I try really hard to be the best that I can. But even though I realized Luther is a creep, I was still…worried."

"Without reason. You're incredible, a beautiful person inside and out."

"Thank you."

Riley smiled at her continued good manners. "Any problems in the sack were his, Red. It was never about you."

"Yes, I know." She stroked his abdomen and sighed. "Especially now. After today, after being with you, I won't worry anymore." Then she turned into his side, wrapped her arms tight around him as if to protect him, and whispered, "But you didn't know, did you? The woman who hurt you—you blame yourself."

Riley tensed. "It's not the same thing, honey."

"Will you tell me what happened? Not for an interview and not for nosiness, but because I care about you, Riley. And I know from experience that it helps to talk."

A good start, Riley thought, then wondered if she'd feel the same when he finished his tale. "I've never told anyone before." He wanted her to know that, to understand the level of his trust. He shuddered at the small kiss she pressed to his chest, right over his heart. "She died, Red."

A strange stillness settled over her. "Your wife?"

"Yes." He was glad Regina kept her face tucked against him, rather than looking at him. He wasn't a coward, but he couldn't remember those awful days of lies and deceit—his and hers—without feeling raw. "She was having an affair with Phil, one of my friends from the SWAT team." With disgust he added, "A man I respected."

The silence felt heavy, almost suffocating Riley before she asked, "How do you know?"

Riley shook his head, once again wishing he could somehow change things. "I caught them in bed together. I came home from work early and found them in my bedroom, in my bed."

"I'm so sorry."

"I always have control, Regina. Always. But when I saw them, I didn't bother using it. I can't claim temporary insanity or a blinding jealous rage. That would be a lie. I was pissed off, completely furious, and I wanted to beat the hell out of Phil, so I did. I coldly, methodically, hurt him. Not permanently, but I did a lot of superficial damage."

"But listen to what you're saying. You could have killed him, Riley. You're more than capable. But you didn't. Instead you just hurt him, as he deserved."

Riley shook his head. "No one got what they deserved that awful day." He had to draw three breaths before he could continue. "My wife flew around me, screaming and crying. Phil... He was good, but he didn't stand a chance against me."

Regina fisted a hand on his chest. "He was in bed with your wife, Riley. Most men would react the way you did."

"Most men aren't me."

"Meaning you fight better than they could?"

He laughed. "There was no fight to it."

"And don't you see? Another man without your control might have killed him, even if he hadn't meant to."

He couldn't deny that. As a cop, he'd seen more than a few crimes of passion. "You know, it was strange, but a good part of my anger was for Phil's wife. She was seven months pregnant at the time."

Regina curled closer, both arms around him, one leg over his. Absently, Riley stroked her shoulder.

"God, Regina, when Phil finally left my house, my wife went with him and..." He hesitated, but she had a right to know. "They both died in a car wreck."

"They made their own decisions, Riley."

"They were both upset. Physically, Phil was in no condition to drive. I should have stopped them. I should have at least stopped her from going along. But I didn't." His throat hurt, but he said it all. "I wanted her out of my sight. I wanted her gone."

"But you didn't want her dead."

She sounded so sure of that. Many times, Riley had remembered that awful day and wondered. He'd been so detached through it all, as if his heart had been anesthetized. "No, I didn't want her dead." Saying it out loud made him finally believe it. He'd reacted, but without the intent of such dire consequences. "Hell, I didn't even want *him* dead. But when I got the call, I dunno, most of my concern was for Phil's wife. I kept seeing her in my mind, how happy she'd been, all the plans she'd been making for them as a family." He glanced down at Regina. "She was cute as hell pregnant and whenever we got together she'd show us the new baby clothes she'd bought or a bassinet or a toy."

"Oh God, how did she take the news about Phil and your wife…."

He shook his head. "I never told her, Red. Not about the cheating. I've never told anyone." He glanced down at her. "Except you."

Regina's eyes were big and soft, filled with understanding. "How did you explain them being in the car together?"

He laughed, but the sound wasn't humorous. "I was CSI—I knew how to cover my tracks. I made sure no one would know I'd been home when he and my wife left together, then I said my wife must have been helping him with a gift for the baby. I told everyone that they'd discussed it, made plans to buy something wonderful because Phil wanted to surprise his wife. No one doubted it. No one questioned me. Hell, no one even noticed my bloody knuckles." He swallowed down his own disgust. "They didn't see the bruises on Phil, either. The wreck was pretty bad and the car caught on fire."

His voice went so quiet, it was barely audible. "Neither of them was all that recognizable."

Riley could feel Regina shivering. "Was anyone else hurt in the wreck?"

"No, thank God. They went off the side of the road, down into a gully. The car flipped and hit a tree. There were no other cars involved."

His stomach started churning; absently he rubbed it, trying to fight off the familiar sickness. Butch appeared, his little furry face so expressive, so concerned. He whined as if he'd sensed Riley's upset, then crawled up onto his chest and curled up under Riley's chin.

Stupidly enough, it helped.

Emotion clogged Riley's throat, but he hugged Regina with one arm, patted Butch with his other hand, and wished the damn story didn't still hurt so much.

Regina was frozen and silent for a long time before asking, "What ever became of Phil's wife?"

"I stuck around until after the birth, trying to help her out. She had a baby boy she named Phil, after his daddy. Phil had a life insurance policy so she's not too bad off financially. After that, I left. I quit my job and moved here. I heard she got remarried about a year ago. Her kid would be... I dunno, almost five now." He stroked his fingers through Regina's hair, taking comfort in her warmth and softness. "I hope she and the kid are happy."

Suddenly Regina sobbed.

Startled, Riley tried to see her face but she pressed herself so close, it felt like she wanted to crawl inside him. Butch panicked, whining at Riley, poking his nose into Regina's cheek.

"Hey. Honey, what's the matter?"

She hiccuped and in a strangled voice said, "I want to give you something, Riley, okay?"

As she spoke, she turned her face up to his and Riley grimaced. She didn't cry well. Already her eyes were watery and red, matching her nose. Her cheeks were blotchy. He smiled. "Yeah, sure. But please, don't cry, baby. I can't stand it."

That made her start sobbing again. She crawled out of the bed, still sniffling, and headed out of the room.

"Regina?"

"I'll be right back," she wailed.

Riley watched her go, enjoying the way his shirttails barely covered her tush. He looked at Butch. "Women." Then he added, "But damn, she looks good in my shirt, doesn't she?" And he murmured, "Even better out of it, though."

She came back into the bedroom, the framed photo in her hand. She plopped into bed, burrowed into Riley's side, and dropped the photo on his lap. "Here, you can have it."

Lip curled in distaste, Riley lifted the smug, smiling face of Senator Welling away from his body and dropped it on the nightstand. "Gee, thanks. Just what I always wanted."

Regina gave a choked laugh, lightly punched him, and then hugged him in a strangle hold. "You asked me earlier why I brought the stupid thing along."

Stupid thing? "Uh, yeah."

"I see the photo and I remember his commitment to his family and how he stands for all the things, I value. It gives me hope that someday I'll have those things, too."

Riley rolled his eyes. "Regina…"

"It gave me hope that some day I'd meet a man like him. But I don't need him for inspiration anymore." She smiled up at Riley and even with the blotchy cheeks, she looked beautiful. "You're the finest man I know, Riley. No one else could ever measure up to you."

Oh hell. It was bad enough when he thought she used Welling as a masculine measuring tape. But if he became the damn tape, she was bound for disappointment. "No, Regina, I'm just a man."

"A good man. A real man. And that's better than a public persona any day."

Riley's heart about stopped. Was it possible she loved him, too? Had he finally gotten through to her? He started to tell her so when his phone rang. Riley reached for the nightstand and snatched up the receiver. "Hello?" And then with foreboding, "Yeah, Dermot. What's up?"

Just as he suspected, Earl had been released. The judge returned not more than a few hours ago, but Earl had made his call and somehow gotten things expedited.

"Thanks for the heads-up. I guess all we can do now is hope he doesn't jump bail." He hung up and rubbed his face. "Looks like we're back to square one unless Senator Welling can remember something vital."

Regina gasped as if someone had pinched her. "Oh no. Senator Welling and the ceremony. We're going to be late."

Riley glanced at the clock and cursed. "We'll make it if we hurry." He threw the covers aside and stood.

Regina remained in bed, her bottom lip caught between her teeth. "Riley? Are you sure we can't just skip it? Somehow, I'm not as excited about seeing him as I had been."

He smiled, caught her under the arms and lifted her

from the bed. "No, we can't skip it. I don't want to miss this chance. If we get there early, we can talk to the senator before the ceremony begins and get it out of the way."

"Then come back here and make love some more?"

Riley feigned a scandalized gasp. "Why, Ms. Foxworth, you surprise me."

She grinned. "When we get home, I'll surprise you even more."

Home. He liked the sound of that. "It's a deal."

CHAPTER TEN

BUTCH PUT ON AN AWFUL, melodramatic fit about being left alone. He was a smart little dog who understood *everything* whenever the mood suited him, and right now he understood that two dressed humans heading for the door meant he'd be alone.

He didn't like it, and he didn't hold back in letting them know his deepest feelings. Not only did he howl pitifully, but he laid flat on his belly and did an army crawl, as if his little legs wouldn't work.

They tried stepping out and waiting to see if he'd calm down. He didn't. He made such a racket that he sounded like a pack of wolves. Riley feared complaints from his neighbors if they left Butch carrying on so enthusiastically.

In the end, since the ceremony would mostly be outdoors, Regina gave in and tucked him away in her satchel. She hooked his leash to his collar as a precaution in case he attempted to escape. She kept the leash wrapped around her hand and the strap of the big bag over her shoulder with Butch close to her side.

He seemed to like that just fine. He curled up and went to sleep like a baby in a knapsack.

"And you said *I'd* spoil him?"

Regina scowled at that accusation. "He's still getting

used to us. There's been no stability in his life yet, what
with me bringing him home, then bringing him here...."

Riley drew her close without mussing her hair, and
pressed a warm kiss to her forehead. "I do understand.
Even cantankerous little dogs need reassuring." Then he
grinned. "Just remember that us old dogs need it, too."

Regina intended to reassure him in a big way as soon
as they returned. She was going to tell him how she felt.
Love was love and it should never be denied. To get it,
you had to give it. That was the argument she'd used
when choosing Butch, and now she'd apply it to Riley.
She'd give him her heart and hope he gave his in return.

It had worked with Butch.

Riley drove his truck to the ceremony. Regina felt
the difference now in just being with him. There was
a new comfort, a new ease that existed between them.
She thought of everything he'd told her, everything he'd
gone through. No wonder he hadn't wanted to get involved again. He had not only the emotional turmoil of
an unfaithful spouse, but he also had a battle with his
professional conscience for being untruthful.

Regina considered his thoughtfulness for Phil's wife
one of the most commendable things she'd ever heard.
Riley had put his own hurt aside to protect someone
else—and that, more than anything, defined the type
of man he was.

Milling crowds filled the lawn in front of the museum center where the Historical Society had planned
the ceremony. Keeping Regina tucked close to his side
with a precautionary, proprietary air, Riley repeatedly
flashed his badge to dispatch a path to the quiet cham-
bers inside the museum where Senator Welling passed

the time until his introduction. In the end though, it was Regina who got them beyond the final barrier of guards.

She gave her name and politely asked them to inform Senator Welling that she would greatly appreciate a moment of his time. One unconvinced guard did as she asked, then returned with a smile, saying Senator Welling would love to see her again.

The guards wouldn't let Riley in, though, and Riley wouldn't let Regina in without him. He was most firm on that issue, so Regina stuck her head in the heavy carved wooden door of the museum's inner sanctum and requested that her escort be given entrance as well.

Senator Welling, smiling and as jovial as the last time she'd seen him, rose from behind a large desk and bid them both inside. "Ms. Foxworth—Regina—how wonderful to see you again."

It was enough of a surprise that he remembered her, but he also sounded sincerely happy to see her. Regina smiled with true pleasure. By rights, the senator should have looked exhausted from his recent travels. The commendation from the Historical Society came at the tail end of a two-week tour. Instead, he looked vital and energetic. "Senator Welling. I hope we're not imposing."

"Of course not. And please, no formality here. Call me Xavier. After all, we're old friends now."

"Why, thank you. I'd be honored."

Another guard came forward to frisk both her and Riley.

"I'm sorry," Xavier said with a wry, philosophical shrug. "They're quite insistent on doing their jobs."

"Oh, I understand. You're a very important man. Of course they have to protect you." Regina held her arms out to her sides and submitted to being patted down. Butch didn't take it well, snapping at the guard and startling him when he peeked inside the bag. The senator, a lover of animals, was merely amused when Butch peeked out at him and growled.

Unlike the others who'd called her dog a rat and worse, Xavier said, "Such distinctive coloring. A purebred Chihuahua?"

"Yes, thank you. I think he's beautiful, too." Regina beamed at Xavier for his exquisite taste in animals.

Riley didn't take the invasion of privacy much better than Butch had, but at least he didn't try to bite anyone. He introduced himself, showed his badge, and still got roughly checked for hidden weapons. Regina watched him warily, unsure what he might do.

When the security check had been completed, he merely nodded. "Senator Welling—"

"Xavier, please," he reminded Riley.

Riley conceded with a nod. "Xavier. Thank you for seeing us."

"It's my pleasure." After sharing a hearty handshake with Riley, he took Regina's hand and winked at her. "We have plenty of time to spare before the ceremony and I've only been sitting here hoping I won't trip over my words."

His charming, self-deprecating grin could win over the worst skeptics, Regina decided. "I'm sure you'll keep them all enthralled."

Laughing, still holding her hand, Xavier turned to Riley. "My biggest fan, or so she tells me."

Riley's mouth flattened. "Yeah, she tells me that, too."

Regina frowned at Riley's tone—and noticed he was

staring at Xavier's hand clasping hers. Could he be jealous? He'd made that comment about old dogs needing reassurance, too. Trying to be inconspicuous, she pulled away from Xavier. "Senator, how is your intern? That lovely young lady I met at the park with you."

His gray brows rose in confusion. "My intern?"

Regina forged on. "I recall she was very quiet, but you told me she worked hard and was very dedicated to you."

Xavier cleared his throat. "Yes, a hard worker. I'm sorry, but you know, I can't keep up with all the interns. They come and go, and…" Suddenly he stopped. He turned to his guards and said, "Wait outside."

The guards shared a look, hesitant to obey.

Xavier frowned and rounded his desk to shoo them away. "Really, I'm quite safe here with the young lady and her friend. Go. I'd like some privacy."

Regina was stunned at the sudden turn of events. Both men were forced out a door at the back of the office, behind where Xavier had been sitting. In a heartbeat, Riley was there, standing mostly in front of her, blocking her with his body. She tried to nudge him aside, but he wouldn't move.

"Riley, really," she whispered.

Glancing over his shoulder, he gave her one brief, hard look that stopped all other protests in her throat.

When Xavier turned back to them, his expression had become strained. "There. Much better, don't you think?" His smile didn't reach his eyes. "Please, take a seat and tell me what you've been up to." Xavier returned to his chair.

Regina started to take the nearest chair opposite the desk, but Riley stopped her by backing further into her.

"With your permission, Senator, I'd like to ask you a few questions about that day in the park."

Xavier's complexion paled. He looked down at his desk a moment, then faced Riley squarely. "Is there a problem?"

Regina could feel the tension in Riley, but she didn't understand it. He seemed braced for an attack, ready to charge. But why?

"Since that day, Regina has been repeatedly threatened by someone. I believe it started with the car that ran her off the road."

Xavier swallowed, and in a murmur said, "Thank God she wasn't injured that day. Terrible, terrible thing to happen to a young woman. She could have been killed."

Riley's arms hung loose at his sides. It was a negligent pose, but Regina had taken enough lessons from him to know he was readying himself, keeping limber, poised.

"Yes, she could have. And that wasn't the only incident. She's been accosted several times. The worst, however, was the fire."

Xavier's head shot up. "A fire?"

"Yes. A deliberate fire, in my opinion. It burned a building to the ground and almost took Regina and her friend with it."

Xavier squeezed his eyes shut and shook his head. "This is dreadful. Just dreadful."

By small degrees, Riley started backing up, forcing Regina toward the door where they'd entered.

The sense of foreboding was so thick in the air, Regina thought she might choke on it. "Senator?"

He shook his head. "I'm only a man, flawed, damn it."

"What the hell does that mean?" Riley demanded.

The senator looked up, then beyond Riley. His face went ashen.

Someone had stepped in the room behind them.

Startled, more than a little frightened, Regina jerked around—and let out a relieved breath. Mrs. Welling stood there, elegantly dressed in a turquoise suit with pearl jewelry.

Riley started to move Regina to his side, but Mrs. Welling reached out and took her hand. "Hello. I heard Xavier had guests."

Flustered, Regina all but gushed. "Mrs. Welling! It's so wonderful to finally meet you. I didn't know you were here, too, but then you always accompany Xavier, don't you?"

"'Xavier'?" She slanted a sardonic look at her husband. "I see you're a close friend, to call him by his first name."

"Oh." Regina felt the heat pulsing in her face. "No, not at all. He just—"

"It's all right. My husband has mentioned you, Ms. Foxworth." Mrs. Welling was tall, softened with age, but still striking in appearance. Her brown hair was stylishly laced with gray, her eyes a stunning, clear blue. She held Regina's hand overlong.

Regina was aware of Xavier slowly standing behind his desk, of Riley stepping aside so that he stood between husband and wife. Regina prayed Riley wouldn't lose his temper and do something outlandish.

She was trying to send him a warning look to behave when the door behind Xavier opened. Regina's view was blocked by Riley, but she heard him curse.

With Mrs. Welling still clasping her hand, she stepped to the side to better see.

A tall man, probably a guard, stood there. He wasn't smiling, and he kept his narrowed, alert gaze on Riley. Slowly he lifted his right arm and pointed a gun.

Regina gasped. Instinctively, she tried to move toward Riley, but Mrs. Welling kept her immobile. "Meet Earl Rochelle, Ms. Foxworth. I believe he's made himself something of a nuisance to you."

Confusion warred with fear. "You…you're the one who broke into my apartment?" Regina had a hard time taking it in. Mrs. Welling seemed so cold, Xavier was rocking back and forth on his heels, muttering to himself and shaking his head. Riley just stood there, as sturdy and unshakable as a stone wall.

Earl nodded at Riley. "Your lover boy roughed me up. But now it's time for payback."

Riley shifted the tiniest bit. "You son of a bitch." His voice was calm, without inflection. "So you're working for the senator?"

Xavier violently shook his head. "No. No, I'd never hurt anyone…."

Mrs. Welling laughed. "Xavier, be truthful. You hurt me all the time." Her lovely face contorted—with pain, with anger. "Every single time you crawl into bed with another woman. But no more, you bloated, pompous ass. I've stuck with you this long, and I'll be damned if I let you ruin our family now."

Regina turned to face her, her brain blank with shock, with disbelief. "Mrs. Welling… I'm sorry. I didn't know."

"Of course you didn't. Along with a good portion of the constituents, you think Xavier is an honorable man, a *family* man. In truth, my dear, he's a lying, cheating pig."

Xavier shook his head, his face now bright pink, his eyes pleading. "No, dear. It was only those few times…."

"I'm not a fool, Xavier. I've known of every single affair. Your intern—who by the way, Ms. Foxworth, is no more than a well-paid prostitute—was only one in a long line of young women. You preach family values, all the while you're paying for sex with a common whore."

Her voice had risen with her ire, and Earl moved closer. "Mrs. Welling, please. Discretion is necessary."

She released Regina to wave away his concerns. "I dismissed the guards for now. I told them to return when it's time for Xavier's introduction. We've at least fifteen more minutes."

Regina suddenly understood. "The photograph." She stared at Mrs. Welling. "It has the intern… I mean, the prostitute, in the picture with the senator. They were…" Aghast, she turned to stare at Xavier. "They were having an affair *in the park?*"

"You begin to understand. The stupid park wasn't due to be open. Xavier knew I was watching him, and he thought he could lose my spies in the woods. But Earl kept a tail on him." She glanced at her husband with loathing. "Earl saw everything, including the damn picture you took. Xavier, the idiot, didn't think it was anything to worry about. He didn't think anyone would put two and two together. I know better. If that picture got out, the whole family would be ruined. I had Earl run you off the road, but you kept the camera around your neck and Xavier came to your aid."

Sadly, his shoulders slumped, Xavier said, "I couldn't let you hurt her."

"The way you hurt me?" Mrs. Welling turned away from him. "At the fire we finally got the camera, but it was filled with new film. Since then, we've been unable to find either the undeveloped film or the photograph."

Riley laughed. "She has it framed and keeps it in her bedside drawer."

Regina gaped at him even as she felt herself enveloped in mortified heat. *"Riley."*

Riley ignored her, moving closer to the desk, casually leaning a hip on the edge. Earl stiffened, but kept quiet.

The senator stared at her in astonishment.

Mrs. Welling's face contorted. "So you've slept with him, too?" she wrongly concluded. Outraged, she shook her head and addressed Riley. "Thank you for letting us know." Her lip curled, destroying her image of a respected and elegant politician's wife. "Retrieving the vile thing will be so much easier now, especially with you two out of the picture."

"And how exactly do you plan to accomplish that?"

At Riley's question, she pulled another gun out of her purse, but this one was odd-shaped, unlike any gun Regina had ever seen. "Why don't you let me worry about that, Mr. Moore?"

Riley shifted again. Regina felt sure he planned to do something, but what, she couldn't guess. She only wished he'd hurry up. She was starting to sweat nervously. Things did not look good. She realized that she should have been worried about him, but she somehow knew he'd handle things.

Then Mrs. Welling made the bad decision to grab

Regina by the hair. She had the odd gun raised when suddenly Butch exploded from the bag with such a feral, wild snarl it sounded like a pack of demon dogs had been unleashed.

He bit Mrs. Welling's hand, her arm, and ran right up to her face where he sank his small sharp teeth into her nose. The woman screamed in reaction and swatted at the dog.

Regina saw red. She hadn't realized she'd learned anything substantial from Riley, but without any real thought she caught her small dog in one arm, grabbed the arm holding the gun in the other and deftly tripped Mrs. Welling to her back. The woman hit her head on the hardwood floor and stayed there, dazed.

Regina jerked the gun from her hand.

Almost at the same time, Riley moved with blinding speed. His leg came up and over the desk, landing his foot squarely in the senator's face. He went down with a grunt. Earl moved, but Riley already had the advantage. He grabbed Earl's gun arm, pulled him forward and delivered his elbow into his throat.

Gagging and gasping, Earl collapsed to his knees. The gun fell from his hand and Riley kicked it aside. Hesitating only a moment to make certain Earl was sufficiently incapacitated, Riley turned and reached for the fallen gun. Both doors exploded open as guards filed in. Riley groaned, his hands lifted in a nonthreatening pose. He started to explain, and finally saw that Dermot and Lanny headed up the cavalry. He actually laughed.

Dermot grinned. "We followed him. You seemed so sure he was up to something more than a break-in."

Lanny nodded. "And you being sure made us sure,

so when the judge returned and we had to release him, we decided it might be smart to keep a close watch."

"Good job," Riley told them and they both puffed up like proud peacocks.

"Explaining to these guys wasn't easy though." Dermot nodded to the hired guards with a scowl.

They ignored him.

One stepped forward and picked up the strange gun by Mrs. Welling. "A tranquilizer gun?"

Regina's knees felt suddenly weak. She trembled from her head to her toes. "She was going to use it on us." Her voice was little more than a breathy squeak. "Then he—" she pointed to Earl "—was going to kill us."

The guards looked at her like she was nuts. Earl shouted denials. Senator Welling stirred just in time for a small bespectacled woman in a black suit to duck her head into the room and say, "Senator, it's time for… your…introduction." Her eyes rounded, looking huge behind her glasses.

One of the guards caught her arm and pulled her completely into the room, then shut and locked the door.

The senator moaned. Mrs. Welling, now sitting on the floor holding her head, said, "Forget it. There'll be no more honors for him."

Regina looked around at the chaos and wanted to cry. It was more than just the scandal that was sure to ensue, the political ramifications, the threat to her and Riley. Something she'd cherished, something she'd believed was real, had just been defiled in the worst possible way.

Her stomach actually cramped. She'd been such an utter fool.

Then Riley was there, his hand closing gently on her upper arm. "Babe, you're crushing Butch. Loosen up."

Regina glanced at Butch, at his bulgy little eyes, and saw it was true. She relinquished her hold on him.

"That's it. Here, let me hold him." Riley balanced the dog in one arm, up close to his chest because Butch seemed more than a little rattled by all that had happened. He was curled in on himself, his eyes still wild, and low growls continually emitted from deep in his throat as he watched everyone and everything. Once Riley held him, he looked less threatened.

With his other arm, Riley gathered Regina protectively into his side. Regina knew everyone was looking at her with varying degrees of expression—virulence from Mrs. Welling, disgrace from Xavier, concern from Lanny and Dermot.

She felt like a spectacle, something she detested, a feeling left over from her childhood. Ashamed, she turned into Riley to hide. "You told them where I kept the picture."

At her agonized whisper, he tightened his hold and his voice became hard. "Only to distract them, to keep them talking until I could best situate myself to react."

"Oh." She supposed that made sense. She'd put them into a situation and he'd had to rescue them because of it.

"Damn it, Red, I would never deliberately do anything to hurt you."

He sounded so outraged, Regina tried to soothe him. "Okay, Riley." The last thing she wanted was another spectacle.

To her surprise, Riley murmured near her ear, "Red, you've made me so proud."

"Proud?" She wasn't expecting that and her laugh was bitter and hurt. "I was a gullible idiot."

"No. You handled yourself well, disarming Mrs. Welling, protecting Butch, helping me."

Had she done all that? She had struck out at the crazy woman, but... "I got us in this situation in the first place by being an idiot."

"No." He turned her to face him, his expression volatile. "You're you, sweet and trusting and sincere, and I happen to love you an awful lot."

She jerked back. The suffocating crowd and her own embarrassment seemed to fade away. Her entire focus was on Riley and those awesome words he'd just uttered. "You what?"

With exasperation, he took her arm and towed her into the farthest corner of the room. It wasn't really far enough, merely a few feet away. The guards were watching them while another phoned a supervisor on his cell phone. The situation was sticky and could explode into an ugly scandal if it wasn't handled quickly and efficiently.

Riley cupped the back of her neck and put his forehead to hers. "Listen to me, Regina. I know the human garbage that exists in our world. Hell, I've dealt with them more times than I care to remember. Rapists, murderers, sadists... They're out there and we all have to be careful. But there are a lot of good people in the world, too, the kind of people you believe in."

"Like you."

"Like *you.*" He looked pained. "I'm not perfect, Red. I'm as flawed as your senator. But I would never cheat on you or deliberately hurt you and I'll always try to make you happy. You have my word on that."

She stared at him.

"I love you for who you are. I don't want you to change, to be jaded by this. I *like* the things you believe in. Hell, I believe in them, too." He bent to see her face. "You still do, don't you? You won't let one creep distort things for you?"

Her smile came slowly, along with sudden insight. The senator wasn't the man she'd believed him to be— but Riley was. True, he wasn't perfect, so he'd likely make mistakes in his life, just as she would. But he was steadfast, solid, a man you could rely on.

A man she could trust with her love.

"No, I won't let him disillusion me." She touched Riley's chest. She knew Riley, so she knew how incredible a person could be. No one could ever change that. "I love you, too, Riley. I fought it, but I knew last night that I'd lost the battle."

He didn't smile, but new warmth darkened his blue eyes. "I've known how I feel for a long while now."

"Buck and Harris and Ethan knew how you felt, too."

"They *what?*"

Nodding, Regina said, "They told me, but I didn't really believe them." Then in a barely there whisper, she confessed, "I thought you only wanted sex."

He rolled his eyes. "Of course I want sex," he answered in the same low whisper, and then added with gentle awe, "Look at you."

At his very private words, she glanced around the room. She knew no one could hear him, but when Lanny winked at her, she blushed. They really should have found some privacy for this chat.

"I was giving you time, Red, and trying to get this mess sorted out so we wouldn't be distracted." He

looked up at the sound of the door opening and two
more men—very official in appearance—stepped in.
"I think the mess just got messier, but at least you're
out of it now. I can concentrate on you."

"On us?" she specified.

He pressed a firm kiss to her mouth. "Yes."

"I do love you, Riley, but now that this is over, I have
no reason to stay with you. I'm not the type of woman
who shacks up."

He went stiff as a board, and Regina said, "Will you
marry me?"

He slumped against her, half in relief, half in amusement. Butch complained until he could squirrel up between their bodies and poke his face out.

"Riley?" Regina prayed he'd said yes.

"Yeah, I'll marry you." He grinned. "It's nice having a very proper woman around. Takes the guesswork
out of things."

With that settled, Regina turned back to face the
room. "What do you think will happen now?"

"I dunno. I don't really care as long as none of them
can ever again threaten you."

A sort of wistful melancholy crept up on her. "It's
strange, but I still think he's a good senator—he's just
not a good husband."

"Maybe. I promise I'll be a good husband." When
she smiled in agreement, Riley hugged her tight. "One
thing, Red."

"What?"

"You remember what I said about babies?"

Regina softened all the way to her toes. Her knees
felt like butter, her heart full and ripe. "Yes."

"I'm a homebody at heart. I want a house—"

"I have the house," she rushed to remind him, just in case he was getting cold feet.

"—and a dog."

"Got the dog, too. A perfect dog. A dog others will envy." She rubbed Butch's oversize ears.

Laughing, Riley hefted Butch up closer to his face and the dog playfully nipped his chin, appearing very pleased with the situation. "I'd really like a few kids *without* tails if you think we can manage that sometime in the misty future."

Tears filled her eyes. All around them was chaos, but the government could work itself out. This was important. "Since we love each other and we're getting married, and we intend to stay married forever, I'd say it would only be right and proper."

RILEY STEPPED through the door, took one look at Regina, and backed out. With the music she had playing on the stereo, she hadn't heard him. He turned to his friends and said, "Wait out here a second."

Buck crossed his arms over his massive chest. "If you're going to leave me hanging in the street just so you can grab a nooner, forget it."

Harris laughed. "Men in love are so predictable."

Rosie shoved him for that inelegant remark. "You'll get yours someday, Harris. Just wait and see."

His horrified expression had both Riley and Ethan chuckling.

Shaking his head, Riley said, "No, it's not that. She's just not ready for you. Two minutes, I swear. That's all I need."

"Two minutes? Talk about a quickie," Harris muttered, then ducked behind Buck before Rosie could reach him.

Riley slipped through the door and locked it behind him. He loved the house that Regina had chosen. It wasn't all that large but it had a real family feel to it, a coziness that she enhanced by her mere presence.

Since she'd already taken care of a sizeable down payment, he'd splurged on most of the furnishings. Between their combined efforts, things were really coming together.

The music continued to play, and Regina still had her delectable rump in the air as she rummaged beneath the couch for Butch's bone. The dog sat beside her, his expression anxious and watchful.

"Can I help?"

She screeched, whipped around to sit on her butt, and stared at him. "You're home early!"

"It ended quicker than I thought." He'd had to testify in court on a burglary, then had stopped by to see his friends. They'd invited themselves over, but obviously Regina wasn't ready for company.

Before he could explain that he had them all with him, she was on her feet and racing Butch to the door to greet him. Both woman and dog appeared thrilled with his arrival.

Dressed in one of his shirts—something she knew he loved seeing—and with her rich hair wound into enormous curlers around her head, Regina launched herself into his arms. Since that day at the Historical Society, she'd grown completely at ease with him. Around others, she remained immeasurably polite and proper, but with Riley she shared every facet of herself, including her less polished moments. Like now.

When the delicious kiss ended, Butch demanded his attention with a yodeling bark. He stretched up to stand on his hind legs, dancing around in what Riley called his circus dog impersonation.

Riley picked him up and treated him to a full body rub before saying to Regina, "Sorry to break it to you, but everyone is with me."

Her hands went to her cheeks and her green eyes widened. "Everyone?"

He nodded toward the door. "Harris and Buck, Rosie and Ethan. They invited themselves over. They're waiting on the porch."

The words no sooner left his mouth than she whipped around and dashed down the hallway to their bedroom. Riley enjoyed the back view of her, watching her long legs and the way his shirttails bounced over her bottom. "I'll keep them entertained while you finish getting ready."

The slamming of the door was her only reply.

Fifteen minutes later Regina emerged dressed in pressed slacks, a beige cotton sweater and a huge smile. "Sorry I kept you all waiting. Usually I'm dressed and ready by this time of the day, but I got behind this morning after Barbara Walters's people called."

Rosie's mouth fell open. Ethan jerked around to face her. Buck, who'd been on the floor playing with Butch, froze. Harris snorted in disbelief.

Riley, the only one with his wits still about him, raised a brow. "Barbara Walters?" He wasn't all that surprised. It seemed everyone in the media wanted the scoop on Senator Welling's sudden withdrawal. With his influence, the senator had put a gag order on the entire event. The guards present that day would never speak a word. Lanny and Dermot had been warned that they could lose their jobs if they released any information to the press.

Riley had assured the senator's people up front that they couldn't use his job to threaten him. All he cared about was that Regina be kept safe. Beyond that stipulation, they could handle the situation as quietly and secretively as they wished. But they *would* have to handle it because he wouldn't tolerate any more threats to Regina. So far, they had things in hand.

Regina was the only one left that could talk—and she wasn't about to.

"What did she want?" Buck asked.

"The same thing the others wanted."

Agog with fascination, Rosie asked, "To hear firsthand what happened with the senator?"

"Right." Regina sat down on Riley's lap, which was the only seat available in the small living room. She leaned back against his chest and smiled. "I told them that they'd just have to find out the nitty-gritty details like everyone else, after the federal investigation ended."

Rosie flopped back against her husband's arm. "Wow. Barbara Walters and you turned her down."

Buck rolled to his back and propped up on his elbows. "I can't believe you don't want revenge after the hell Welling's wife put you through."

Regina shrugged. "What good would revenge do? The senator has lost a lot of credibility with his constituents. They apparently don't like secrets, but with his wife under indictment and his own blame in the whole thing, what else can he do but keep quiet?"

"He could have not cheated in the first place," Harris

grouched with feeling, then looked blank when everyone stared at him. "What? I have morals, too, ya know."

Regina sighed. "They have two children, and I think
the kids have been through enough. Even with his wife
blaming everything on Earl, her involvement is bound
to make headlines eventually. The whole family is going
to suffer. I won't take part in that."

Harris nodded, giving her a look full of admiration.
"You're something else, Regina, you know that?"

Riley scowled at his tender tone, but Harris blew it by
saying, "And here I thought you were a nosy reporter."

"I am." Regina gave them all an evil grin. "But I
still like the more personal and upbeat human-interest
stories." She hesitated just long enough to add impact,
then announced, "That's why I told Walters's retinue
that if they wanted a real scoop they should bring their
TV crew to Chester and check out the local heroes."

Riley choked on his own breath.

Ethan groaned as if in mortal pain.

"You'd never get them here for something like that,"
Rosie said. "They like stories of worldwide appeal."

"Oh, I dunno. What could be more appealing to the
world than the local heroes who keep us safe?" She
slanted Rosie a look. "I specifically mentioned Harris and Buck."

Buck bolted upright. "I'm no hero! Hell, I just own
a lumberyard."

"You were right there by Riley the day he caught
Earl. You may not have a hero's occupation, but you
have the soul of a hero."

"I don't!"

"Yes, you do," she insisted. "Think of the interview
as free advertising for your business."

Harris said, *"Oh gawd,"* with great disgust. "That's weak, Regina. Very weak."

She didn't seem the least upset by the criticism. "When I told them two of the men were still single, they sounded pretty interested. They told me they're doing this whole segment on singles in America, and heroes would naturally be prime fodder for the piece. They want me to call them back with more information."

Buck and Harris stared at each other, their Adam's apples bopping in panic.

"You wouldn't."

"You didn't."

Riley started to laugh. "I can tell you unequivocally that she would. For some insane reason, she thinks the two of you epitomize all that is good in mankind."

"They're your and Ethan's friends," Regina said with prim regard. "And you two are definitely heroic."

"Hear, hear," Rosie agreed.

"So of course they're good men. And since they won't let me interview them…" She left the sentence dangling with loaded suggestion.

"Hey, I put up with it," Ethan pointed out.

"Me, too," Riley added. His own interview had been carefully edited by Regina. Anything that might have been too personal or hurtful had been omitted.

It was still embarrassing, especially because the love she felt for him had shone through and Harris and Buck had harassed him for days afterward, pretending to swoon, blowing him kisses and asking for his autograph. But the public had gobbled it up, his chief was thrilled with the positive P.R. for the department and Regina had thanked him oh so sweetly, so he was glad he'd given in.

Buck finally said, "Regina, be reasonable. You have to call off Walters."

Her nose lifted. "I could do that—*if* you agree to give me a story." Her gaze slanted to Harris. "Both of you."

With hardy groans and a lot of grumbling, they surrendered to the inevitable. "Deal."

Regina relaxed. "I'll return their call after dinner. But I need the interviews before our wedding next week."

"Why the rush?" Harris asked, looking somewhat stricken by the whole idea of being in the limelight.

"After the wedding, I plan to be busy for a while—with my own personal hero."

Riley hugged her close. He knew the truth: Regina was the heroic one. With her big heart and unwavering faith in human nature, she had filled his soul. He intended to keep her safe for the rest of their lives. If that made him a hero, too, at least in her eyes, then he'd gladly live with the label.

* * * * *

*Don't miss the next book in Lori Foster's
sizzling new* LOVE UNDERCOVER *series!
Turn the page for a sneak peek of* BARE IT ALL,
coming soon from Harlequin HQN!

CHAPTER TWO

ALICE STOOD THERE lost in thought for far too long before she remembered that she had coffee to make.

Never had she thought to have a man in her apartment. Certainly not her hunky police detective neighbor, and most definitely not overnight. It made sense for her to be off-kilter.

She no sooner finished preparing the coffee than she decided Reese might also like something to eat. It was lunchtime for her, but he hadn't even had breakfast yet.

Maybe he hadn't had dinner the night before, either. His work as a detective had literally landed on his doorstep, and she doubted he'd had time to relax, much less enjoy a real meal. A man his size likely required a lot of sustenance.

Yesterday had consisted of bad guys coming and going, good guys sneaking in, gunshots and arrests, deaths and ambulances... Shivering, Alice wrapped her arms around herself.

The life-or-death scenario had been unsettling for her, too. Having Reese on her couch, near at hand, gave her a sense of security that no weapon could. Even having Cash underfoot was reassuring. People still left her ill at ease, but animals were so nonjudgmental, so welcoming, she naturally took comfort from them.

Reese didn't know it, but being Cash's dog-sitter was

the greatest gift. Until he'd proposed the arrangement a few days ago, she hadn't realized what a difference it made to have another living, breathing creature nearby.

She sighed, realized several minutes had passed, and decided she'd ask Reese what he'd like to eat.

Picking up her keys, Alice locked the door behind her. Never again would she take any chances when it came to security. On her way out, she glanced up the steps at Reese's apartment door. Unlike in the movies, there was no dramatic caution tape draping the door, but yesterday Reese had said they preferred for him to stay out until they finished gathering their forensic evidence or taking photos or whatever they had to do. She really had no idea of police procedure. Other than Reese, she'd never known a good officer.

Sure, she'd been acquainted with a few shady men who claimed the badge but not the honor that should have been inherent in the job. Yesterday, she'd met good cops.

She'd learned the hard way to recognize the difference.

Remembering the day before made her palms sweat. Yes, Reese had only come to her because of the destruction in his place, but she was glad for any reason. While she hopefully put up a brave front, no way had she wanted to stay alone.

As she'd done so many times, she pushed the unpleasant memories to the back of her mind and went down the steps to the glass, double entry doors.

Before she stepped out, she saw Reese standing there in the shade, Cash's leash held loosely in his hand.

Two neighbor ladies, one a beautiful blonde with

oversize breasts, the other a very cute and petite brunette, stared at him adoringly while chatting.

They wore jogging shorts and sports bras and had a lot of skin showing. They stood far too close to him for mere conversation.

Alice didn't think about it, didn't even have time to process her reaction before she found herself striding out to the yard and right up to Reese and Cash. She snatched the dog's leash from his hand, startling him.

Lifting one eyebrow, he looked down at her. "Alice."

Her heart punched painfully against her breastbone. Unfair that a man with morning rumpled hair and whiskers could still manage to look so good. "The coffee's done." She stared at the women while thrusting the keys out to him. "I can wait with Cash until he finishes up if you'd like to go on in and get a cup."

Slowly his expression shifted from surprise to amusement. "Why thank you, Alice." With a knowing grin, he accepted her key ring. "Your hospitality knows no bounds."

She had no idea how to reply to that.

With a pleased smile, Reese touched her cheek, bid good day to the other ladies, and headed inside. The bright sunshine gleamed on his shoulders and gilded his fair hair. Though barefoot, he didn't pick his way across the grounds; he strode like a confident man in control of himself and those around him.

When Alice realized that she wasn't the only one noticing, she cleared her throat, loudly.

The blonde laughed. "Sorry, honey, but you know, I just can't pull my eyes away. He's an awful lot of man."

The brunette agreed. She looked at Alice, and asked with palpable doubt, "So, you two have a thing?"

A thing…? Understanding sank in. "What? No!" Alice looked down at herself, too. No, she wasn't cute and petite like the brunette, and she certainly didn't have the curves that the blonde flaunted. She was just herself, plain, understated, most times all but invisible.

Hadn't she been told that often enough?

And thank God for it.

"We're only neighbors."

"Uh-huh, sure you are." The friendly blonde continued to smile. "I wish I was that type of neighbor, too. I've suggested it, but I swear, Reese is a squirrely one, always dodging me."

"You've actually suggested…?"

"That we hook up, sure. And believe me, I haven't been subtle!" She laughed. "I figured he turned me down because we're too close for comfort, being in the same apartment building and all that. But if he's spending the night with you, then that must not be an issue for him."

The women stared at her, waiting for an explanation. Why hadn't she left well enough alone? She had no claim on Reese, so she should have kept her nose out of it.

But she had butted in, behaving like a territorial girlfriend, given them reason for speculation. Walking away now would be both rude and fodder for gossip.

"Do you both live here?" she asked while trying to decide how to proceed.

"Upper floor," the brunette said. "She's on one side of Reese, and I'm on the other."

"Doesn't that sound naughty?" The blonde laughed again. "We've known Reese awhile now."

Alice's temples pounded. "How…nice."

The blonde performed introductions. "I heard Reese call you Alice. I'm Nikki, and she's Pam."

"Hello." Until Reese, Alice had managed to keep her distance from all of her neighbors. Now she had Reese's admirers curious about her.

Knowing she'd just complicated her life, Alice turned her attention to Cash. Perhaps she could distract the women by playing with the dog?

But no, Cash flopped down in a ray of sunshine and looked so comfortable, she hated to disturb him. There was no help for it. She smiled at the women. "If you live that close to Reese, then you already know what happened yesterday."

Pam lifted both brows. "You mean between the two of you?"

"No!" Good grief. Such a suggestion. "Really, nothing happened between us."

Nikki grinned some more.

"I was talking about the police conflict that took place in his apartment."

"We were out late," Pam said.

"And much of the morning, too," Nikki added. "What happened?"

Hoping to extricate herself soon, Alice did her best to summarize. "Yesterday, I saw a person going into Reese's apartment, so I called him."

"You have his number?" Pam asked with disbelief.

"I…yes." Alice wanted to groan. Pam and Nikki looked ready to pounce on her every word. She nodded toward Cash. "I watch his dog for him while he works, so it was necessary to exchange numbers."

The women peered at Cash with disdain. Nikki said, "He pees *everywhere*."

"I know." Alice smiled with affection. "Cash has already marked every inch of my apartment."

"Oh my God, you're kidding?" Pam shuddered. "I'd send him to the pound for that."

Feeling very protective of the dog, Alice scowled. "He's a puppy still. He's learning."

Nikki couldn't quite uncurl her lip. "So he's actually Reese's dog? I assumed he was yours since you're the one I usually see bringing him outside."

"I pet-sit for him. Reese only recently got him, but being a detective, his hours can be…unconventional. And right now Cash needs a lot of attention, not to mention structure."

"So yesterday, when you said someone went into his place?" Nikki dismissed the dog. "Reese was getting robbed?"

"Not exactly. It was just…" Unsure how much she should actually tell, Alice fudged the truth. "A conflict of sorts, that's all. It ended well enough when yet another detective showed up. But Reese's apartment got a little…messy."

With bullet holes. Blood. A dead body on the floor.

She shook her head. "Reese had a lot to do once they made arrests, a lot of follow-up work, so he got in late." Or rather, early. "His apartment is still considered a crime scene."

Dismissing all of that, Pam asked in disbelief, "And so he came to *you?*"

Alice shrugged. "He slept on my couch."

"Your couch?" Nikki put a hand to her heart in dramatic fashion. "I would have *dragged* him into the bedroom."

"Or joined him on the couch." Pam grinned.

"I don't know," Nikki added. "He's awfully big to play with on a couch."

They both laughed.

Through tight lips, Alice explained, "We don't have that type of relationship." In fact, she wasn't sure what type of relationship they had. A couple of times now Reese had hinted about an attraction, but was it just teasing?

And if it wasn't, what then?

"Oh, honey," Nikki commiserated. "That must've been torturous for you, having a man like him so close but still not getting the advantages."

"It's great news for us, though." Pam elbowed her friend. "He's still up for grabs."

Alice couldn't fathom their attitudes. "So you're each interested in Reese?" How would that work? Neither of the women felt possessive?

Pam shrugged. "I do my best to get him to notice me, but Reese is a master at being polite without encouraging too much."

Nikki agreed. "I'd be on him in a heartbeat if he'd give me a signal. He's so delectably big and brawny."

Big and brawny were not attributes that Alice generally admired. Not in a man who showed too much intimate interest in her.

But for whatever reason, Reese was different, and her heart raced every time he got near.

"He's very compassionate," Alice said, then suffered through some curious expressions from Nikki and Pam. "It's true. He saved Cash. Someone had put the dog in a cardboard box and left him in the middle of the street."

"Probably because he pees everywhere!"

Nikki laughed at Pam and agreed.

Alice didn't find it at all funny. How could anyone
be that heartless? Luckily, Reese had cared enough to
investigate when he saw the box, and once he'd discov-
ered Cash, he'd taken him to the vet, adopted him, and
loved him. True, Reese spent too much time away, but
he assured the dog had proper care.

With her.

She sighed. "Reese is one of the kindest men I've
ever met."

Nikki grinned at her. "Yeah, and despite his big hard
body and that incredible face, I'm sure it was his *kindness* that you noticed first, right?"

No, that quality might not be what first drew her attention to Reese, but it was definitely what got past her
defensive walls.

"He's also a police detective, honest and protective
of others."

Pam snickered. "And with as long as we've been talking, the big, bad cop just might be in the shower right
now." She gave Alice's shoulder a pat and started away
with Nikki. "If I was you, I'd hurry in and join him."

"Have some fun for me, Alice." Nikki smiled as she
followed Pam. "We want to hear all the juicy details
tomorrow!"

Alice was too frozen to say her goodbyes. Until
Pam's parting remark it hadn't sunk in that she'd left
Reese Bareden, a *detective,* alone in her apartment.

Oh, Good Lord.

There was no telling what he'd find if he decided to
snoop. And for a detective, snooping no doubt came
naturally.

"Cash, come on, boy. Let's go!"

Ears lifted, his eyes bright, the dog jumped up, always ready for some excitement.

Good thing, because it seemed to her wherever Reese Bareden went, excitement definitely followed.

WHILE ALICE HUNG OUTSIDE, saying God knew what, Reese did a quick surveillance of her apartment. Her bedroom was plain to the point of painful, not at all like most ladies' bedrooms. In lieu of a frilly comforter she had a simple beige quilt over a full-size bed. Utilitarian curtains were pulled back to allow in the warm summer breeze. Not a single piece of clothing showed out of place. Other than one photograph sitting on her dresser, she kept her surfaces clutter-free. He approached the picture for a better look.

She'd had shorter hair when the photo was taken, and beside her sat a girl some years younger. A sister? They shared the same eyes, hair color, and the same lush mouth. Alice looked happy in a way that Reese hadn't yet seen.

Carefree.

Relaxed.

The Alice he knew never looked quite that tranquil, and seeing the contrast in the photo bothered him.

He strode to her closet to look inside.

Her very basic wardrobe hung in a tidy, organized way with her shoes lined up side by side on the floor. A shoebox on top of a shelf drew his attention and he lifted it down.

Inside he found the heavy Glock that she'd carried into his apartment yesterday. Again he remembered the weapon in her hand, and the look in her eyes.

"Shit." He returned the box to the top of her closet

and closed the door. He started to leave the room, hesitated, and instead looked under her bed.

Not a speck of dust, but he did find a lethal retractable baton. Scowling, he opened her nightstand and saw a Taser.

"Son of a bitch." How many people did she expect to fend off? And what the hell had happened to her to make her think all the weapons were necessary?

None of it gelled. Alice was a first-class introvert. Painfully solemn and withdrawn. Sort of…quietly dignified. She reminded him of his third-grade teacher, minus the bun and support hose. He curled his lip, disliking that description a lot—especially given how she turned him on.

There had to be something twisted in that.

At first, Alice-something-or-other—he really needed to learn her last name—had felt like a challenge. He didn't want to think himself conceited, but women didn't ignore him, so her disregard had piqued his interest.

Then he'd noticed her odd intensity, the extreme way she focused whenever she ventured outside, almost like she watched for the boogeyman. Why would a young, middle-class woman in a good neighborhood need to be so over-the-top cautious, even in broad daylight?

Her softness felt like a lure. Big dark eyes. Baby-fine brown hair.

And that soft, full mouth…

The first time he saw her smile—*at his dog*—something had sparked. Reese couldn't explain it any more than he could dismiss it, but something about her turned him on at a gut level.

He saw that tempting smile of hers and he got hard.

Knowing she could come back in any moment, Reese searched through her bathroom, but in his cursory exploration he found only the usual female products. No meds other than a few OTCs like aspirin and cold pills.

In the spare bedroom set up as her office he struck gold. With enough time to dig around, he could probably uncover all kinds of info on that elaborate computer network. Paper files filled a rack on the corner of the desk. She had an external drive set up. Mail filled a basket, meaning he could learn her last name with a simple peek. Everything was so neatly organized that going through it would be a breeze.

But that would be such a huge invasion of her privacy.

Worse than peeking in closets and under beds.

God, it was tempting…

In a belated bid for integrity, Reese shut the door. He'd talk to Alice. He'd ask questions and hopefully get answers, and then he'd decide how to proceed.

Right now, after seeing the guns, Taser and baton, he really did need that coffee.

A few minutes later, he'd just sat down at the table with his second cup when the front door flew open and Alice charged in, Cash hot on her heels.

Reese half rose from his seat. "What's wrong?"

She halted comically, still breathing fast. Cash looked at her, looked at Reese, and twitched his ears as if awaiting further instruction.

"Alice?"

After blowing out a breath, Alice shook her head. "Nothing is wrong." She closed the door, and simply… stood there.

"Just felt like taking a wind sprint, huh?" Would he ever understand her?

Damn straight he would.

"I had no idea you could move so quickly." Coffee in hand, he left the table. "I believe your temples are dewy. Did you run all the way in?"

She looked blank for only a moment, then visually searched the apartment as if seeking signs of his intrusion.

Let her look. He'd folded up his blankets. Put his clothes near the door. He'd even buttoned his slacks.

No way would he put on a shirt, though, not when he enjoyed her appreciation. And thinking of her appreciation...

He started toward her.

She locked her gaze to his. "What are you doing?"

Her uncertainty cut deep. "Greeting my dog." Gently, Reese took the leash from her small hand and unhooked Cash. He knelt down. "Did you miss me, Cash? Did you?"

Alice stared down at him. "You talk to him like he's a baby."

"He likes it." And then, to drive home that point, he said in his most ridiculous voice, "Don't you, boy? Yes, you do."

Alice blurted, "I'm sorry I intruded."

Huh. What was that about? Slowly, so he wouldn't make her any jumpier, Reese stood. "Let's go to the kitchen. This is my second cup, but as foggy as I am today, I might need the whole pot."

"All right." She marched ahead of him. "I was going to offer you breakfast. Or lunch." At the sink, she pivoted to face him. "What do you feel like?"

Such a loaded question, and being male, so many inappropriate comments came to mind. But given all her weaponry and secrets, he got right to the point instead of teasing.

"I feel like an explanation." Or two or three. He helped himself to another cup of coffee, which put him within touching distance of her, and started with her last apology. "When did you intrude?"

"Outside. With your lady friends."

Ah. What justification would she give for that little display? "You wanted me to get my coffee." He saluted her with his cup. "Much appreciated."

"Actually...no." She rubbed her forehead. "I mean, yes, I did want you to have your coffee, of course. But I...I don't really understand what I was thinking. I saw you out there with those women and the next thing I knew, I was behaving like a jealous wife."

Wow. Reese stared at her, flabbergasted. She threw that out there like it was nothing. No reserve at all.

No sense of self-protection, either.

"Again," she said, her tone still very no-nonsense, "I'm sorry."

Shaking off the surprise, Reese opened her refrigerator. "No problem." He withdrew her carton of eggs.

She frowned. "They're both very attractive."

"Nikki and Pam?"

The frown intensified. "Don't be deliberately obtuse."

"All right." If she wanted to dish it out, he could dish it right back. "They're both sexy as hell." He grinned. "And they know it, too."

Alice reached around him and pulled out bacon. "This is awkward."

She didn't act discomfited. She acted like it was routine to have such an odd conversation. "Nothing with me should be awkward."

She eyed him, moved around to get out a pan. "I understand they were...trying to hook up?"

"With those two, always. They're relentless in their pursuits." He put just enough complaint in his tone to sound comically pitiful.

"Oh, poor you. How awful it must be to have *sexy as hell* women hitting on you."

The bite of her sarcasm was so totally unexpected, he loved it. "Since I don't want to get involved with either of them, even for a one-night stand, it gets tedious."

"So you really have turned them down?" She quickly added, "That's what they said. That they kept trying and you kept dodging them."

He crossed his heart.

"Is it the proximity? That was Nikki's guess."

Since proximity would also put Alice off-limits, he denied it. "That might have factored in a little. But they're both drinkers and heavy partiers."

"And you're not?"

"When was the last time you saw me head to a party?"

"I haven't kept track of your agenda, one way or the other."

Bull. Alice was far too aware of everyone and everything not to have noticed him. But even without her keen observation, few would miss a man of his size. Thanks to a good draw from the family gene pool, he had both height and strength.

Men and women alike made note of him. But it

wasn't until Cash that Alice had acknowledged his existence.

He turned on a burner to get the skillet hot. "I work too many hours, and when I get some downtime, I like to kick back with my friends, which usually means watching sports, fishing, that sort of thing." He opened a drawer and found an egg turner. "And I like to hit up the gym a couple of times a week just to unwind."

"You look…" She coughed lightly. "…physically fit."

"Thanks." He was in prime condition, but if she wanted to understate it, he wouldn't debate it with her.

She got out bread for toast. It was interesting how easily they moved together to prepare breakfast.

"Another strike against Pam and Nikki, they're not dog people." He smiled at how Alice maneuvered around Cash without complaint, giving him the occasional pat or stroke without even thinking about it.

"That matters to you?"

"The dog and I are a package deal now." He began laying bacon in the skillet. "Love me, love my dog."

Silence filled the air. Had the "love" word thrown her when likening herself to a jealous wife hadn't? The mysteries added up. "So Alice, while we prepare breakfast, why don't we have that talk?"

"All right." She took down glasses and poured orange juice. "Before we get into that, though, would you like to tell me what you found while snooping?"

He went still, unsure whether she bluffed, or if she—

"I know you did, Reese."

"You assume—"

"I *know*."

Giving up, he said, "You're loaded down with weapons. Want to tell me why?"

One shoulder lifted. "Self-protection."

"Most people cover that with one gun."

She avoided his gaze by turning the bacon with a fork. "So what did you find?"

"Glock in bedroom closet, Taser in nightstand—"

"You got into my nightstand?"

Interesting reaction. "Long enough to see the Taser, yes." He studied her frown. "I also saw the baton under your bed."

Mouth tight, she asked, "Is that it?"

No fucking way. "There's more?"

With only the slightest hesitation, she lowered the heat under the bacon, took his hand, and led him out of the kitchen and down the hall.

Reese was so astounded by her touch that he barely noticed Cash trotting along behind them. It seemed that wherever Alice went, the dog followed.

She veered into the bathroom, released him and gestured behind the toilet. Frowning, Reese leaned around her to see...a revolver strapped to the tank. It was hidden from view so that only someone who knew where to look would find it.

He started to say something, but Alice walked out, so he followed, as did Cash. She went into her office, pulled her chair out from her desk, and tipped it back to show another Taser and a spare cell phone attached underneath.

"Jesus." Reese rubbed a hand over his head. "What else?" Because somehow, he just knew there was more.

She marched back into the kitchen, opened a cabinet drawer, and one by one, set out a flashlight, another spare cell phone, a big knife, mace and finally a stun gun. "I prefer a Taser so I won't have to get close, but the stun gun is here just in case."

Muscles knotted, tension mounting from her dispassionate explanation and overabundance of weapons, Reese growled out, *"Why?"* She had a damned fortress going on, and there must be a reason.

"I don't want to be hurt."

In contrast to his tone, hers was soft, and a little chilling because of it. It wrecked him, imagining what might have instilled so much caution.

His worst fears were confirmed when her big dark eyes lifted to his, and she said softly, "Again."

USA TODAY bestselling author

CHRISTIE RIDGWAY

introduces a sizzling new series set in Crescent Cove, California, where the magic of summer can last forever....

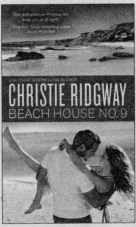

When book doctor Jane Pearson arrives at Griffin Lowell's beach house, she expects a brooding loner. After all, his agent hired her to help the reclusive war journalist write his stalled memoir. Instead, Jane finds a tanned, ocean-blue-eyed man in a Hawaiian shirt, hosting a beach party and surrounded by beauties. Faster than he can untie a bikini top, Griffin lets Jane know he doesn't want her. But she desperately needs this job and digs her toes in the sand.

Griffin intends to spend the coming weeks at Beach House No. 9 taking refuge from his painful memories—and from the primly sexy Jane, who wants to bare his soul. But warm nights, moonlit walks and sultry kisses just may unlock both their guarded hearts....

Available wherever books are sold!

LORI FOSTER

77708	THE BUCKHORN LEGACY	___ $7.99 U.S.	___ $9.99 CAN.
77695	RUN THE RISK	___ $7.99 U.S.	___ $9.99 CAN.
77656	A PERFECT STORM	___ $7.99 U.S.	___ $9.99 CAN.
77647	FOREVER BUCKHORN	___ $7.99 U.S.	___ $9.99 CAN.
77612	BUCKHORN BEGINNINGS	___ $7.99 U.S.	___ $9.99 CAN.
77582	SAVOR THE DANGER	___ $7.99 U.S.	___ $9.99 CAN.
77575	TRACE OF FEVER	___ $7.99 U.S.	___ $9.99 CAN.
77571	WHEN YOU DARE	___ $7.99 U.S.	___ $9.99 CAN.
77491	UNBELIEVABLE	___ $7.99 U.S.	___ $9.99 CAN.
77444	TEMPTED	___ $7.99 U.S.	___ $9.99 CAN.

(limited quantities available)

TOTAL AMOUNT	$ _____
POSTAGE & HANDLING	$ _____
($1.00 FOR 1 BOOK, 50¢ for each additional)	
APPLICABLE TAXES*	$ _____
TOTAL PAYABLE	$ _____

(check or money order—please do not send cash)

To order, complete this form and send it, along with a check or money order for the total above, payable to Harlequin HQN, to: **In the U.S.:** 3010 Walden Avenue, P.O. Box 9077, Buffalo, NY 14269-9077; **In Canada:** P.O. Box 636, Fort Erie, Ontario, L2A 5X3.

Name: _____
Address: _____ City: _____
State/Prov.: _____ Zip/Postal Code: _____
Account Number (if applicable): _____

075 CSAS

*New York residents remit applicable sales taxes.
*Canadian residents remit applicable GST and provincial taxes.

HARLEQUIN®HQN™
™www.Harlequin.com

PHLF0213BL